CW01643399

In 1793, at the tender age of just seventeen, Horatio Hornblower was forced to find his sea legs as a midshipman. After suffering his first bout of seasickness, the hapless doctor's son quickly rose through the ranks to become Admiral of the Fleet Lord Hornblower. In between, Hornblower must sail back and forth along the coasts of Europe and the Americas, repeatedly engaging or eluding the mighty ships of Napoleon and Spain. His heroic exploits in the French revolutionary war and his many other adventures in service of his country have made the name Horatio Hornblower into legend.

C. S. Forester was born in Cairo in 1899, where his father was stationed as a government official. He studied medicine at Guy's Hospital, and after leaving Guy's without a degree he turned to writing as a career. His first success was *Payment Deferred*, a novel written at the age of twenty-four and later dramatized and filmed with Charles Laughton in the leading role. In 1932 Forester was offered a Hollywood contract, and from then until 1939 he spent thirteen weeks of every year in America. On the outbreak of war he entered the Ministry of Information and later he sailed with the Royal Navy to collect material for *The Ship*. He then made a voyage to the Bering Sea to gather material for a similar book on the United States Navy, and it was during this trip that he was stricken with arteriosclerosis, a disease which left him crippled. However, he continued to write and in the Hornblower novels created the most renowned sailor in twentieth-century fiction. He died in 1966.

Bernard Cornwell is the bestselling author of the Sharpe series of novels.

Lord Hornblower

C. S. FORESTER

Introduction by Bernard Cornwell

PENGUIN BOOKS

PENGUIN BOOKS

Published by the Penguin Group
Penguin Books Ltd, 80 Strand, London WC2R 0RL, England
Penguin Group (USA) Inc., 375 Hudson Street, New York, New York 10014, USA
Penguin Group (Canada), 90 Eglinton Avenue East, Suite 700, Toronto, Ontario, Canada M4P 2Y3 (a division of Pearson Penguin Canada Inc.)
Penguin Ireland, 25 St Stephen's Green, Dublin 2, Ireland (a division of Penguin Books Ltd)
Penguin Group (Australia), 250 Camberwell Road, Camberwell, Victoria 3124, Australia (a division of Pearson Australia Group Pty Ltd)
Penguin Books India Pvt Ltd, 11 Community Centre, Panchsheel Park, New Delhi – 110 017, India
Penguin Group (NZ), cnr Airborne and Rosedale Roads, Albany, Auckland 1310, New Zealand (a division of Pearson New Zealand Ltd)
Penguin Books (South Africa) (Pty) Ltd, 24 Sturdee Avenue, Rosebank, Johannesburg 2196, South Africa

Penguin Books Ltd, Registered Offices: 80 Strand, London WC2R 0RL, England

www.penguin.com

First published by Michael Joseph 1946
Published in Penguin Books 1964
This edition published 2006
12

Set in 11/13 pt Monotype Dante by
Palimpsest Book Production Limited, Polmont, Stirlingshire
Printed in England by Clays Ltd, St Ives plc

ISBN-13: 978-1-405-92463-4

www.greenpenguin.co.uk

MIX
Paper from responsible sources
FSC™ C018179

Penguin Books is committed to a sustainable future for our business, our readers and our planet. This book is made from Forest Stewardship Council™ certified paper.

Introduction

Lord Hornblower was the fifth book to be written in the series but falls ninth in chronological order. It was published in 1946, fairly hard on the heels of *The Commodore*. Horatio Hornblower, who began as a frightened midshipman, seasick aboard HMS *Justinian*, begins this book as Sir Horatio Hornblower, Knight of the Most Honourable Order of the Bath, and ends it as Lord Hornblower of Smallbridge. It has been a swift series of promotions, which was probably why the next few books that Forester wrote after *Lord Hornblower* filled the gaps in our hero's earlier career.

Lord Hornblower takes the series through to the conclusion of the Napoleonic wars, ending with the news of Waterloo. It begins, though, with a splendid small-ship action. The crew of HMS *Flame*, an eighteen-gun brig, has mutinied and is threatening to hand the ship over to the French. Hornblower is ordered to retake the *Flame*, but how? If he appears to threaten the *Flame* then the mutinous crew will give the brig to the nearby French, yet if he refrains from attacking then the mutiny will appear to have succeeded, and that is unthinkable. Hornblower seems to be in an utterly impossible quandary, and it is no part of my duty to reveal how he succeeds in extracting himself, except to say that the solution is brilliantly and typically ingenious.

Lord Hornblower was not the last book in the series,

but it does have an air of finality about it. Forester, in the months after the Second World War, found himself preoccupied by thoughts of the fall of empires. The British empire was tottering, the French empire in the Far East was on life-support, the German and Japanese empires were shattered and the victors were conducting war-crimes trials. All these things influenced *Lord Hornblower*. It is a story of the chaos that follows war, of betrayal and sadness. I suspect Forester could happily have abandoned Hornblower after this book because, by 1947, he was a sick man. He had settled in California, where he was diagnosed with arteriosclerosis so severe that his doctors ordered him to do nothing. He found that an impossible order to obey and, after the diagnosis, wrote two Hornblower novels in quick succession, this one being the second. But he had other books he wanted to write and in the next three years he was to produce *The Sky and the Forest* and *Randall and the River of Time*, both books more ambitious than much of his other fiction. He did return to Hornblower, but *Lord Hornblower* still reads like a summation.

Forester, even if he had never written Hornblower, would be remembered as one of the great adventure-writers of the twentieth century. He is the author of *The African Queen*, of *Death to the French*, of *The Gun* and of *Brown on Resolution*, all of them astonishingly good books. He was, one suspects, a born writer. As a child he had been an avid reader, but as a young man his early career was frustrating. It is fortunate for us that his weak heart prevented him joining the army in 1917, though it was a disappointment for Forester, who felt he had somehow failed by not serving in the First World War. He enrolled as a medical student in Guy's Hospital instead, but never finished his training, concluding that he was not cut out to be a doctor. He wanted to be a writer. His first novel was rejected, but he persevered and was only twenty-five when he was first published. Two years later he had his first success with *Payment Deferred*, a murder story that became a stage play in London and, later, a film. The square peg had found the square hole and Forester the writer was off and running.

Hornblower was, of course, his greatest creation, and what makes him great is Hornblower's character. This difficult, honest, self-doubting, supremely decent man who 'looked on himself as a coward' yet is a great naval warrior. Forester was interested in the phenomenon of a 'man alone', a man who must make difficult decisions without benefit of orders or advice, and in *Lord Hornblower* he makes his hero take some extraordinarily difficult decisions. At any time in the Napoleonic wars a naval captain could find himself isolated and faced with the need to make a crucial choice, and he had to make it on the basis of his own intelligence and instinct, depending, as Forester put it in *Mr Midshipman Hornblower*, on his 'internal compass'. Such a man could not seek orders because it would take too long for a ship to find a superior officer, and so he was alone. Hornblower is repeatedly in that quandary, and in *Lord Hornblower*, even though he is close to the pinnacle of his career, he is still besieged by self-doubt. He regards himself as a 'fortunate plodder', not an inspired leader, despite all the evidence of his career to the contrary. There is a telling moment in this book when, after a triumph, his crew begin to cheer him and he orders them to be silent. Forester probably drew the incident from a similar occurrence in the life of the Duke of Wellington, though it is hard to think of the first Duke as a man tortured by too many doubts. Yet one day, having rescued a British brigade from a nasty predicament, the men began to cheer the Duke, who angrily demanded silence. 'Why, Your Grace?' an aide enquired. 'Because if you allow them to cheer you one day,' the Duke replied, 'they will jeer you the next.' I doubt that Hornblower would have worried about the jeers. What worried him was the mistaken idea that he did not deserve the cheers. Yet of course he did. He is the supreme military hero of adventure fiction and it is time, once more, to sail into battle under his judicious command.

I

The chapel stall of carved oak on which Sir Horatio Hornblower was sitting was most uncomfortable, and the sermon which the Dean of Westminster was preaching was deadly dull. Hornblower fidgeted like a child, and like a child he peered round the chapel and at the congregation to distract his mind from his physical troubles. Over his head soared the exquisite fan tracery of what Hornblower soberly decided was the most beautiful building in the world; there was something mathematically satisfactory in the way the spreading patterns met and remet, a sort of inspired logic. The nameless workmen who had done that carving must have been far-sighted, creative men.

The sermon was still going on, and Hornblower feared that when it was finished there would be some more singing, more of those high-pitched noises from the surpliced choir boys which would distress him painfully again, more painfully than the sermon or the oaken stall. This was the price he had to pay for having a ribbon and star to wear, for being a Knight of the Most Honourable Order of the Bath; as he was known to be on sick leave in England – and fully convalescent – he could not possibly evade attendance at this, the most important ceremonial of the Order. Certainly the chapel looked effective enough, the dull sunshine which made its way through the windows being reflected and multiplied into a soul-stirring glow by the knights' crimson mantles and flashing orders. There was at least this to be said for this pomp and vanity; it was certainly beautiful in a strange, effective way, even without regard to historical associations. Maybe the stall on which he sat had in earlier years caused the same discomfort to Hawke or Anson; maybe Marlborough, in crimson and white similar to his own, had fidgeted and fretted through a similar sermon.

The important-looking person over there with a silver gilt crown on his head and velvet tabard embroidered in the royal arms was merely Bath King-at-Arms, some well-connected fellow who had this well-paid sinecure and could doubtless comfort himself, while sitting through the sermon, with the thought that he was earning his living by doing so once a year. Beside him was the Prince Regent, the Sovereign of the Order, his scarlet face at odds with the crimson of his mantle. And there were soldiers, generals, and colonels, with whose faces he was unfamiliar. But elsewhere in the chapel there were men with whom he was proud to share the brotherhood of the Order – Lord St Vincent, huge and grim, the man who took his fleet down into the heart of a Spanish squadron twice its strength; Duncan, who destroyed the Dutch Navy at Camperdown; and a dozen more of admirals and captains, some of them even junior to him in the Navy List – Lydiard, who captured the *Pomona* off Havannah; Samuel Hood, who commanded the *Zealous* at the Nile; and Yeo, who stormed the fort at El Muro. There was something pleasant and heartwarming at being a member of the same chivalrous Order as men like these – ridiculous, but true. And there were three times as many heroes as these, brother-knights also still at sea (for the ones present here were only those with shore appointments or on leave) making the final desperate effort to tear down the Napoleonic Empire. Hornblower felt a surge of patriotic emotion within him; his spirit soared, and then he incontinently began to analyse this wave of emotion and to wonder how much of it was due to the romantic beauty of his surroundings.

A uniformed naval lieutenant had made his way into the chapel, and stood hesitating for a moment before discovering Lord St Vincent and hastening to him, offering him the large dispatch (whose seals were already broken) which he held in his hand. No one was paying any attention to the sermon now – the cream of the Royal Navy were all craning round, peering at St Vincent as he read the dispatch, which had clearly arrived from the Admiralty at the other end of Whitehall. The Dean's voice wavered, and then he rallied gamely, droning on to deaf ears, and ears which remained deaf for a long time, for St Vincent, having read the dispatch through once without any change of expression in his craggy face, immediately turned back to the beginning and read it through again. St Vincent who had so boldly risked the fate of England on a single prompt decision at the battle which gave him his title was nevertheless not a man to plunge hastily into action where there was time to think.

He finished his second reading, folded the dispatch, and then swept his gaze round the chapel. Two score Knights of the Bath stiffened with excitement and hoped to catch his eye. St Vincent rose to his feet and clasped his crimson cloak about him; he threw a word to the waiting lieutenant, and then, seizing his plumed hat, proceeded to hobble stiffly out of the chapel. Attention immediately transferred itself to the lieutenant, who was watched by every eye as he walked across the transept, and Hornblower stirred uncomfortably, his heart beating fast, as he realized that the lieutenant was heading straight for him.

'His Lordship's compliments, sir,' said the lieutenant, 'and he would like a word with you immediately.'

Now it was Hornblower's turn to fasten his mantle and to remember to pick up his plumed hat. He must at all costs appear nonchalant, and give to the assembled Knights no chance to smile at him for appearing flustered at this summons from the First Lord. He must look as if he was accustomed to this sort of thing every day. He stepped negligently out of his stall; his sword made its way between his legs and only by the mercy of Providence was he saved from tumbling headlong. He recovered himself with a clatter of spurs and scabbard, and set himself to stalk with slow dignity down the aisle. Every eye was on him; the Army officers present must be feeling merely a disinterested curiosity, but the Navy – Lydiard and the others – must be wondering what new fantastic turn the naval war had taken, and envying him the adventures and distinction which must await him. At the back of the chapel, in the seats reserved for the privileged public, Hornblower caught sight of Barbara making her way out of her pew to meet him. He smiled nervously at her – he could not trust himself to speak with all those eyes on him – and gave her his arm. He felt the firm touch of her hand upon it, and heard her clear, incisive voice; of course Barbara would not be awed by the fact that everyone was watching them.

'Further trouble, I suppose, dear?' said Barbara.

'I suppose so,' mumbled Hornblower.

Beyond the door St Vincent was awaiting them, the little wind tossing the ostrich feathers of his hat and ruffling the crimson cloak of silk. His massive legs bulged the white silk trunk hose; and he was pacing up and down on huge, gouty, deformed feet that distorted the white silk shoes. But the fantastic costume in no way detracted from the grim dignity of the man. Barbara slipped her arm out of Hornblower's and discreetly dropped back to allow the two men to converse in private.

'Sir?' said Hornblower, and then, remembering – he was not used yet to dealings with the peerage – 'My lord?'

'You're ready for active service now, Hornblower?'

'Yes, my lord.'

'You'll have to start tonight.'

'Aye aye, sir – my lord.'

'When they bring my damned coach up I'll take you to the Admiralty and give you your orders.' St Vincent lifted his voice in a bellow that had hailed the maintop in West Indian hurricanes. 'Haven't they got those damned horses in *yet*, Johnson?'

St Vincent caught sight of Barbara over Hornblower's shoulder.

'Your servant, ma'am,' he said; he took off the plumed hat and held it across his breast as he bowed; age and gout and a lifetime at sea had not deprived him of the courtly graces, but the business of the country still had first call upon his attention, and he turned back immediately to Hornblower.

'What is the service, my lord?' asked the latter.

'Suppression of mutiny,' said St Vincent grimly. 'Damned bloody mutiny. It might be '94 over again. Did you ever know Chadwick – Lieutenant Augustine Chadwick?'

'Midshipman with me under Pellew, my lord.'

'Well, he's – ah, here's my damned coach at last. What about Lady Barbara?'

'I'll take my own carriage back to Bond Street,' said Barbara 'and I'll send it back for Horatio at the Admiralty. Here it comes now.'

The carriage, with Brown and the coachman on the box, drew up behind St Vincent's coach, and Brown sprang down.

'Very good, then. Come on, Hornblower. Your servant, ma'am, again.'

St Vincent climbed in heavily, with Hornblower beside him, and the horses' hoofs clashed on the cobbles as the heavy vehicle crawled forward. The pale sunlight flickered through the windows on St Vincent's craggy face as he sat stoop-shouldered on the leather seat; some urchins in the street caught sight of the gaily attired individuals in the coach and yelled 'Hooray', waving their tattered caps.

'Chadwick had *Flame*, eighteen-gun brig,' said St Vincent. 'The crew's mutinied in the Bay of the Seine and are holding him and the other officers hostage. They turned a master's mate and four loyal hands adrift in the gig with an ultimatum addressed to the Admiralty. The gig made Bembridge last night, and the papers have just reached me – here they are.'

St Vincent shook in his gnarled hand the dispatch and the enclosures which he had clasped since he received them in Westminster Abbey.

'What's the ultimatum, my lord?'

'Amnesty – oblivion. And hang Chadwick. Otherwise they turn the brig over to the French.'

'The crazy fools!' said Hornblower.

He could remember Chadwick in the *Indefatigable*; old for a midshipman then, twenty years ago. He must be in his fifties now, and only a lieutenant. He had been a vile-tempered midshipman; after being passed over continually for promotion he must be a worse-tempered lieutenant. He could make a little vessel like the *Flame*, in which probably he was the only commissioned officer, a perfect hell if he wanted to. That might be the basis of the mutiny. After the terrible lessons of Spithead and the Nore, after Pigott had been murdered in the *Hermione*, some of the worst characteristics of the naval service had been eliminated. It was still a hard, cruel life, but not one to drive men into the suicidal madness of mutiny unless there were some special circumstances involved. A captain both cruel and unjust, a determined and intelligent leader among the men – that combination might make a mutiny. But whatever the cause, mutiny must be suppressed instantly, visited with extreme punishment. Smallpox or the plague were no more infectious and no more fatal than mutiny in a fighting service. Allow one mutineer to escape punishment, and he would be remembered by every next man with a grievance, and his example followed.

And England was at the very climax of her struggle with the French despotism. Five hundred ships of war at sea – two hundred of them ships of the line – were striving to keep the seas clear of enemies. A hundred thousand men under Wellington were bursting over the Pyrenees into southern France. And all the motley armies of eastern Europe, Russians and Prussians, Austrians and Swedes, Croats and Hungarians and Dutch, were being clothed and fed and armed by England's exertions. It seemed as if England could not put forth one single further effort in the struggle; even as if she must falter and break down under the dreadful strain. Bonaparte was fighting for his life, with all the cunning and ferocity one might expect of him. A few more months of constancy, a few more months of fierce exertion, might bring him crashing down and restore peace to a mad world; a moment's wavering, a breath of doubt, and tyranny might be clamped upon mankind for another generation, for uncounted generations to come.

The coach was wheeling into the Admiralty yard, and two wooden-legged naval pensioners were stumping out to open the doors. St Vincent climbed out, and he and Hornblower, in their brilliant crimson and white silk, walked through to the First Lord's room.

'There's their ultimatum,' said St Vincent, throwing a paper upon the desk.

Written in a poor hand, was Hornblower's first mental note – not the work of some bankrupt tradesman or lawyer's clerk caught by the press gang.

On board HMS Flame off Havre
7 October 1813

We are all loyal hearts and true here, but Lieutenant Augustine Chadwick has flogged us and starved us, and has turned up all hands twice a watch for a month. Yesterday he said that today he would flog every third man of us and the rest of us as soon as the others was healed. So we have him under lock and key in his cabin, and there's a whip rove at the foreyardarm waiting for him for he ought to be strung up after what he did to the boy James Jones, he killed him and we think he said in his report that he died of fever. We want their Lordships at the Admiralty to promise us to try him for his crimes and give us new officers and let bygones be bygones. We want to fight on for England's liberties for we are loyal hearts and true like we said but France is under our lee and we are all in this together and we are not going to be hanged as mutineers and if you try to take this vessel we shall run him up to the yardarm and go in to the French. We are all signing this.

Humbly and respectfully yours,

All round the margin of the letter were the signatures, seven of them, and several score of crosses, with a note against each cross – 'Henry Wilson, his mark'; 'William Owen, his mark', and so on; they indicated the usual proportion of literates and illiterates in an average ship's company. Hornblower looked up at St Vincent when he finished examining the letter.

'Mutinous dogs,' said St Vincent.

Maybe they were, thought Hornblower. But they had a right to be, he also thought. He could imagine perfectly well the sort of treatment to which they had been subjected, the unending wanton cruelty added to the normal hardship of life in a ship on blockading service; miseries which only death or mutiny could bring to an end – no other way out at all.

Faced with the certainty of a flogging in the immediate future, they had risen in mutiny, and he could not blame them. He had seen enough backs cut to ribbons; he knew that he himself would do anything, literally anything, to avoid such torture for himself if he were faced with the prospect of it. His flesh crept as he made himself seriously consider how he would feel if he knew he were to be flogged next week. The men had moral right on their side; it was not a matter of justice, but one of expediency, that they should be punished for their justifiable crime. The national existence of the country depended greatly on seizing the mutineers, hanging the ringleaders, flogging the rest; cauterizing before the disease could spread farther this new plague spot which had appeared in England's right arm. They must be hanged, morally innocent or not – it was a part of war, like the killing of Frenchmen who were possibly admirable husbands and fathers. But it would be as well not to let St Vincent guess at his sentiments – the First Lord obviously hated mutineers just as mutineers, without troubling to think more deeply about their case.

'What orders do you have for me, my lord?' asked Hornblower.

'I'll give you *carte blanche*,' replied St Vincent. 'A free hand. Bring *Flame* back safe and sound, and the mutineers along with her, and you can set about it any way you choose.'

'You will give me full powers – to negotiate, for instance, my lord?'

'I didn't mean that, damn it,' replied St Vincent. 'I meant you could have any force you asked for. I could spare you three ships of the line, if you want them. A couple of frigates. Bomb-vessels. There's even a rocket-vessel if you think you could use it – this fellow Congreve wants to see his rockets in action again.'

'It doesn't appear to be the kind of situation in which great force would be of much use, my lord. Ships of the line would seem to be superfluous.'

'I know that too, damn it.' The struggle in St Vincent's mind was evident in his massive face. 'Those insolent rascals can slip into the Seine's mouth in two shakes of a duck's tail at the first sign of danger to themselves. It's brains that are needed here, I know. That's why I sent for *you*, Hornblower.'

A nice compliment. Hornblower preened himself a little; he was talking here on terms almost of equality to one of the greatest admirals who had ever hoisted his flag, and the sensation was extraordinarily pleasant. And the internal pressure which was mounting inside the First Lord suddenly forced out of him a yet more astonishing statement.

'And the men like you, Hornblower,' exploded St Vincent. 'Damn it, I don't know a man who doesn't. They'll follow you and listen to you. You're one of the officers the men talk about among themselves. They trust you and expect things of you – so do I, damn it, as you can see.'

'But if I talk to the men it will imply that I am negotiating with them, my lord.'

'No negotiations with mutineers!' blared St Vincent, striking the desk with a fist like a leg of mutton. 'We had enough of that in '94.'

'Then the *carte blanche* that you give me is no more

than the usual naval officer's orders, my lord,' said Hornblower.

This was a serious matter; he was being sent out on an extremely difficult task, and would have to bear all the odium of failure should he be unsuccessful. He had never imagined himself bandying arguments with a First Lord, yet here he was actually doing so, impelled by sheer necessity. He realized in a moment of clairvoyance that he was not arguing on behalf of himself, after all; he was not trying to safeguard his own interests. He was debating purely impersonally; the officer who was to be sent out to recapture *Flame* and whose future might depend upon the powers given him was not the Hornblower sitting in this carved chair, dressed in crimson and white silk, but some poor devil he was sorry for and whose interests he had at heart because they represented the national interests. Then the two beings merged together again, and it was he, Barbara's husband, the man who had been at Lord Liverpool's dinner party last night and had a slight ache in the centre of his forehead today in consequence, who was to go out on this unpleasant task, where not a ha'porth of glory or distinction was to be won and the gravest risk was to be run of a fiasco which might make him the laughing-stock of the Navy and an object of derision through the country.

He studied St Vincent's expression again attentively; St Vincent was no fool and there was a thinking brain behind that craggy brow – he was fighting against his prejudices, preparing to dispense with them in the course of his duty.

'Very well then, Hornblower,' said the First Lord at

length. 'I'll give you full powers. I'll have your orders drawn up to that effect. You will hold your appointment as Commodore, of course.'

'Thank you, my lord,' said Hornblower.

'Here's a list of the ship's company,' went on St Vincent. 'We have nothing here against any of them. Nathaniel Sweet, bosun's mate – here's his signature – was first mate of a Newcastle collier brig once – dismissed for drinking. Maybe he's the ringleader. But it may be any of 'em.'

'Is the news of the mutiny public?'

'*No*. And please God it won't be until the court martial flag is hoisted. Holden at Bembridge had the sense to keep his mouth shut. He put the master's mate and the hands under lock and key the moment he heard their news. *Dart*'s sailing for Calcutta next week – I'll ship 'em out in her. It'll be months before the story leaks out.'

Mutiny was an infection, carried by words. The plague spot must be isolated until it could be cauterized.

St Vincent drew a sheaf of papers to himself and took up his pen – a handsome turkey-feather with one of the newfangled gold nibs.

'What force do you require?'

'Something handy and small,' said Hornblower.

He had not the remotest idea how he was going to deal with this problem of recovering a vessel which had only to drop two miles to leeward to be irrecoverable, but his pride made him assume an appearance of self-confidence. He caught himself wondering if all men were like himself, putting on a brave show of moral courage when actually they felt weak and helpless – he remembered Suetonius' remark about Nero, who believed all men to be privately as polluted as himself although they did not admit it publicly.

'There's *Porta Coeli*,' said St Vincent, raising his white eyebrows. 'Eighteen-gun brig – sister to *Flame*, in fact. She's at Spithead, ready to sail. Freeman's in command – he had the cutter *Clam* under your command in the Baltic. He brought you home, didn't he?'

'Yes, my lord.'

'Would she serve?'

'I think so, my lord.'

'Pellew's commanding the mid-Channel squadron. I'll send him orders to let you have any help you may request.'

'Thank you, my lord.'

Here he was, committing himself to a difficult – maybe an impossible – enterprise without any attempt to leave himself an avenue of retreat, neglecting utterly to sow any seed of future excuses which might be reaped to advantage in case of failure. It was utterly reckless of him, but that ridiculous pride of his, he knew, was preventing him. He could not use 'ifs' or 'buts' to men like St Vincent or to any man at all, for that matter. He wondered if it was because the First Lord's recent compliments had gone to his head, or maybe it was because of the casual remark that he could 'request' help of Pellew, a commander-in-chief, who had been his captain twenty years ago when he was a midshipman. He decided it was not either of these reasons. Just his nonsensical pride.

'Wind's nor'westerly and steady,' said St Vincent, glancing up at the dial which repeated the indications of the weathervane on the Admiralty roof. 'Glass is dropping, though. The sooner you're off the better. I'll send your orders after you to your lodgings – take this chance to say goodbye to your wife. Where's your kit?'

'At Smallbridge, my lord. Almost on the road to Portsmouth.'

'Good. Noon now. If you leave at three; po'chaise to Portsmouth – you can't ride post with your sea chest. Eight hours – seven hours, the roads aren't poached yet at this time o' year – you can be under way at midnight. I'll send Freeman his orders by post this minute. I wish you luck, Hornblower.'

'Thank you, my lord.'

Hornblower gathered his cloak round him, hitched up his sword, and took his leave. Before he had quitted the room a clerk had entered at the summons of St Vincent's jangling bell to take dictation of his order. Outside the north-westerly wind of which St Vincent had spoken blew freshly, and he felt chilled and forlorn in his gay crimson and white silk. But the carriage was there waiting for him, as Barbara had promised.

2

She was waiting for him when he arrived at Bond Street, steady of eye and composed of feature, as was to be expected of one of a fighting race. But she could only trust herself to say a single word.

'Orders?' she asked.

'Yes,' answered Hornblower, and then gave vent to some of the powerful mixed emotions within him. 'Yes, dear.'

'When?'

'I sail tonight from Spithead. They're writing my orders now – I must leave as soon as they reach me here.'

'I thought it would be like that, from the look on St Vincent's face. So I sent off Brown to Smallbridge to pack your kit. It'll be ready for you when we get there.'

Capable, far-sighted, level-headed Barbara! Yet 'Thank you, dear,' was all he could say. There were often these difficult moments even now, after all this time with Barbara; moments when he was overflowing with emotion (maybe that was the reason) and yet could not find words.

'May I ask where you are going, dear?'

'I cannot tell you if you do,' said Hornblower, forcing a smile. 'I'm sorry, dear.'

Barbara would say no word to anyone, nor convey by any hint or sign upon what kind of mission he was setting out, but, all the same, he could tell her nothing.

Then if news of the mutiny leaked out Barbara could not be held responsible; but that was not the real reason. It was his duty to keep silent, and duty allowed of no exceptions. Barbara smiled back at him with the brightness that duty demanded. She turned her attention to his silken cloak, and draped it more gracefully over his shoulders.

'A pity,' she said, 'that in these modern days there are so few opportunities for men to dress beautifully. Crimson and white sets off your good looks, dear. You are a very handsome man – did you know that?'

Then the brittle artificial barrier between them broke and vanished as utterly as a punctured soap bubble. His was a temperament that longed for affection, for the proofs of love; but a lifetime of self-discipline in an unrelenting world had made it difficult, almost impossible, for him to let the fact appear. Within him there was always the lurking fear of a rebuff, something too horrible to risk. He always was guarded with himself, guarded with the world. And she; she knew those moods of his, knew them even while her pride resented them. Her stoic English upbringing had schooled her into distrusting emotion and into contempt for any exhibition of emotion. She was as proud as he was; she could resent being dependent on him for her life's fulfilment just as he could resent feeling incomplete without her love. They were two proud people who had made, for one reason or another, self-centred self-sufficiency a standard of perfection to abandon which called for more sacrifice than they were often prepared to make.

But in these moments, with the shadow of separation looming over them, pride and resentment vanished, and they could be blessedly natural, each stripped of the numbing armour the years had built about them. She was in his arms, and her hands under his cloak could feel the warmth of his body through the thin silk of his doublet. She pressed herself against him as avidly as he grasped at her. In that uncorseted age she was wearing only the slightest whalebone stiffening at the waist of her gown; in his arms he could feel her beautiful body limp and yielding despite the fine muscles (the product of hard riding and long walking) which he had at last educated himself to accept as desirable in woman, whom he had once thought should be soft and feeble. Warm lips were against warm lips, and then eyes smiled into eyes.

'My darling! My sweet!' she said, and then lip to lip again she murmured the endearment of the childless woman to her lover. 'My baby. My dear baby!'

The dearest thing she could say to him. When he yielded to her, when he put off his protective armour, he wanted to be her child as well as her husband; unconsciously he wanted the reassurance that, exposed and naked as he was, she would be true and loyal to him like a mother to her child, taking no advantage of his defenceless condition. The last reserve melted; they blended one into the other in that extremity of passion which they could seldom attain. Nothing could mar it now. Hornblower's powerful fingers tore loose the silken cord that clasped his cloak; the unfamiliar fastenings of his doublet, the ridiculous strings of his trunk hose – it did not break into his mood to have to deal with them. Some time Barbara found herself kissing his hands, the long beautiful fingers whose memory sometimes haunted her nights when they were separated, and it was a gesture of the purest passion without symbolism. They were free for each other, untrammelled, unhindered, in love. They were marvellously one, and one even when it was all over; they were complete and yet not sated. They were one even when he left her lying there, when he glanced into the mirror and saw his scanty hair madly tousled.

His uniform hung on the dressing-room door; Barbara had thought of everything during the time he had been with St Vincent. He washed himself in the hand-basin, sponging his heated body, and there was no thought of washing away impurity – the act was one of simple pleasure. When the butler knocked at the door he put his dressing gown over his shirt and trousers and came out. It was his orders; he signed the receipt for them, broke the seal, and sat down to read them through to make sure there were no misunderstandings which ought to be cleared up before he left London. The old, old formulas – 'You are hereby requested and required'; 'You are therefore strictly charged' – the same ones under whose authority Nelson had gone into action at Trafalgar and Blake at Tenerife. The purport of the orders was plain, and the delegation of power unequivocating. If read aloud to a ship's company – or to a court martial – they would be readily understood. Would he ever have to read them aloud? That would mean he had opened negotiations with mutineers. He was entitled to do so, but it would be a sign of weakness, something that would mean lifted eyebrows throughout the Navy, and which would cast a shadow of disappointment over St Vincent's craggy face. Somehow or other he had to fool and trick a hundred English seamen into his power, so that they could be hanged and flogged for doing something he knew very well he would have done himself in the same circumstances. He had a duty to do; sometimes it was his duty to kill Frenchmen and sometimes it might be another duty. He would prefer to have to kill Frenchmen if someone had to be killed. And how in Heaven's name was he to set about this present task?

The door to the bedroom opened and Barbara came in, radiant and smiling. Their spirits rushed together as their eyes met; the imminence of physical separation, and Hornblower's contemplation of his new distasteful duty, were not sufficient to disrupt the mental accord between them. They were more united than they had ever been before, and they knew it, the fortunate pair. Hornblower rose to his feet.

'I shall be ready to leave in ten minutes,' he said. 'Will you come with me as far as Smallbridge?'

'I was hoping you would ask me to do so,' said Barbara.

3

It was the blackest imaginable night, and the wind, backing westerly, was blowing half a gale and promising to blow harder. It blew round Hornblower, flapping his trouser-legs about his knees above his sea boots and tugging at his coat, while all round and above him in the blackness the rigging shrieked in an insane chorus, as though protesting at the madness of mankind in exposing frail man-made equipment to the violence of the world's forces. Even here, in the lee of the Isle of Wight, the little brig was moving in lively fashion under Hornblower's feet as he stood on the tiny quarterdeck. Somewhere to windward of Hornblower someone – a petty officer, presumably – was cursing a seaman for some unknown error; the filthy words reached Hornblower's ears in gusts.

A lunatic, thought Hornblower, must know these mad contrasts, these sudden changes of mood, these violent alterations in the world about him; in the one case it was the lunatic who changed, but in his own case it was his surroundings. This morning, hardly more than twelve hours ago, he had been sitting in Westminster Abbey with the Knights of the Bath, all dressed in crimson and white silk; he had dined with the Prime Minister the night before. He had been in Barbara's arms; he had been living in Bond Street luxury, with every whim that might arise ready to be satisfied at the mere pulling of a bell-cord. It was a life of self-indulgent ease; a score of servants would be genuinely shocked and upset if the slightest thing occurred to disturb the even way of the life of Sir Horatio – they ran those two words together, of course, making a curious bastard word like Surroratio out of them. Barbara had watched over him all through the summer, to make sure that the last seeds of the Russian typhus which had brought him home sick were eradicated. He had wandered in the sunshine through the gardens at Smallbridge hand in hand with little Richard, with the gardeners backing respectfully away and pulling at their hats. There had been that golden afternoon when he and Richard had lain side by side on their bellies beside the fish pond, trying to catch golden carp with their hands; returning to the house with the sunset glowing all about them, muddy and wet and gloriously happy, he and his little child, as close together as he had been with Barbara that morning. A happy life; too happy.

At Smallbridge this afternoon, while Brown and the post-boy were carrying out his sea chest to the chaise, he had said goodbye to Richard, taking hold of his hand to shake it as man to man.

'Are you going back to fight, Father?' Richard asked.

He said one more goodbye to Barbara; it was not easy. If he had good fortune, he might be home again in a week, but he could not tell her that, for it might reveal too much about the nature of his mission. That little bit of deception helped to shatter the mood of unity and union; it made him a little cold and formal again. Hornblower had had a strange feeling as he turned away from her of something lost for ever. Then he had climbed into the chaise with Brown beside him and rolled away, skirting the autumnal Downs to Guildford in the gathering evening, and then down the Portsmouth Road – the road along which he had driven on so many momentous occasions – through the night. The transition was brief from luxury to hardship. At midnight he set foot in the *Porta Coeli*, welcomed by Freeman, square, stocky, and swarthy as ever, with black hair hanging to his cheeks, gipsy-fashion; one noted almost with surprise that there were no rings in his ears. Not more than ten minutes was necessary to tell Freeman, under seal of secrecy, the mission upon which the *Porta Coeli* was to be dispatched; in obedience to his orders received four hours earlier Freeman already had the brig ready for sea, and at the end of that ten minutes the hands were at the capstan getting in the anchor.

'It's going to be a dirty night, sir,' said Freeman out of the darkness beside him. 'Glass is still dropping.'

'I expect it will be, Mr Freeman.'

Freeman suddenly raised his voice to one of the loudest bellows that Hornblower had ever heard – that barrel-shaped chest could produce a surprising volume of sound

'Mr Carlow! Have all hands shorten sail. Get that maintopmast-stays'l in! Another reef in the tops'ls! S'uth-east by south, quartermaster.'

'South-east by south, sir.'

The deck under Hornblower's feet vibrated a little with the rush of the hands over the planking; otherwise there was nothing to show him in the darkness that Freeman's orders were being obeyed; the squeal of the sheave-pulleys in the blocks was swept away in the wind or drowned in the howling of the cordage, and he could see nothing of the rush of the men up the rigging to reef the topsails. He was cold and tired after a day which had begun – unbelievably, it seemed now – with the arrival of the tailor to dress him in the ceremonial costume of a Knight of the Bath.

'I'm going below, Mr Freeman,' he said. 'Call me if necessary.'

'Aye aye, sir.'

Freeman slid back the sliding hatch that covered the companionway – *Porta Coeli* was flush-decked – and a faint light emerged, revealing the stair; a faint light, but dazzling after the intense blackness of the night. Hornblower descended, bowing almost double under the deck-beams. The door to his right opened into his cabin, six feet square and four feet ten high; Hornblower had to crouch down on his haunches to survey it by the wavering light of the lantern swinging from the deck above. The crampedness of these, the finest quarters in the brig, was nothing compared with the conditions in which the other officers lived, he knew, and twenty times nothing compared with the conditions in which the hands lived. Forward the height between decks was just the same as this – four feet ten – and there the men slept in two banks of hammocks, one suspended above the other, with the noses of the men of the upper tier scraping the deck above and the tails of the men in the lower tier bumping the deck below, and noses meeting tails in the middle. The *Porta Coeli* was the best fighting machine of her tonnage that could sail the seas; she carried guns that could smash any opponent of her own size; she had magazines that could supply those guns during hours or days of fighting; she carried provisions enough to enable her to keep the sea for months without touching land; she was staunch and stout enough to face any weather that blew; the only thing that was wrong with her was that to achieve these results in 190 tons the human beings who lived in her had to be content with living conditions to which no careful farmer would ever subject his livestock. It was at the cost of human flesh and blood that England maintained the countless small vessels which kept the seas safe for her under the protecting shield of the ponderous ships of the line.

The cabin, small though it was, housed a prodigious stink. The first thing the nostrils noticed was the sooty, stuffy smell of the lamp, but they immediately became aware of a whole gamut of supplementary odours. There was the flat bilge smell, tolerable, in fact almost unnoticed by Hornblower, who had smelt bilge for twenty years. There was a penetrating smell of cheese, and as if to set that off there was a perceptible smell of rats. There was a smell of wet clothing, and finally there was a mixture of human odours, the long-confined body odour of unwashed men predominating.

And all this mixture of smells was balanced by a battery of noises. Every timber resonated the shrieking of the rigging; to be inside the cabin was to be like a mouse inside a violin while it was being played. Overhead the continual footfalls on the quarterdeck and the clatter of ropes being thrown down made it seem – to continue the analogy – as if someone else were tapping the body of the violin at the same time with small mallets. The wooden sheathing of the brig creaked and crackled with the vessel's motion in the water like a giant's knuckles rapping on the exterior; and the shot in the racks rolled just a trifle with each movement, too, thumping solemnly and unexpectedly just at the end of the roll as they fetched up.

Hornblower had hardly entered his cabin when the *Porta Coeli* suddenly heeled over unexpectedly far; apparently as she was just emerging into the open Channel the full force of the westerly breeze caught her and laid her. Hornblower was taken by surprise – it always was a slow process recovering his sea legs after a long stay ashore – and was precipitated forward, fortunately towards the cot, on which he was thrown face downward, and as he lay spreadeagled upon the cot his ears caught the assorted noises as the various loose objects always not properly secured at the outset of a voyage cascaded to the decks at this, the first big roll. Hornblower squirmed round on to the cot, bumped his head on the deck-beams above as another roll took him by surprise again, and fell back on to the coarse pillow, sweating in the wet stuffiness of the cabin both as a result of his exertions and with the beginnings of seasickness. He was cursing feebly and yet with all his heart; an intense hatred for this war, the more bitter for being completely hopeless, surged up inside him. What peace might be like he could hardly imagine – he had been a mere child when last the world was at peace – but he longed with uncontrollable yearning for peace as a cessation from war. He was weary of war, overweary of it, and his weariness was accentuated and embittered by the experiences of the last year. The news of the complete destruction of Bonaparte's army in Russia had early roused hopes of immediate peace; but France had shown no signs of wavering, had raised new armies, and had stemmed the torrent of the Russian counter-attack far from any vital point of the Empire. The wiseacres had pointed to the severity and all-embracing nature of Bonaparte's conscription, to the harshness of the taxation he exacted, and predicted an early upheaval in the interior of the Empire, backed maybe by a revolt of the generals. Ten months had elapsed since those predictions began generally to be made, and there was not a sign as yet of their coming true. When Austria and Sweden joined the ranks of Bonaparte's enemies, men looked again for immediate victory. They hoped that when Bonaparte's unwilling allies – Denmark, Holland, and the rest – fell away from their allegiance this presaged a prompt breaking-up of the Empire, and they were disappointed each time. For long it had been predicted by thoughtful men that when the tide of war washed back into the Empire itself, when Bonaparte should be compelled to make war support war on the soil of his subjects and not on that of his enemies or tributaries, the struggle would end almost automatically. Yet three months had elapsed since Wellington with a hundred thousand men had swept over the Pyrenees within the sacred frontiers, and still he was locked in a death grapple in the far south, still seven hundred miles from Paris. There seemed to be no end to Bonaparte's resources or determination.

To Hornblower in his present despairing mood it seemed as if the struggle must continue until every last man in Europe was dead, until the whole of England's substance was irrevocably consumed; and for himself that until old age should set him free he would be condemned, on account of the mad determination of one single man, to the loss of his liberty, to spending his days and his nights in hideous surroundings like the present, torn from his wife and his son, seasick and cold, depressed and unhappy. For almost the first time in his life he began to wish for a miracle, or for some unsought turn of good fortune – that a stray bullet should kill Bonaparte, or that some prodigious mistake would permit the gaining of an indisputable and decisive victory; that the people of Paris should rise successfully against the tyrant, that the French harvest should fail utterly, that the Marshals, to preserve their fortunes, should declare against the Emperor and succeed in inducing their soldiers to follow them. And none of these things, as he knew, was in the least likely; the struggle must go on and on, and he must remain a seasick prisoner in the chains of discipline until his hair turned white.

He opened his tightly closed eyes to find Brown standing over him.

'I knocked, sir, but you didn't hear me.'

'What is it?'

'Is there anything I can get for you, sir? They're just goin' to douse the galley fire. A cup o' coffee, sir? Tea? A hot grog?'

A good stiff dose of liquor might put him to sleep, would drown his morbid and gloomy thoughts, give him some respite from the black depression which was engulfing him. Hornblower found himself actually dallying with the temptation, and was genuinely shocked at himself. That he, who had not drunk to make himself drunk for nearly twenty years, who detested intoxication in himself even more than in other people, should give even a moment's favourable consideration to such a thought startled him in addition to appalling him. It was a new depravity that he had never known existed in him, made worse by the knowledge that he was on a secret mission of great importance, where a clear head and ready judgement would be vitally necessary. He spurned himself in bitter self-contempt.

'No,' he said. 'I shall go back on deck.'

He swung his legs down from the cot; the *Porta Coeli* was now well clear of the land, and was rolling and plunging like a mad thing in the choppy waters of the Channel. The wind on her quarter was laying her over so that as Hornblower rose to his feet he would have slid down to the opposite bulkhead if Brown had not put out a brawny hand and saved him. Brown never lost his sea legs; Brown was never sick; Brown had the vast physical strength that Hornblower had always coveted. He stood on his straddled legs like a rock, quite unmoved by the antics of the brig, while Hornblower swayed uncertainly. He would have hit his head against the swinging lamp if Brown's firm hand on his shoulder had not deflected him.

'A dirty night, sir, an' it'll be a long sight worse afore it's better.'

Job had the same sort of comforters. Hornblower snarled sidelong at Brown in pettish bad temper, and the bad temper was only made worse by seeing Brown being philosophical about it. It was infuriating to be treated like a child in a tantrum.

'Best wear that scarf Her Ladyship made you, sir,' went on Brown, unmoved. ''Twill be mortal cold by morning.'

In a single movement he flipped open a drawer and produced the scarf. It was a square of priceless silk, light and warm, maybe the most costly thing Hornblower had ever owned, even taking into account his hundred-guinea sword. Barbara had embroidered upon it, with infinite pains – she detested fiddling with needle and thimble, and the fact that she had done so was the prettiest compliment she could pay him. Hornblower put it round his neck inside the collar of his pea-jacket, and was reassured by it, by its warmth and softness and by the memories of Barbara that it conjured up. He steadied himself, and then plunged for the door and up the five steps to the quarterdeck.

It was utterly dark up there, and Hornblower was blinded, emerging from even the miserable light of his cabin. All round him the wind roared hugely; he had to bend his head to meet it. The *Porta Coeli* was lying right over on her side, even though the wind was not abeam but over her quarter. She was both rolling and pitching. Spray and spindrift mixed with the rain that flew across her deck, stinging Hornblower's face as he clawed his way up to the weather bulwarks. Even when his eyes had grown accustomed to the darkness he could hardly make out the dim narrow rectangle of the reefed maintopsail. The little vessel leaped under his feet madly, like a horse; the sea was violent – even through the din of the gale Hornblower could hear the groan of the tiller-ropes as the quartermaster at the wheel fought to keep her from falling away into the trough.

Hornblower sensed the presence of Freeman somewhere near him, and ignored him. There was nothing to say, and even if there had been anything to say the violence of the wind would have made it difficult. He hitched his elbow on the hammock-netting to steady himself and gazed into the darkness. Just overside the white top of each advancing wave was momentarily visible before the *Porta Coeli* lifted to it. Forward the hands were at work on the pumps; Hornblower's ear could catch the flat clatter of them at intervals. There was nothing surprising at that, because with the violent working of the vessel in the waves the seams must be gaping and closing like mouths. Somewhere in this black night ships would be sailing, worn down by the gale; somewhere ships would be driving ashore, and seamen would be dying in the surf with this pitiless wind howling over them. Anchors would be dragging and lines parting. And this wind would be blowing over the miserable bivouacs of embattled Europe, too. The million anonymous peasant soldiers huddled round the campfires which they could hardly keep alight would curse the wind and the rain as they lay sleepless and hungry awaiting tomorrow's battle. It was strange to think that upon them, upon these inconsiderable unknowns, depended, to a large part, his release from his present thraldom. He vomited excruciatingly into the scuppers as his seasickness reached a climax.

Freeman was speaking to him with unintelligible words. He could not understand them, and Freeman had to yell louder.

'It seems as if I shall have to heave-to, sir.'

Freeman had spoken in a moderate tone at first, a trifle embarrassed. It was a difficult position for Freeman; by the law and custom of the sea he was captain of this ship and Hornblower, although so far superior in rank, was no more than a passenger. Only an admiral could take command out of the hands of the officer appointed for that purpose, without a long and difficult process; a captain, even one who held commodore's rank as did Hornblower, could not do so. Legally, and under the rulings of the Articles of War, Hornblower could only direct the *Porta Coeli*'s operations; Freeman was solely responsible for the manner in which Hornblower's orders were carried out. Legally it was entirely for Freeman to decide whether to heave-to or not; but no mere lieutenant commanding an eighteen-gun brig could happily disregard the wishes of a commodore on board, especially when the commodore happened to be Hornblower, with his reputation of impatience of delay and eagerness to set about the tasks before him – no lieutenant with a thought for his own future could do so, at any rate. Hornblower grinned to himself through his nausea at Freeman's dilemma.

'Heave-to if you wish, Mr Freeman,' he bellowed back, and as soon as he had said the words Freeman was shouting his orders through his speaking-trumpet.

'Heave-to! Get the foretops'l in! Set the maint'mast-stays'l. Quartermaster, bring her to.'

'Bring her to, sir.'

The furling of the foretopsail eased her, and the staysail steadied her, and then she came to the wind. Until now she had fought against it; now she yielded to it, like a woman giving way at last to an importunate lover. She rose to an even keel, turning her starboard bow to the choppy seas, rising and falling to them with something of rhythm instead of her previous unpredictable plunges over the quartering waves. The starboard mainshrouds gave something of a lee to Hornblower where he stood against the starboard bulwark, so that even the force of the wind seemed to be a little moderated.

4

Everything was much more comfortable, no doubt, much safer. There was no danger now of the *Porta Coeli* losing spars or canvas or working her seams considerably open. But it did not bring her any nearer to the *Flame* and her mutinous crew; on the contrary; it meant that every moment she was drifting farther away, and to leeward. To leeward! Hornblower's mind, like that of every sailor, was obsessed with the importance of keeping to windward of one's destination. He grudged bitterly every yard of leeway made, far more bitterly than any miser grudged paying out his pieces of gold. Here in the Channel in the late autumn, where westerly gales were to be expected daily, any drift to the eastward might have to be bought back at compound interest. Every hour of leeway would have to be regained when the wind moderated, by two or three hours of beating back to windward, unless the wind should come easterly, which one could not expect.

And every hour might count; no one could guess what might be the next mad action of the desperate men on board *Flame*. At any moment they might be led by panic to hand themselves over to the French; or the ringleaders might abandon the vessel and seek refuge in France, never to be regained for the hangman's rope. And at any moment the news might begin to seep through the Navy that a king's ship had successfully thrown off the bonds of discipline, that downtrodden seamen were negotiating, as one power with another, with the Lords of the Admiralty. Hornblower could guess only too well what might be the effect of that news. The sooner *Flame* was dealt with in exemplary fashion the better; but he was still without any idea as to how to deal with her. This present gale would hardly discommode her – she would be able to ride it out in the lee of the Normandy peninsula. A vessel of her tonnage could venture anywhere in the Bay of the Seine; on the one hand she could run for Le Havre, on the other to Caen river.

The batteries of the Cotentin coast would protect her; the *chasse-marées* and the Seine gunboats would be ready to come to her aid. Both at Cherbourg and at Le Havre there were French frigates and ships of the line, half-manned and unready for sea, but always able at a pinch to push out a few miles from port and cover the escape of the *Flame*. At the approach of superior force she would certainly run; she might stand and fight an equal, such as this *Porta Coeli*, but Hornblower found himself hesitating at the prospect of meeting on equal terms a British ship manned by English sailors filled with the courage of despair. Victory would be dearly bought – what a triumphant clamour Bonaparte would raise through Europe at the news of a battle between two British ships! There would be many dead – what would be the effect on the Navy at the news of British sailors killing each other? What would be the results in Parliament? And the chances were certainly large that the two brigs would cripple each other so badly as to fall easy victims to the *chasse-marées* and gunboats. And worse than that, there was the chance of defeat. Equal ships, equal crews; a chance as arbitrary as the spin of a coin might decide the action. No, only as a last resort, perhaps not even then, would he fight a simple action against the *Flame*. But what the devil was he to *do*?

Hornblower shook himself into consciousness of the world about him, backing out of the blind alley of thought in which he had found himself. The wind was still shrieking round him, but it was no longer an avalanche of darkness. Before his eyes the lean rectangle of the reefed maintopsail was distinctly visible against the sky. There was a faint grey light about him; the white-flecked waves over which the brig was uneasily rising were plain to his sight. Morning was coming. Here he lay, hove-to in mid-Channel, out of sight of land. And it was still less than twenty-four hours since he had sat in silks amid the Knights of the Bath in Westminster Abbey, and much less than twenty-four hours since Barbara had – that was another line of thought from which he had hastily to shake himself free. It was raining again, the chill drops blowing into his face. He was cold through and through; as he moved he felt Barbara's scarf about his neck sopping wet with the water that had run down from his face. Freeman was beside him; the day-old beard that sprouted on Freeman's cheeks was an additional convincing touch in his gipsy appearance.

'The glass stays low, sir,' said Freeman. 'No sign of the weather moderating.'

'I can see none myself,' said Hornblower.

There was scanty material for conversation, even if Hornblower had wanted to enter into conversation with his subordinate. The grey sky and the grey sea, the shrieking wind, the chill that enveloped them, the pessimistic gloom which clouded Hornblower's thoughts, all these helped Hornblower to maintain the deliberate taciturnity which he had so long cultivated.

'Have me called at the first sign of a change, Mr Freeman,' he said.

He walked over to the hatchway; it was only with an effort that he could set one foot before the other, and he could hardly bend at all to get his hands on the hatch coaming as he descended. His joints groaned as he crept under the threatening deck-beams into his cabin. He was utterly numb with cold and fatigue and seasickness. He was just conscious, resentfully, that he must not fall, as he longed to do, fully clothed upon his cot – not for fear of rheumatism, but because there might be no chance for days of drying the cot's bedding if once he made it wet. And then here came Brown, materializing suddenly at his side – he must have been alert in the wardroom pantry on the watch for him.

'Let me take your coat, sir,' said Brown. 'You're cold, sir. I'll untie that scarf. Those buttons, sir. Sit down now and I'll be able to get those boots off, sir.'

Brown was stripping him of his wet clothes as if he were a baby. He produced a towel as if by magic, and chafed Hornblower's ribs with it; Hornblower felt life returning through his veins at the touch of the coarse material. Brown slipped a flannel nightshirt over his head, and then knelt on the swaying deck to chafe his legs and feet. Through Hornblower's dazed mind there passed a momentary amazement at Brown's efficiency. Brown was good at everything to which he turned his hand; he could knot and splice, and he could drive a pair of horses; he could carve model ships for Richard, and be tutor and nursemaid to the boy as well; heave the lead, hand and reef, and wait at table; take a trick at the wheel or carve a goose; undress a weary man and – just as important – know when to cut off his flow of soothing remarks and lay him down in silence and pull the blankets over him, leaving him alone without any trite or irritating words about hoping he slept well. In Hornblower's last tumultuous thoughts before exhaustion plunged him into sleep he decided that Brown was a far more useful member of society than he himself was; that if in his boyhood Brown had been taught his letters and his figures, and if chance had brought him to the quarterdeck as a king's letter-boy instead of to the lower deck as a pressed man, he would probably be a captain by now. And, significantly, hardly a trace of envy tinged Hornblower's thoughts of Brown; he was mellow enough by now to admire without resentment. Brown would make some woman a fine husband, as long as there was no other woman within reach. Hornblower smiled at that, and went on smiling in his sleep, seasickness and the plunging of the *Porta Coeli* over the short seas notwithstanding.

He woke later feeling refreshed and hungry, listened benevolently to the tumult of the noisy ship about him, and then poked his head out of the blankets and shouted for Brown. The sentry outside the cabin door took up the cry, and Brown came in almost immediately.

'What's the time?'

'Two bells, sir.'

'In which watch?'

'Afternoon watch, sir.'

He might have known that without asking. He had

been asleep for four hours, of course – nine years as a captain had not eradicated the habits acquired during a dozen years as a watchkeeping officer. The *Porta Coeli* stood up first on her tail and then on her nose as an unusually steep sea passed under her.

'The weather hasn't moderated?'

'Still blowin' a full gale, sir. West-sou'west. We're hove-to under maintopmast-stays'l and maintops'l with three reefs. Out o' sight o' land, an' no sail visible neither, sir.'

This was an aspect of war to which he should have grown used; endless delay with peril just over the horizon. He felt marvellously fortified by his four hours' sleep; his depression and his yearning for the end of the war had disappeared, not eradicated but overlain by the regained fatalism of the veteran. He stretched luxuriously in his heaving cot. His stomach was decidedly squeamish still, but, rested and recumbent as he was, it was not in active rebellion, whatever it might promise should he become active. And there was no need to be active! There was nothing for him to do if he should rise and dress. He had no watch to keep; by law he was merely a passenger; and until this gale blew itself out, or until some unforeseen danger should develop, there was nothing about which he need trouble his head. He had still plenty of sleep to make up; probably there were anxious and sleepless nights ahead of him when he should come to tackle the duty to which he had been assigned. He might just as well make the most of his present languor.

'Very good, Brown,' he said, imparting to his voice the flat indifference after which he always strove. 'Call me when the weather moderates.'

'Breakfast, sir?' The surprise in Brown's voice was apparent and most pleasurable to Hornblower; this was the one reaction on his restless captain's part which Brown had not anticipated. 'A bite o' cold beef an' a glass o' wine, sir?'

'No,' said Hornblower. His stomach would not keep them down, he feared, in any case.

'Nothing, sir?'

Hornblower did not even deign to answer him. He had shown himself unpredictable, and that was really something gained. Brown might at any time grow too proprietorial and too pleased with himself. This incident would put him in his place again, make him not quite so sure of his acquaintance with all his captain's moods. Hornblower believed he could never be a hero to Brown; he could at least be quirky. He gazed placidly up at the deck-beams over his nose until the baffled Brown withdrew, and then he snuggled down again, controlling an expostulatory heave of his stomach. Contented with his lot, he was satisfied to lie and doze and daydream. At the back of the west wind a brig full of mutineers awaited him. Well, although he was drifting away from them at a rate of a mile or two in the hour, he yet was approaching them as fast as it was in his power to do so. And Barbara had been so sweet.

He was sleeping so lightly at the end of the watch that he was roused by the bosun's calls turning out the watch below, a sound to which he should have been thoroughly used by now. He shouted for Brown and got out of bed, dressing hurriedly to catch the last of the daylight. Plunging out on deck, his eyes surveyed the same desolate scene as he had expected – an unbroken grey sky, a grey sea flecked with white, furrowed into the short steep rollers of the Channel. The wind still blew with gale force, the officers of the watch bending into it with their sou'westers pulled low over their eyes, and the watch crouching for shelter under the weather bulwarks forward.

Hornblower was aware, as he looked about him, of the commotion aroused by his appearance on deck. It was the first opportunity the ship's company of the *Porta Coeli* had had of seeing him in daylight. The midshipman of the watch, at a nudge from the master's mate, dived below, presumably to report his appearance to Freeman; there were other nudges observable among the hands forward. The huddle of dark tarpaulins showed a speckling of white as faces turned towards him. They were discussing him; Hornblower, who sank the *Natividad* in the Pacific, and fought the French fleet in Rosas Bay, and last year held Riga against all Boney's army.

Nowadays Hornblower could contemplate with a certain equanimity the possibility of being discussed by other people. There were undeniable achievements on his record, solid victories for which he had borne the responsibility and therefore deservedly wore the laurels. His weaknesses, his seasickness, and his moodiness, could be smiled at now instead of being laughed at. The gilded laurels were only tarnished to his own knowledge, and not to that of others. They did not know of his doubts and his hesitations, not even of his actual mistakes – they did not know, as he did, that if he had only called off the bomb-vessels at Riga five minutes earlier – as he should have done – young Mound would be still alive and a distinguished naval officer. Hornblower's handling of his squadron in the Baltic had been described in Parliament as 'the most perfect example in recent years of the employment of a naval force against an army'; Hornblower knew of the imperfections, but apparently other people could be blind to them. He could face his brethren in the profession, just as he could face his social equals. Now he had a wife of beauty and lineage, a wife with taste and tact, a wife to be proud of and not a wife he could only gloweringly dare the world to criticize – poor Maria in her forgotten grave in Southsea.

Freeman came climbing out of the hatchway, still fastening his oilskins; the two of them touched their hats to each other.

'The glass has begun to rise, sir,' shouted Freeman, his hands making a trumpet before his mouth. 'This'll blow itself out soon.'

Hornblower nodded, even while at that moment a bigger gust flogged his oilskins against his legs – the gustiness itself was a sign that the gale was nearing its end. The light was fast fading out of the grey sky; with sunset perhaps the wind would begin to moderate.

'Will you come round the ship with me?' yelled Hornblower, and this time it was Freeman's turn to nod. They walked forward, making their way with difficulty over the plunging, dripping decks, with Hornblower looking keenly about him. Two long guns forward – six-pounders; the rest of the armament twelve-pounder carronades. The breachings and preventer tackles were in good shape. Aloft, the rigging, both standing and running, was properly set up and cared for; but the best proof that the vessel was in good order lay in the fact that nothing had carried away during the weather of the last twenty-four hours. Freeman was a good captain; Hornblower knew that already. But it was not the guns, not even the vessel's weatherly qualities, which were of first importance in the present expedition. It was the human weapons that most mattered; Hornblower darted quick glances from side to side under his brows as he inspected the material of the brig – taking pains to observe the appearance and demeanour of the men. They seemed patient, not sullen, thank God. They were alert, seemingly ready for any duty. Hornblower dived down the fore-hatchway into the unspeakable din and stink of the battened-down 'tween-decks. There were sailors asleep in the fantastic fashion of the British tarpaulin – snoring heavily as they lay on the bare deck, despite the din about them. There were men huddled in gaming groups. He saw sleeves tugged and thumbs pointed as men caught sight of him – their first sight of the almost legendary Hornblower. An exchange of a nod and a wink. Hornblower, shrewdly estimating the feeling about him, guessed with pleasure that there was expectancy rather than resignation or reluctance.

It was an odd fact, but one whose existence could not be doubted, that men were pleased at the prospect of serving under him, Hornblower; the Hornblower, that is (qualified Hornblower), whom they thought existed, not the real actual Hornblower who wore the coat and trousers he was wearing. They hoped for victory, excitement, distinction, success; the poor fools. They did not stop to think that men died where Hornblower took command. The clear-headedness resulting from seasickness and an empty stomach (Hornblower could not remember when last he had eaten) allowed free play to a whole conflict of emotions within him; pleasure at being so gladly followed, pity for the thoughtless victims; a thrill of excitement at the thought of future action, and a wave of doubt regarding his ability to pluck success this time from the jaws of chance; pleasure, reluctantly admitted, at finding himself at sea and in command again, and regret, bitter and soul-searching, for the life he had just left, for Barbara's love and little Richard's trusting affection. Hornblower, noting his inward turmoil, cursed himself for a sentimental fool at the very moment when his sharp eye picked out a seaman who was knuckling his forehead and bobbing and grinning with embarrassed pleasure.

'I know you,' said Hornblower, searching feverishly through his memory. 'Let me see now. It must have been in the old *Indefatigable*.'

'That's right, sir. We was shipmates then, sir. And you worn't more'n a nipper, then, sir, beggin' your pardon, sir. Midshipman of the foretop, you was, sir.'

The seaman wiped his hand on the leg of his trousers before gingerly accepting the hand which Hornblower held out to him.

'Harding's your name,' said Hornblower, his memory coming to his rescue, with a tremendous effort. 'You taught me long splicing while we were off Ushant.'

'That's right, sir. 'Deed you're right, sir. That were ninety-two, or wore it ninety-three?'

'Ninety-three. I'm glad to know you're on board, Harding.'

'Thank you kindly, sir, I'm sure. Thank you kindly.'

Why should the whole vessel buzz with pleasure because he had recognized an old shipmate of twenty years back? Why should it make a ha'porth of difference? But it did; Hornblower knew it and felt it. It was hard to say whether pity or affection for his weak fellow-men held first place in the new complex of emotions which the incident aroused. Bonaparte might be doing the same thing at that same moment, recognizing in some German bivouac some old comrade-in-arms in the ranks of the Guard.

They had reached the after part of the brig now, and Hornblower turned to Freeman.

'I am going to dine, now, Mr Freeman,' he said. 'Perhaps after that we may be able to make some sail on the brig. I shall come on deck to see, in any case.'

'Aye aye, sir.'

Dinner; eaten seated on the small locker against the bulkhead. Cold salt beef – quite a good cut, tasty to a palate long accustomed to it and yet deprived of it for the last eleven months. 'Rexam's Superfine Ships' Biscuits' from a lead-lined box discovered and provided by Barbara – the best ships' bread which Hornblower had ever tasted, costing maybe twenty times as much as the weevily stuff he had eaten often enough before. A bite of red cheese, tangy and seasoned, admirably suited to accompany the second glass of claret. It was quite absurd that he should feel any satisfaction at having to lead this sort of life again, and yet he did. Undeniably, he did.

He wiped his mouth on his napkin, climbed into his oilskins, and went up on deck.

'The wind's dropped a little, Mr Freeman, I fancy.'

'I fancy it has, sir.'

In the darkness the *Porta Coeli* was riding to the wind almost easily, with a graceful rise and swoop. The seas overside could not be nearly as steep as they had been, and this was rain, not spray, in his face, and the feel of the rain told him that the worst of the storm was over.

'With the jib and the boom-mains'l both reefed, we can put her on the wind, sir,' said Freeman, tentatively.

'Very well, Mr Freeman. Carry on.'

There was a special skill about sailing a brig, especially, of course, on a wind. Under jib and staysails and the boom-mainsail she could be handled like a fore-and-aft rigged vessel; Hornblower knew it all theoretically, but he also knew that his practice would be decidedly rusty, especially in the dark and with a gale blowing. He was well content to remain in the background and let Freeman do what he would. Freeman bellowed his orders; with a mighty creaking of blocks the reefed boom-mainsail rose up the mast while men on the dizzy yard got in the maintopsail. The brig was hove-to on the starboard tack, and as the effect of the jib made itself felt she began to pay off a little.

'Mains'l sheets!' bellowed Freeman, and to the man at the wheel, 'Steady as you go!'

The rudder met and counteracted the tendency of the *Porta Coeli* to fall off, and the boom-mainsail caught the wind and forced her forward. In a moment the *Porta Coeli* changed from something quiescent and acquiescent into something fierce and desperate. She ceased to yield to wind and sea, ceased to let them hurtle past her; now she met them, she fought against them, battled with them. She was like some tigress previously content to evade the hunters by slinking from cover to cover, but now hurling herself on her tormentors mad with fighting fury. The wind laid her over, the spray burst in sheets across her bows. Her gentle rise and swoop were transformed into an illogical jerky motion as she met the steep waves with immovable resolution; she lurched and she shuddered as she battered her way through the waves. The forces of the world, the old primitive powers that had ruled earth and water since the creation, were being set at defiance by man, weak, mortal man, who by virtue of the brain inside his fragile skull was able not merely to face the forces of the world but to bend them to his will, compel them to serve him. Nature sent this brisk westerly gale up the Channel; subtly and insidiously the *Porta Coeli* was making use of it to claw her way westward – a slow, painful, difficult way, but westward all the same. Hornblower, standing by the wheel, felt a surge of exultation as the *Porta Coeli* thrashed forward. He was like Prometheus stealing fire from the gods; he was the successful rebel against the blind laws of nature; he could take pride in being a mere mortal man.

5

Freeman bent over the tallow that armed the bottom of the lead; a seaman held a lantern at his shoulder so as to let the light fall upon it. The master's mate and midshipman of the watch completed the group, a vignette of blackness and light in the massive darkness all around. Freeman was not hasty in reaching his decision; he peered at the sample brought up from the bottom of the sea first from one angle and then from another. He sniffed at it; he applied a forefinger to it and then carried the finger to his tongue.

'Sand and black shell,' he mused to himself.

Hornblower held back from the group; this was something Freeman could do better than he, although it would be nearly blasphemy to say so in public, seeing that he was a captain and Freeman a mere lieutenant.

'Maybe we're off Antifer,' said Freeman at length. He looked out of the light into the darkness towards where Hornblower was standing.

'Lay her on the other tack, if you please, Mr Freeman. And keep the lead going.'

Creeping about in the night off the treacherous Normandy coast was a nervous business, even though in the past twenty-four hours the wind had moderated to nothing more than a strong breeze. But Freeman knew what he was about; a dozen years spent in handling vessels in the soundings round the fringes of Europe had given him knowledge and insight obtainable in no other way. Hornblower had to trust Freeman's judgement; he himself with compass and lead and chart might do a good workmanlike job, but to rate himself above Freeman as a Channel pilot would be ridiculous. 'Maybe,' Freeman had said; but Hornblower could value that 'maybe' at its true worth. Freeman was confident about it. The *Porta Coeli* was off Cape Antifer, then, a trifle farther to leeward than he wished to be when dawn should come. He still had no plan in his head about how to deal with the *Flame* when he met her; there was no way round, as far as he could see, the simple geometrical difficulty that the mutineers, with Le Havre open to them on one side and Caen on the other, could not be cut off from taking refuge with the French if they wished to; for that matter, there were a dozen other inlets on the coast, all heavily protected by batteries, where the *Flame* could find a refuge. And any forcing of the matter might result easily enough in Chadwick being hoisted up to his yardarm, to dangle there as a dead man – the most horrible and dangerous incident in the history of the Navy since the murder of Pigott. But contact had to be made with the mutineers – that was clearly the first thing to do – and there was at least no harm in trying to make that contact at a point as advantageous as possible. Some miracle might happen; he must try and put himself across the course of wandering miracles. What was it that Barbara had said to him once? 'The lucky man is he who knows how much to leave to chance.' Barbara had too good an opinion of him, even after all this time, but there was truth in what she said.

The *Porta Coeli* went smartly about, and reached to

the north-westward, close-hauled to the south-westerly wind.

'The tide starts to make about now, Sir Horatio,' said Freeman, beside him.

'Thank you.'

That was an additional bit of data in the problem of the morrow which was not yet fully revealed to him. War was as unlike spherical trigonometry as anything could be, thought Hornblower, grinning at the inconsequence of his thoughts. Often one approached a problem in war without knowing what it was one wanted to achieve, to prove, or construct, and without even knowing fully what means were available for doing it. War was generally a matter of slipshod, makeshift, hit-or-miss extemporization. Even if it were not murderous and wasteful it would still be no trade for a man who enjoyed logic. Yet maybe he was taking too flattering a view of himself; maybe some other officer – Cochrane, say, or Lidyard – would, if in his position, already have a plan worked out for dealing with the mutineers, a plan that could not fail to bring satisfactory results.

Four bells rang out sharply; they had been over half an hour on this tack.

'Kindly go about on the other tack, Mr Freeman. I don't want to get too far from land.'

'Aye aye, sir.'

If it was not for the war, no captain in his senses would dream for a moment of plunging about in the darkness on this shoal coast, especially when he was extremely doubtful of his exact position – their present estimate was the sum of a series of guesses, guesses about the leeway made while hove-to, guesses at the effects of the tides, guesses at the correspondence between soundings taken overside and soundings marked on the chart.

'What do you think the mutineers will do, sir, when they sight us?' asked Freeman.

The fact that Hornblower had unbent enough to give an explanation of why he wanted to go about must have encouraged Freeman to this familiarity; Hornblower was irritated, but most of all because he had no thoughts on the matter.

'There's no profit in asking questions which time will surely answer, Mr Freeman,' he said, tartly.

'Yet speculation is a fascinating thing, Sir Horatio,' replied Freeman, so unabashed that Hornblower stared at him in the darkness. Bush, if Hornblower had spoken to him in that fashion, would have retired wounded into his shell.

'You may indulge yourself in it if you so desire, Mr Freeman. I have no intention of doing so.'

'Thank you, Sir Horatio.'

Now was there, or was there not, a hint of mockery behind the hint of subservience in that reply? Was it possible that Freeman could actually be smiling inwardly at his superior officer? If so, he was running a fearful risk; a suggestion of dissatisfaction in Hornblower's future report to the Admiralty would put Freeman on the beach for life. But Hornblower knew, the moment the thought came into his head, that he would do no such thing. He could never blast an able man's career just because that man had not treated him with slavish respect.

'Water's shoaling fast, sir,' said Freeman, suddenly –

both he and Hornblower had subconsciously been listening to the cry of the leadsman in the chains. 'I should like to go about again.'

'Certainly, Mr Freeman,' said Hornblower, formally.

They were creeping round Cape de la Hève, the northerly point of the Seine estuary, just within which lies Le Havre. There was a chance, a tiny one, that they might find themselves at dawn both to leeward of the *Flame* and between her and France so that she would have no means of escape at all. And the night was wearing on; it would not be long now before daylight.

'You have a good man at the masthead, Mr Freeman?'

'Yes, Sir Horatio.'

He would have to tell the hands about the mission on which they had been sent, even though that meant violating the secrecy surrounding the mutiny. Normally there would be little enough need to confide in the hands; British seamen, fatalistic after twenty years of war, would fire into Frenchmen or Americans or Dutchmen without much thought about the rights or wrongs; but to ask them to fight against a sister-ship, to fire into a British vessel, which might, for all he knew, still be wearing her commissioning pendant and her White Ensign, might cause hesitation if he called upon them to do so without some preliminary warning. A careful officer would in ordinary circumstances never breathe the word 'mutiny' to his men; no lion-tamer would ever remind the lion that the lion was stronger than he. It was almost daylight.

'Would you be so good as to turn up the hands, Mr Freeman? I wish to address them.'

'Aye aye, sir.'

The pipes wailed through the brig, and the watch below came streaming up through the hatchway, pouring sleepily aft; the poor devils were losing an hour of sleep because of the inconsiderate way in which dawn did not correspond with the end of the watch. Hornblower looked round for some point of vantage from which he could address them; in a flush-decked vessel like the *Porta Coeli* he had not the advantage of speaking down into a waist from a quarterdeck. He swung himself up on to the weather bulwark, balancing himself with a hand on the mainbackstay.

'Men,' he said, 'are you wondering what has sent you out here?'

Maybe they were, but the rather sleepy, apathetic, breakfastless lines before him showed little sign of it.

'Are you wondering what has sent me out to sea with you?'

By God, they *were* wondering that. There must have been speculation on the lower deck as to why a full commodore – and not only a commodore, but Hornblower of the legendary past – should have been sent to sea in a mere eighteen-gun brig. It was flattering to see a movement of interest in the lines, a lifting of heads, even while Hornblower cursed at fate for having to make use of rhetorical tricks, and more for having to exploit his own personal renown.

'There is villainy afloat,' said Hornblower. 'British seamen have disgraced themselves. They have mutinied in the very presence of the enemy.'

He had the men's interest now, without a doubt. He had said the word 'mutiny' to these slaves of the lash and the whistle. Mutiny, the remedy for all their ills, which would give them freedom from the hardship of their lives, the cruelty and the danger, the foul food and the severance from all the amenities of life. One crew had mutinied. Why should not they do so too? He would have to tell them about the *Flame*, remind them that close at hand lay the shores of France, where Bonaparte would gladly heap wealth and luxury upon any British seaman who brought a British ship of war over to him. Hornblower let a note of contempt creep into his voice.

'The crew of the *Flame*, our own sister-ship, has done this thing. Now they are sheltering here in this very Bay of the Seine. Every man's hand is against them. The French have no use for mutineers, and it is our mission to dig these rats from their holes. They have betrayed England, forgotten their duty to King and Country. I expect most of them are honest but stupid, led astray by a few designing villains. It is those villains who must pay the price of their villainy, and we must see they have no chance of escape. If they are mad enough to offer fight, then we must fight them. If they surrender without bloodshed, that fact will be remembered in their favour when they are brought to trial. I want no bloodshed if I can help it – you know as well as I do that a cannon shot will kill a man without stopping to ask whether he is a villain or just a fool. But if they want bloodshed, then we shall let them have it.'

Hornblower ended his speech, and looked over to Freeman to dismiss the men. It was a cheerless business making a speech to hungry men in a grey dawn, but Hornblower, darting glances at the men as they went about their business, saw that there was nothing to fear from the ship's company. They were buzzing with talk, of course, but news of mutiny would set any crew a-buzz, just as a village would be set a-buzz by news of a local murder. But it was only gossipy talk, he could see; the men were not making any deductions from the news. He had presented the case to them in such a way as to make it obvious to them that he expected them to obey his orders for dealing with the mutineers, and he had let no hint creep into his speech of his fear that they should be tempted to follow their example. That had not occurred to them yet – but it might, if they were allowed to ruminate over it. He must see that they were kept busy; the ordinary ship's routine was attending to that at the moment, for they were at work on the opening business of every naval day, washing down the decks before being piped to breakfast.

'Land!' yelled a voice from the masthead. 'Land on the port bow.'

It was rather thick weather, typical Channel weather for the end of the year, but in the growing light Hornblower could see the dark line against the grey. Freeman was scrutinizing the coast through his glass.

'That's the south shore of the Bay,' said Freeman. 'There's the Cane river.'

Hornblower was only just beginning to realize that Freeman was anglicizing the pronunciation of 'Caen' when Freeman trained his telescope round and gave a string of more surprising examples still of what an Englishman can do to French names.

'Yes, there's Cape dee lay Heave, and Harbour-Grace,' he said.

The growing light revealed the *Porta Coeli's* position,

over towards the southern shore of the estuary of the Seine.

'That was an excellent piece of navigation last night, Mr Freeman.'

'Thank you, Sir Horatio.'

Hornblower would have added more words of warmer praise, if it had not been for Freeman's rather chilling manner; he supposed Freeman was entitled to be short-tempered before breakfast if he wished. And any capable lieutenant was entitled to be jealous of a captain; in the opinion of every ambitious lieutenant a captain was just a lieutenant who had been lucky and who would continue to be lucky, drawing three times a lieutenant's pay and prize money, reaping the harvest of the lieutenant's labours, and secure in the knowledge that time would make an admiral of him in the end while the lieutenant's promotion still depended on the whims of his superiors. Hornblower could remember feeling just the same when he was a lieutenant; for Freeman to show it was natural even though foolish.

The leadsman's cry in the chains indicated that the water was shoaling again; they had left the middle ground far behind them and had now crossed the southerly channel of the estuary. There was still plenty of water for the *Porta Coeli*; she had been expressly designed for this very purpose of penetrating into inlets and estuaries, carrying the war as close to Bonaparte's shores as might be. Bonaparte's dominion stopped short at the line which the shot from his shore batteries could reach, and beyond that line England ruled supreme and unchallenged.

'Sail on the lee bow!' yelled the lookout.

Freeman swung himself up to the lee mainshrouds with the agility of an ape; braced against the ratlines, he trained his glass forward.

'A brig, sir,' he hailed down to Hornblower, and a few seconds later 'That's *Flame* all right, sir.'

'Put the helm up and we'll bear down on her, Mr Freeman, if you please.'

Flame was exactly where one would expect to find her, close up under the lee of the land, sheltered from any gale from north-west round to the east; and free to consult her own safety whether attacked by British or French. Soon Hornblower's own glass picked her out from the grey murk. A trim, beautiful little vessel, lying hove-to on the edge of the shoals. She showed no signs, at that distance at least, of any disorder on board. Hornblower wondered how many telescopes there were being trained upon the *Porta Coeli*, what anxious debate was being held on board by men recognizing the new arrival as the first move on the part of their lordships of the Admiralty in reply to their suicidal ultimatum. Those men had ropes round their necks.

'She's waiting for us to come down to her,' said Freeman.

'I wonder for how long,' answered Hornblower.

'What are you men standing chattering there for?' suddenly blared out Freeman, addressing a group of excited seamen lining the bulwark forward. 'Master-at-arms! Master-at-arms! Take those men's names and bring them to me at the end of the watch! You bosun's mate, there! Collier! Keep those men of yours at work! This is a King's ship, not a blasted school for young ladies!'

A thin beam of watery sunshine broke through the greyness and lit up the *Flame* as she lay in the circle of Hornblower's glass. He suddenly saw her yards swing round; she put herself before the wind and began to move in the direction of Honfleur. Her foretopsail was conspicuously patched – a light cross against the darker material, as if she were some Crusading ship.

'They won't stand and wait for us,' said Freeman.

'Sail ho!' yelled the lookout again. 'Sail on the lee quarter!'

Telescopes swung round as if all were actuated by a single machine. A big ship with all plain sail set to the royals had appeared out of the mist beyond the middle ground, on a course rapidly diverging from that of the *Porta Coeli*. Hornblower recognized her instantly for what she was, and did not need Freeman's identification.

'French West Indiaman,' said Freeman. 'With a clear run to Harbour-Grace.'

One of the rare ships to run the continental blockade, bearing an invaluable cargo of grain and sugar to ease Bonaparte's distress; she had taken advantage of the recent gale, which had blown the blockading squadrons from their stations, to dash up the Channel. A cargo delivered into the Seine, where centred the Imperial power, and whence diverged the whole road and canal systems, was worth two brought into some isolated inlet on the Biscay coast. The small British vessels of war, like the *Porta Coeli* and the *Flame*, had been constructed and stationed to prevent this very thing.

'There'll be no catching her before she reaches Harbour-Grace,' muttered Freeman.

'Let her go, Mr Freeman,' said Hornblower, loudly.

'Our duty's with *Flame* at present. There goes ten pounds a man prize money.'

There were enough hands within earshot to hear that speech; they would repeat it to the rest of the crew. No one who thought of the lost prize money would feel any better disposed towards the mutineers.

Hornblower turned his attention back to the *Flame*; she was standing steadily and without hesitation on a course which would take her into Honfleur. It would not be long before she was in French power, and it would be foolish to press matters to such an extreme, even though it was a bitter pill to swallow, to admit a check.

'Oh, heave-to, Mr Freeman, please. Let's see what she does then.'

The *Porta Coeli* came up into the wind in response to sail and helm, Hornblower training round his glass to keep *Flame* under observation. The moment the *Porta Coeli's* manoeuvre became apparent, the *Flame* imitated it, coming up into the wind and lying motionless, the white cross conspicuous on her foretopsail.

'Try bearing down on them again, Mr Freeman.'

Flame turned away instantly towards France.

'A wink's as good as a nod, Mr Freeman. Heave-to again.'

Clearly the mutineers had no intention of allowing the *Porta Coeli* to come any nearer than she was at present, well beyond cannonshot. She would hand herself over to the French sooner than permit any closer approach.

'Mr Freeman, will you be so good as to have a boat hoisted out for me? I'll go and parley with the villains.'

That would be a sign of weakness, but the mutineers could be in no doubt about the weakness of his position and the corresponding strength of their own. It would be telling them nothing they did not know already, that they held Hornblower and the Lords of the Admiralty and the British Empire itself in a cleft stick. Freeman showed no signs of his doubts regarding the advisability of a valuable captain putting himself in the power of mutineers. Hornblower went below to pocket his orders; it might even be necessary to show the mutineers the full powers with which he had been entrusted – but it would be only in the last resort that he would do so; that would be letting the mutineers too much into Their Lordships' confidence. The boat was overside with Brown at the tiller when Hornblower came on deck again; Hornblower went down the side and settled himself into the sternsheets.

'Give way!' ordered Brown; the oars bit the water and the boat began to crawl towards the *Flame*, dancing over the little waves of the estuary.

Hornblower watched the brig as they approached; she lay hove-to, but Hornblower could see that her guns were run out and her boarding-nettings rigged, and she had clearly no intention of being taken by surprise. The hands were at their guns, there were lookouts aloft, a warrant officer aft with a telescope under his arm – not a sign in the world of mutiny on board.

'Boat ahoy!' came the hail across the water.

Brown held up his four fingers, the universal signal that there was a captain in the boat – four fingers for the four sideboys demanded by ceremonial.

'Who are ye?' hailed the voice.

Brown looked around at Hornblower, received a nod from him, and hailed back.

'Commodore Sir Horatio Hornblower, KB.'

'We'll allow Commodore Hornblower on board, but no one else. Come alongside, and we've cold shot here to drop into you if you play any tricks.'

Hornblower reached for the mainchains and swung himself up into them; a seaman raised the boarding-nettings so that he could struggle under them to the deck.

'Kindly tell your boat to sheer off, Commodore. We're taking no risks,' said a voice.

It was a white-haired old man who addressed him, the telescope under his arm marking him out as officer of the watch. White hair fluttered about his ears; sharp blue eyes in a wrinkled face looked at Hornblower from under white brows. The only thing in the least bizarre about his appearance was a pistol stuck in his belt. Hornblower turned and gave the required order.

'And now may I ask your business here, Commodore?' asked the old man.

'I wish to speak to the leader of the mutineers.'

'I am captain of this ship. You can address yourself to me, Nathaniel Sweet, sir.'

'I have addressed myself to you as far as I desire, unless you are also the leader of the mutineers.'

'Then if you have done so, you can call back your boat and leave us, sir.'

An impasse already. Hornblower kept his eyes on the blue ones of the old man. There were several other men within earshot, but he could sense no wavering or doubt among them; they were prepared to support their captain. Yet it might be worth while speaking to them.

'Men!' said Hornblower, raising his voice.

'Belay that!' rapped out the old man. He whipped the pistol out of his belt and pointed it at Hornblower's stomach. 'One more word out of turn and you'll get an ounce of lead through you.'

Hornblower looked steadily back at him and his weapon; he was curiously unafraid, feeling as if he were watching move and counter-move in some chess game, without remembering that he himself was one of the pawns in it with his life at stake.

'Kill me,' he said with a grim smile, 'and England won't rest until you're swinging on a gallows.'

'England has sent you here to swing me on a gallows as it is,' said Sweet, bleakly.

'No,' said Hornblower. 'I am here to recall you to your duty to King and Country.'

'Letting bygones be bygones?'

'You will have to stand a fair trial, you and your confederates.'

'That means the gallows, as I said,' replied Sweet. 'The gallows for me, and I should be fortunate compared with some of these others.'

'A fair and honest trial,' said Hornblower, 'with every mitigating circumstance taken into consideration.'

'The only trial I would attend,' replied the old man, 'would be to bear witness against Chadwick. Full pardon for us – a fair trial for Chadwick. Those are our terms, sir.'

'You are foolish,' said Hornblower. 'You are throwing away your last chance. Surrender now, with Mr Chadwick unbound and the ship in good order, and those circumstances will weigh heavily in your favour at your trial. Refuse, and what have you to look for? Death. That is all. Death. What can save you from our country's vengeance? Nothing.'

'Begging your pardon, Captain, but Boney can,' interposed the old man, drily.

'You trust Bonaparte's word?' said Hornblower, rallying desperately before this unexpected counter-attack. 'He'd like to have this ship, no doubt. But you and your gang? Bonaparte won't encourage mutiny – his power rests too much on his own army. He'll hand you back for us to make an example of you.'

It was a wild shot in the dark, and it missed its bull's-eye by an unmeasurable distance. Sweet stuck his pistol back into his belt and produced three letters from his pocket, waving them tauntingly in front of Hornblower.

'Here's a letter from the Military Governor of Harbour-Grace,' he said. 'That only promises us welcome. And here's a letter from the Prefect of the Department of the Inferior Seine. That promises us provisions and water should we need them. And here's a letter from Paris, sent down to us by post. It promises us immunity from arrest, civil rights in France, and a pension for every man from the age of sixty. That is signed "Marie Louise, Empress, Queen, and Regent". Boney won't go back on his wife's word, sir.'

'You've been in communication with the shore?' gasped Hornblower. It was quite impossible for him to make any pretence at composure.

'We have,' said the old man. 'And if *you* had the chance before you, Captain, of being flogged round the fleet, you would have done the same.'

It was hopeless to continue the present discussion. At least at the moment, the mutineers were unassailable. The only terms to which they would listen would be their own. There was no sign of doubt or dissension on board. But maybe if they were allowed more time to think about it, maybe if they had a few hours in which to consider the fact that Hornblower himself was on their trail, doubt might creep in. A party might form determined to save their necks by recapturing the ship; they might get at the liquor – Hornblower was completely puzzled by the fact that a mutinous British crew was not all roaring drunk – *something* might happen. But he must make a fighting retreat, not ignominiously crawl overside with his tail between his legs.

'So you are traitors as well as mutineers?' he blared. 'I might have expected it. I might have guessed what kind of curs you are. I won't foul my lungs by breathing the same air as you.'

He turned to the side and hailed for his boat.

'We're the kind of curs,' said the old man 'who will let you go when we could clap you down below in the orlop with Chadwick. We could give you a taste of the cat, Commodore Sir Horatio Hornblower. How would you like *that*, sir? Remember, tomorrow, that the flesh is still on your ribs because *we* spared you. Good morning to you, Captain.'

There was sting and venom in those last words; they called up pictures in Hornblower's imagination that made his flesh creep. He did not feel in the least dignified as he wriggled under the boarding-netting.

The *Flame* still rode peacefully to the wind as the boat danced back over the waves. Hornblower gazed from the *Flame* to the *Porta Coeli*, the two sister-ships, identical in appearance save for the white cross-shaped patch on the *Flame*'s foretopsail. It was ironical that not even a trained eye could see any difference in appearance between the brig that was loyal to the King and the brig that was in open rebellion against him. The thought increased his bitterness; he had failed, utterly and completely, in his first attempt to win over the mutineers. He did not think there was the least possibility of their abating their terms; he would have to choose between agreeing to them, between promising the mutineers a free pardon and driving them into the hands of Bonaparte. In either case he would have failed in his mission; the merest least experienced midshipman in the Navy could have done as much. There was still some time to spare, for there was still little chance of news of the mutiny leaking out, but unless time brought dissension among the mutineers – and he saw no chance of that – it would be merely wasted time as far as he could see.

The boat was now halfway between the two brigs; with those two vessels under his command he could wage a lively war against the Normandy coast; he felt in his bones that he could set the whole Seine estuary in an uproar. His bitterness surged up stronger still, and then abruptly checked itself. An idea had come to him, and with the idea all the well-known old symptoms, the dryness in his throat, the tingling in his legs, the accelerated heartbeat. He swept his glance back and forth between the two brigs, excitement welling up inside him: calculations of wind and tide and daylight already formulating themselves, unsummoned, in his mind.

'Pull harder you men,' he said to the boat's crew, and they obeyed him, but the gig could not possibly travel fast enough to satisfy him in his new mood.

Brown was looking at him sidelong, wondering what plan was evoking itself in his captain's brain; Brown himself – as well aware of the circumstances as Hornblower was – could see no possible way out of the situation. All he knew was that his captain looked back over his shoulder time and time again at the mutinous brig.

'Oars!' growled Brown to the boat's crew, as the officer of the watch gave the signal to the boat to come alongside; the bowman hooked on to the chains, and Hornblower went up the brig's side with a clumsy impetuosity that he could not restrain. Freeman was waiting for him on the quarterdeck, and Hornblower's hand was still at his hat when he gave his first order.

'Will you pass the word for the sailmaker, Mr Freeman? And I shall want his mates, and every hand who can use a needle and palm.'

'Aye aye, sir.'

Orders were orders, even when they dealt with such extraneous matters as making sails while negotiating with a mutinous crew. Hornblower stared over at the *Flame*, still lying hove-to out of gunshot. The mutineers held a strong, an unassailable position, one which no frontal attack could break, and whose flanks were impregnable. It would be a very roundabout route that could turn such a position; maybe he had thought of one. There were some odd circumstances in his favour, fortunate coincidences. It was his business to seize upon those, exploit them to the utmost. He would have to take reckless chances, but he would do everything in his power to reduce the chances against him. The lucky man is he who knows how much to leave to chance.

A stoop-shouldered seaman was awaiting his attention, Freeman at his side.

'Swenson, sailmaker's mate, sir.'

'Thank you, Mr Freeman. You see that patched foretops'l? Swenson, look at it well through this glass.'

The Swedish sailmaker took the telescope in his gnarled hands and levelled it to his eye.

'Mr Freeman, I want *Porta Coeli* to have a foretops'l just like that, so that no eye can see any difference between the two. Can that be done?'

Freeman looked at Swenson.

'Aye aye, sir, I can do that,' said Swenson, glancing from Freeman to Hornblower and back again. 'There's a bolt o' white duck canvas, an' with the old foretops'l – I can do it, sir.'

'I want it finished and ready to bend by four bells in the afternoon watch. Start work on it now.'

A little group had formed behind Swenson, those members of the crew whom inquiry had ascertained to have sailmaking experience. There were broad grins on some of their faces; Hornblower seemed to be conscious of a little wave of excitement and anticipation spreading through the crew like a ripple over a pond set up by the stone dropped into it in the form of Hornblower's unusual request. No one could see clearly as yet what was in Hornblower's mind, but they knew that he intended some devilment. The knowledge was a better tonic to discipline and the happiness of the ship than any ordinary ship's routine.

'Now see here, Mr Freeman,' said Hornblower, moving towards the rail. 'What I propose is this – *Flame* and *Porta Coeli* are as like as two peas and they'll be liker yet as soon as we have that foretops'l set. The mutineers have been in communication with the shore; they told me so, and, what's more, Mr Freeman, the place they've had dealings with is Le Havre – Harbour-Grace, Mr Freeman. Boney and the governor have promised them money and immunity to bring the *Flame* in. We'll go in instead. There's that West Indiaman we saw come in this morning.'

'We'll bring her out, sir!'

'Maybe we will. God knows what we'll find inside, but we'll go in ready for anything. Pick twenty men and an officer, men you can rely on. Give each one his orders about what he is to do if we have a chance to take a prize – heads'ls, tops'ls, wheel, cutting the cable. You know about all that as well as I do. It'll be just at dusk that we stand in, if the wind doesn't change, and I don't think it will. It'll be strange if in the dark we don't contrive something to annoy the Frogs.'

'By God, sir, an' they'll think it's the mutineers! They'll think the mutiny was just a sham! They'll –'

'I hope they will, Mr Freeman.'

6

It was late afternoon when the *Porta Coeli*, apparently unable to reach any decision, stood away from the *Flame* and crossed the broad estuary with the wind blowing briskly on her port beam. The thick weather still persisted; she was far enough both from *Flame* and from Le Havre for the details to be quite obscure when she took in her foretopsail and substituted for it the patched one which an enthusiastic gang of toilers had made ready on deck abaft the foremast. Hurried work with paint-brush and paint erased one name and substituted the other; Hornblower and Freeman wore their plain pea-jackets over their uniforms, concealing their rank. Freeman kept his glass trained on the harbour as they stood in.

'That's the Indiaman, sir. At anchor. And there's a lighter beside her. O' course, they wouldn't unload her at the quay. Not here, sir. They'd put her cargo into lighters an' barges, and send 'em up the river, to Rouen and Paris. O' course they would. I ought to ha' thought o' that before.' Hornblower had already thought of it. His glass was sweeping the defences of the town; the forts of Ste Adresse and Tourneville on the steep cliff above the town; the twin lighthouses on Cape de la Hève – which for a dozen years had not shown a light – the batteries on the low ground beside the old jetty. These last would be the great danger to the enterprise; he hoped that the big forts above would not know of what was going on down below in time to open fire.

'There's a lot of shipping farther in, sir,' went on Freeman. 'Might even be ships of the line. They haven't their yards crossed. I've never been in as close as this before.'

Hornblower turned to look at the western sky. Night was fast falling, and the thick weather on the horizon showed no signs of clearing. He wanted light enough to find his way, and darkness enough to cover him on his way out.

'Here's the pilot lugger standing out, sir,' said Freeman. 'They'll think we're *Flame* all right.'

'Very good, Mr Freeman. Set the men to cheering at the ship's side. Secure the pilot when he comes on board. I'll con her in.'

'Aye aye, sir.'

It was just the sort of order to suit the temperament of British seamen. They entered wholeheartedly into the spirit of the thing, yelling like lunatics along the bulwarks, waving their hats, dancing exuberantly, just as one would expect of a horde of mutineers. The *Porta Coeli* backed her maintopsail, the lugger surged alongside, and the pilot swung himself into the mainchains.

'Lee braces!' roared Hornblower, the maintopsail caught the wind again, the wheel went over, and the *Porta Coeli* stood into the harbour, while Freeman put his shoulder between the pilot's shoulder blades and shot him neatly down the hatchway where two men were waiting to seize and pinion him.

'Pilot secured, sir,' he reported.

He, too, was obviously carried away by the excitement of the moment, infected even by the din the hands were making; his pose of amused irony had completely disappeared.

'Starboard a little,' said Hornblower to the helmsman. 'Meet her! Steady as you go!'

It would be the last word in ignominy if all their high hopes were to come to an end on the sandbanks guarding the entrance. Hornblower wondered if he would ever feel cool again.

'A cutter standing out to us, sir,' reported Freeman.

That might be a committee of welcome, or orders telling them where to berth – both at once, probably.

'Set the hands to cheering again,' ordered Hornblower. 'Have the boarding party secured as they come on board.'

'Aye aye, sir.'

They were nearing the big Indiaman; she lay, her sails loose, swinging to a single anchor. There was a lighter beside her, but obviously little enough had been done so far towards unloading her. In the fading light Hornblower could just make out a dozen of her seamen standing at the ship's side gazing curiously at them. Hornblower backed the maintopsail again, and the cutter came alongside, and half a dozen officials climbed onto the *Porta Coeli's* deck. Their uniforms proclaimed their connexion with the navy, the army, and the customs service, and they advanced slowly towards Hornblower, looking curiously about them as they did so. Hornblower was giving the orders that got the *Porta Coeli* under way again, and as she drew away from the cutter in the gathering darkness he wore her round and headed her for the Indiaman. Cutlasses suddenly gleamed about the new arrivals.

'Make a sound and you're dead men,' said Freeman.

Somebody made a sound, beginning to protest volubly. A seaman brought a pistol butt down on his head and the protests ended abruptly as the protester clattered on the deck. The others were hustled down the hatchway, too dazed and startled to speak.

'Very well, Mr Freeman,' said Hornblower, drawling the words so as to convey the impression that he felt perfectly at home here in the middle of a hostile harbour. 'You may hoist out the boats. Maintops'l aback!'

The shore authorities would be watching the brig's movements by what little light was left. If the *Porta Coeli* did anything unexpected, they would wonder idly what unknown condition on board had caused the harbour-master's representative – now gagged and bound under hatches – to change his plans. The *Porta Coeli*'s motion died away; the sheaves squealed as the boats dropped into the water, and the picked crews tumbled down into them. Hornblower leaned over the side.

'Remember men, don't fire a shot!'

The oars splashed as the boats pulled over to the Indiaman. It was practically dark by now; Hornblower could hardly follow the boats to the Indiaman's side fifty yards away, and he could see nothing of the men as they swarmed up her side. Faintly he heard some startled exclamations, and then one loud cry; that might puzzle the people on shore, but would not put them on their guard. Here were the boats returning, each pulled by the two men detailed for the work. The tackles were hooked on and the boats swayed up; as the sheaves squealed again Hornblower heard a crunching sound from the Indiaman, and a dull thump or two – the hand detailed to cut the cable was doing his work, and had actually remembered to carry the axe with him when he went up the ship's side. Hornblower felt the satisfaction of a job well done; his careful instruction of the boarding party in the afternoon, his methodical allocation of duties to each individual man, and his reiteration of his orders until everyone thoroughly understood the part he had to play were bearing fruit.

Against the misty sky he saw the Indiaman's topsails changing shape; the men allotted to the task were sheeting them home. Thank God for a few prime seamen who, arriving in darkness in a strange ship, could find their way to the right places and lay their hands on the right lines without confusion. Hornblower saw the Indiaman's yards come round; in the darkness he could just see a black blur detach itself from her side, the lighter, cut adrift and floating away.

'You can square away, Mr Freeman, if you please,' he said. 'The Indiaman will follow us out.'

The *Porta Coeli* gathered way and headed for the south-eastern exit of the harbour, the Indiaman close at her stern. For several long seconds there was no sign of any interest being taken in these movements. Then came a hail, apparently from the cutter which had brought the officials aboard. It was so long since Hornblower had heard or spoken French that he could not understand the words used.

'*Comment?*' he yelled back through the speaking-trumpet.

An irascible voice asked him again what in the name of the Devil he thought he was doing.

'Anchorage – mumble – current – mumble – tide,' yelled Hornblower in reply.

This time the unknown in the cutter invoked the name of God instead of that of the Devil.

'Who in God's name is that?'

'Mumble mumble mumble,' bellowed Hornblower back again, and quietly to the helmsman, 'Bring her slowly round to port.'

Carrying on a conversation with the French authorities while taking a vessel down an involved channel – however well he had memorized the latter on the chart – taxed his resources.

'Heave-to!' yelled the voice.

'Pardon, Captain,' yelled Hornblower back. 'Mumble – anchor-cable – mumble – impossible.'

Another loud hail from the cutter, full of menace.

'Steady as you go,' cried Hornblower to the helmsman. 'Mr Freeman, a hand at the lead, if you please.'

He knew there was no chance of gaining any more precious seconds; by the time the leadsman was calling the depths and revealing the brig's design of evasion the shore authorities would be fully alert. A pinpoint of light stabbed the thin mist and the sound of a musket-shot came over the water; the cutter was taking the quickest method of attracting the attention of the shore batteries.

'Stand by to go about!' rasped Hornblower; this was the most ticklish moment of the outward passage.

The brig's canvas volleyed as she came round, and simultaneously there was a bigger tongue of red flame in the darkness and the sound of the cutter's six-pounder bow-chaser, cleared away and loaded at last. Hornblower heard no sound of the ball. He was busy looking back at the Indiaman, dimly showing in the minute light of the brig's wake. She was coming about neatly. That master's mate – Calverly – whom Freeman had recommended for the command of the boarding party was a capable officer, and must be highly praised when the time should come to send in a report.

And then from the jetty came a succession of flashes and a rolling roar; the big thirty-two-pounders there had opened fire at last. The sound of the last shot was instantly followed by the noise of a ball passing close by; Hornblower had time somehow to note how much he hated that noise. They were having to round the jetty, and would be within range for several minutes. There was no sign of damage either to the brig or the Indiaman as yet – and there was nothing in favour of returning the fire, for the brig's little six-pounders would make no impression on the solid battery, while the flashes would reveal the vessel's position. He took note of the cry of the leadsman; it would be some minutes before he could tack again and stand directly away from the jetty. It was a long time, on the other hand, before the battery fired again. Bonaparte must have stripped his shore defences of seasoned gunners in order to man the artillery of his army in Germany; untrained recruits, called upon suddenly to man their guns, and working in darkness, would naturally be unhandy. Here it came, the flash and the roar, but this time there was no sound of any shot passing – maybe the gunners had lost all sense of direction and elevation, which was easy enough in the darkness. And the flashes from the guns were convenient in enabling Hornblower to check his position.

A yell came from the lookout in the bows, and Hornblower, looking forward, could just make out the dark square of the top of the pilot-lugger's mainsail, close in on their starboard bow. They were making an effort to impede the brig's escape.

'Steady!' said Hornblower to the helmsman.

Let the weakest go to the wall; there was a shattering crash as brig and lugger met, starboard bow to starboard bow. The brig shuddered and lurched and drove on, the lugger rasping down her side. Something caught and tore loose again, and there came, as the vessels parted, a thin despairing yell from the lugger. The little vessel's bows must have been smashed in like an eggshell by that shock, and the water must be pouring in. The cries died away; Hornblower distinctly heard one wailing voice abruptly cut short, as if water was pouring into the mouth of the despairing swimmer. The Indiaman was still holding her course in the brig's wake.

'By the mark eight!' called the leadsman.

He could lay her on the other tack now, and as he gave the order the battery at the jetty again roared harmlessly. They would be out of range by the time the gunners could reload.

'A very good piece of work, Mr Freeman,' said Hornblower, loudly. 'All hands did their duty admirably.'

Somebody in the darkness began to cheer, and the cry was taken up throughout the brig. The men were yelling like madmen.

'Horny! Good old Horny!' yelled somebody, and the cheering redoubled.

Even from astern they could hear the exiguous prize crew of the Indiaman joining in; Hornblower felt a sudden smarting of the eyes, and then experienced a new revulsion of feeling. He felt a little twinge of shame at being fond of these simpletons. Besides –

'Mr Freeman,' he said, harshly, 'kindly keep the hands quiet.'

The risk he had run had been enormous. Not merely the physical danger, but the danger to his reputation. Had he failed, had the *Porta Coeli* been disabled and captured, men would not have stopped to think about his real motive, which was to make the French authorities believe that the *Flame*'s mutiny was merely a ruse to enable the brig to enter the harbour. No; men would have said that Hornblower had tried to take advantage of the mutiny to feather his own nest, had thrown away the *Porta Coeli* and had left the mutineers unmolested merely to grab at an opportunity to acquire prize money. That was what they would have said – and all the appearances would have borne out the assumption – and Hornblower's reputation would have been eternally tarnished. He had risked his honour as well as his life and liberty. He had gambled everything in hare-brained fashion, thrown colossal stakes on the board for a meagre prize, like the fool he was.

Then the wave of black reaction ebbed away. He had taken a calculated risk, and his calculation had proved exact. It would be a long time before the mutineers could clear up their misunderstanding with the French authorities – Hornblower could imagine the messengers hurrying at this moment to warn the coastal defences at Honfleur and Caen – even if eventually they should succeed in doing so. He had turned the mutineers' position, cut off their retreat. He had bearded Bonaparte under the batteries of his own capital river. And there was the prize he had taken; at least a thousand pounds, his share would be, when the prize money came to be reckoned up, and a thousand pounds was a welcome sum of money, a gratifying sum. Barbara and he would find it useful.

Emotion and excitement had left him tired. He was about to tell Freeman that he was going below, and then he checked himself. It would be an unnecessary speech; if Freeman could not find him on deck he would know perfectly well that he was in his cabin. He dragged himself wearily down to his cot.

7

'Mr Freeman's respects, sir,' said Brown, 'an' he said to tell you that day's just breaking, fairly clear, sir. Wind's backed to sou'-by-west, sir, during the night, blowin' moderate. We're hove-to, us an' the prize, an' it's the last of the flood-tide now, sir.'

'Very good,' said Hornblower, rolling out of his cot. He was still heavy with sleep, and the tiny cabin seemed stuffy, as well as chilly, although the stern window was open.

'I'll have my bath,' said Hornblower, reaching a sudden decision. 'Go and get the wash-deck pump rigged.'

He felt unclean; although this was November in the Channel he could not live through another day without a bath. His ear caught some surprised and jocular comments from the hands rigging the pump as he came up through the hatchway, but he paid them no attention. He threw off his dressing gown, and a puzzled and nervous seaman, in the half-light, turned the jet of the canvas hose upon him while another worked the pump. The bitterly cold seawater stung as it hit his naked skin, and he leaped and danced and turned about grotesquely, gasping. The seamen did not realize it when he wanted the jet stopped, and when he tried to escape from it they followed him up across the deck.

'Avast, there!' he yelled in desperation, half frozen and

half drowned, and the merciless stream stopped.

Brown threw the big towel round him, and he scrubbed his tingling skin, while he jumped and shivered with the stimulus of the cold.

'I'd be frozen for a week if I tried that, sir,' said Freeman, who had been an interested spectator.

'Yes,' said Hornblower, discouraging conversation.

His skin glowed delightfully as he put on his clothes in his cabin with the window shut, and his shivering ceased. He drank thirstily of the steaming coffee which Brown brought him, revelling in the pleasant and unexpected feeling of well-being that filled him. He ran light-heartedly on deck again. The morning was already brighter; the captured Indiaman could now be made out, hove-to half a gunshot to leeward.

'Orders, Sir Horatio?' said Freeman, touching his hat.

Hornblower swept his glance round, playing for time. He had been culpably negligent of business; he had given no thought to his duty since he woke – since he went below to sleep, for that matter. He should order the prize back to England at once, but he could not do that without taking the opportunity of sending a written report back with her, and at this moment he simply hated the thought of labouring over a report.

'The prisoners, sir,' prompted Freeman.

Oh God, he had forgotten the prisoners. They would have to be interrogated and note made of what they had to say. Hornblower felt bone-lazy as well as full of well-being – an odd combination.

'They might have plenty to say, sir,' went on Freeman, remorselessly. 'The pilot talks some English, and we had him in the wardroom last night. He says Boney's been licked again. At a place called Leipzig, or some name like that. He says the Russians'll be over the Rhine in a week. Boney's back in Paris already. Maybe it's the end of the war.'

Hornblower and Freeman exchanged glances; it was a full year since the world had begun to look for the end of the war, and many hopes had blossomed and wilted during that year. But the Russians on the Rhine! Even though the English army's entrance upon the soil of France in the south had not shaken down the Empire, this new invasion might bring that about. Yet there had been plenty of forecasts – Hornblower had made some – to the effect that the first defeat of Bonaparte in the open field would bring to an end at the same time both his reputation for invincibility and his reign. These forecasts about the invasion of the Empire might be as inaccurate.

'Sail-ho!' yelled the lookout, and in the same breath 'She's the *Flame*, sir.'

There she was, as before; the parting mist revealed her for only a moment before closing round her again, and then a fresh breath of wind shredded the mist and left her in plain sight. Hornblower reached the decision he had so far been unable to make.

'Clear the ship for action, Mr Freeman, if you please. We're going to fetch her out.'

Of course, it was the only thing to do. During the night, within an hour of the cutting-out of the French Indiaman, the word would be sent flying round warning all French ports in the neighbourhood that the British brig with the white cross on her foretopsail was playing a double game, and only masquerading as a mutinous vessel. The news must have reached this side of the estuary by midnight – the courier could cross on the ferry at Quilleboeuf or elsewhere. Everyone would be on the watch for the brig to attempt another *coup*, and this bank of the river would be the obvious place. Any delay would give the mutineers a chance to reopen communication with the shore and to clear up the situation; if the authorities on shore were once to discover that there were two brigs, sister-ships, in the Bay of the Seine the mutineers might be saved that trouble. Not an hour ought to be lost.

It was all very clear and logical, yet Hornblower found himself gulping nervously as he stood on the quarterdeck. It could only mean a hammer-and-tongs battle – he would be in the thick of it in an hour. This deck which he trod would be swept by the grapeshot of the *Flame*'s carronades; within the hour he might be dead; within the hour he might be shrieking under the surgeon's knife. Last night he had faced disaster, but this morning he was facing death. That warm glow which his bath had induced in him had vanished completely, so that he found himself on the point of shivering in the chill of the morning. He scowled at himself in frantic self-contempt, and forced himself to pace brightly and jerkily up and down the tiny quarterdeck. His memories were unmanning him, he told himself. The memory of Richard trotting beside him in the sunset, holding his finger in an unbreakable clutch; the memory of Barbara; the memory even of Smallbridge or of Bond Street – he did not want to be separated from these things, to 'leave the warm precincts of the cheerful day'. He wanted to live, and soon he might die.

Flame had set more sail – boom-mainsail and jibs; close-hauled she could fetch Honfleur without ever coming within range of the *Porta Coeli*'s guns. Hornblower's fears withdrew into the background as his restless mind, despite itself, interested itself in the tactical aspects of the problem before it.

'See that the hands have some breakfast, if you please, Mr Freeman,' he said. 'And it would be best if the guns were not run out yet.'

'Aye aye, sir.'

It might be a long, hard battle, and the men should have their breakfast first. And running out the guns would tell the people in *Flame* that the *Porta Coeli* expected a fight, and that would warn them that maybe their escape into French protection might not be easy. The more perfect the surprise, the greater the chance of an easy victory. Hornblower glowered at the *Flame* through his glass. He felt a dull, sullen rage against the mutineers who had caused all this trouble, whose mad action was imperilling his life. The sympathy he had felt towards them when he was seated in the safety of the Admiralty was replaced now by a fierce resentment. The villains deserved hanging – the thought changed his mood so that he could smile as he met Freeman's eyes when the latter reported the brig cleared for action.

'Very good, Mr Freeman.'

His eyes were dancing with excitement; he looked over at *Flame* again just as a fresh hail came from the masthead.

'Deck, there! There's a whole lot of small craft putting out from the beach, sir. Headin' for *Flame* it looks like, sir.'

The mutineers' brig was going through the same performance as yesterday, heading towards the French coast just out of gunshot of the *Porta Coeli*, ready to take refuge sooner than fight; the mutineers must think the small craft a welcoming deputation, coming to escort them in. And there was thick weather liable to close in on them again at any moment. *Flame* was spilling the wind from her mainsail, her every action denoting increasing hesitation. Probably on her quarterdeck there was a heated argument going on, one party insisting on keeping out of range of the *Porta Coeli* while another hesitated before such an irrevocable action as going over to the French. Maybe there was another party clamouring to turn and fight – that was quite likely; and maybe even there was a party of the most timid or the least culpable who wished to surrender and trust to the mercy of a court martial. Certainly counsel would be divided. She was hauling on her sheet again now, on a straight course for Honfleur and the approaching gunboats; two miles of clear water separated her from the *Porta Coeli*.

'Those gunboats are closing in on her, sir,' said Freeman, glass to eye. 'And that *chasse-marée* lugger's full of men. Christ! There's a gun.'

Someone in the *Flame* had fired a warning shot, perhaps to tell the French vessels to keep their distance until the debate on her deck had reached a conclusion. Then she wore round, as if suddenly realizing the hostile intent of the French, and as she wore the small craft closed in on her, like hounds upon a deer. Half a dozen shots were fired, too ragged to be called a broadside. The gunboats were heading straight at her, their sweeps out, six a side, giving them additional speed and handiness. Smoke spouted from their bows, and over the water came the deep-toned heavy boom of the twenty-four-pounders they mounted – a sound quite different from the higher-pitched, sharper bang of the *Flame*'s carronades. The lugger ran alongside her, and through his glass Hornblower could see the boarders pouring on to the *Flame*'s deck.

'I'll have the guns run out, Mr Freeman, if you please,' he said.

The situation was developing with bewildering rapidity – he had foreseen nothing like this. There was desperate fighting ahead, but at least it would be against Frenchmen and not against Englishmen. He could see puffs of smoke on the *Flame*'s deck – some, at least, of the crew were offering resistance.

He walked forward a few yards, and addressed himself to the gunners.

'Listen to me, you men. Those gunboats must be sunk when we get in among 'em. One broadside for each will do that business for 'em if you make your shots tell. Aim true, at the base of their masts. Don't fire until you're sure you'll hit.'

'Aye aye, sir,' came a few voices in reply.

Hornblower found Brown beside him.

'Your pistols, sir. I loaded 'em afresh, an' primed 'em with new caps.'

'Thank you,' said Hornblower. He stuck the weapons into his belt, one on each side, where either hand could grasp them as necessary. It was like a boy playing at pirates, but his life might depend on those pistols in five minutes' time. He half drew his sword to see that it was free in its sheath, and he was already hastening back to take his stand by the wheel as he thrust it in again.

'Luff a little,' he said. 'Steady!'

Flame had flown up into the wind and lay all aback – apparently there was no one at the helm at the moment. The lugger was still alongside her, and the four gunboats, having taken in their sails, were resting on their oars, interposing between the *Porta Coeli* and the pair of ships. Hornblower could see the guns' crews bending over the twenty-four-pounders in their bows.

'Hands to the sheets, Mr Freeman, please. I'm going between them – there. Stand to your guns, men! Now, hard down!'

The wheel went over, and the *Porta Coeli* came about on the other tack, handily as anyone could desire. Hornblower heard the thunder of a shot close under her bows, and then the deck erupted in a flying shower of splinters from a jagged hole close to the mainmast bitts – a twenty-four-pound shot, fired upwards at close elevation, had pierced the brig's frail timbers, and, continuing its flight, had burst through the deck.

'Ready about! Hard over!' yelled Hornblower, and the *Porta Coeli* tacked again into the narrow gap between two gunboats. Her carronades went off in rapid succession on both sides. Looking to starboard, Hornblower had one gunboat under his eye. He saw her there, half a dozen men standing by the tiller aft, two men at each sweep amidships tugging wildly to swing her round, a dozen men at the gun forward. A man with a red handkerchief round his head stood by the mast, resting his hand against it – Hornblower could even see his open mouth as his jaw dropped and he saw death upon him. Then the shots came smashing in. The man with the red handkerchief disappeared – maybe he was dashed overboard, but most likely he was smashed into pulp. The frail frame of the gunboat – nothing more than a big rowing-boat strengthened forward for a gun – disintegrated; her side caved in under the shots as though under the blows of some vast hammer. The sea poured in even as Hornblower looked; the shots, fired with extreme depression, must have gone on through the gunboat's bottom after piercing her side. The dead weight of the gun in her bows took charge as her stability vanished, and her bows surged under while her stern was still above water. Then the gun slid out, relieving her of its weight and the wreck righted itself for an instant before capsizing. A few men swam among the wreckage. Hornblower looked over to port; the other gunboat had been as hard hit, lying at that moment just at the surface with the remains of her crew swimming by her. Whoever had been in command of those gunboats had been a reckless fool to expose the frail vessels to the fire of a real vessel of war – even one as tiny as the *Porta Coeli* – as long as the latter was under proper command. Gunboats were only of use to batter into submission ships helplessly aground or dismasted.

The *chasse-marée* and the *Flame*, still alongside each other, were close ahead.

'Mr Freeman, load with canister, if you please. We'll run alongside the Frenchman. One broadside, and we'll board her in the smoke.'

'Aye aye, sir.'

Freeman turned to bellow orders to his crew.

'Mr Freeman, I shall want every available hand in the boarding party. You'll stay here –'

'Sir!'

'You'll stay here. Pick six good seamen to stay with you to work the brig out again if we don't come back. Is that clear, Mr Freeman?'

'Yes, Sir Horatio.'

There was still time for Freeman to make the arrangements as the *Porta Coeli* surged up towards the Frenchman. There was still time for Hornblower to realize with surprise that what he had said about not coming back was sincere, and no mere bombast to stimulate the men. He was most oddly determined to conquer or die, he, the man who was afraid of shadows. The men were yelling madly as the *Porta Coeli* drew up to the Frenchman, whose name – the *Bonne Celestine* of Honfleur – was now visible on her stern. Blue uniforms and white breeches could be seen aboard her; soldiers – it was true, then, that Bonaparte's need for trained artillerymen had forced him to conscript his seamen, replacing them with raw conscript soldiers. A pity the action was not taking place out at sea, for then they would most of them be seasick.

'Lay us alongside,' said Hornblower to the helmsman. There was confusion on the decks of the *Bonne Celestine*; Hornblower could see men running to the guns on her disengaged port side.

'Quiet, you men!' bellowed Hornblower. 'Quiet!'

Silence fell on the brig; Hornblower had hardly to raise his voice to make himself heard on the tiny deck.

'See that every shot tells, you gunners,' said Hornblower. 'Boarders, are you ready to come with me?'

Another yell answered him. Thirty men were crouching by the bulwarks with pikes and cutlasses; the firing of the broadside and the dropping of the mainsail would set free thirty more, a small enough force unless the broadside should do great execution and the untrained landsmen in the *Bonne Celestine* should flinch. Hornblower stole a glance at the helmsman, a grey-bearded seaman, who was coolly gauging the distance between the two vessels while at the same time watching the mainsail as it shivered as the *Porta Coeli* came to the wind. A good seaman, that – Hornblower made a mental note to remember him for commendation. The helmsman whirled the wheel over.

'Down mains'l,' roared Freeman.

The *Bonne Celestine*'s guns bellowed deafeningly, and Hornblower felt powder grains strike his face as the smoke eddied round him. He drew his sword as the *Porta Coeli*'s carronades crashed out, and the two vessels came together with a squealing of timber. He sprang upon the bulwark in the smoke, sword in hand; at the same moment a figure beside him cleared the bulwark in a single motion and dropped upon the *Bonne Celestine*'s deck – Brown, waving a cutlass. Hornblower leaped after him, but Brown stayed in front of him, striking to left and right at the shadowy figures looming in the smoke. Here there was a pile of dead and wounded men, caught in the blast of canister from one of the *Porta Coeli*'s carronades. Hornblower stumbled over a limb, and recovered himself in time to see a bayonet on the end of a musket lunging at him. A violent twisting of his body evaded the thrust. There was a pistol in his left hand, and he fired with the muzzle almost against the

Frenchman's breast. Now the wind had blown the cannon smoke clear. Forward some of the boarders were fighting with a group of the enemy cornered in the bow – the clash of the blades came clearly to Hornblower's ears – but aft there was not a Frenchman to be seen. Gibbons, master's mate, was at the halliards running down the tricolour from the masthead. At the starboard side lay the *Flame*, and over her bulwarks were visible French infantry shakoes; Hornblower saw a man's head and shoulders appear, saw a musket being pointed. It shifted its aim from Gibbons to Hornblower, and in that instant Hornblower fired the other barrel of his pistol, and the Frenchman fell down below the bulwarks, just as a fresh wave of boarders came pouring on board from the *Porta Coeli*.

'Come on!' yelled Hornblower – it was desperately important to make sure of the *Flame* before a defence could be organized.

The brigs stood higher out of the water than did the *chasse-marée*; this time they had to climb upward. He got his left elbow over the bulwark, and tried to swing himself up, but his sword hampered him.

'Help me, damn you!' he snarled over his shoulder, and a seaman put his shoulder under Hornblower's stern and heaved him up with such surprising goodwill that he shot over the bulwarks and fell on his face in the scuppers on the other side, his sword slithering over the deck. He started to crawl forward towards it, but a sixth sense warned him of danger, and he flung himself down and forward inside the sweep of a cutlass, and cannoned against the shins of the man who wielded it. Then a wave of men burst over him, and he was kicked and trodden on and then crushed beneath a writhing body with which he grappled with desperate strength. He could hear Brown's voice roaring over him, pistols banging, sword-blades clashing before sudden silence fell round him. The man with whom he was struggling went suddenly limp and inert, and then was dragged off him. He rose to his feet.

'Are you wounded, sir?' asked Brown.

'No,' he answered. Three or four dead men lay on the deck; aft a group of French soldiers with a French seaman or two among them stood by the wheel, disarmed, while two British sailors, pistol in hand, stood guard over them. A French officer, blood dripping from his right sleeve, and with tears on his cheeks – he was no more than a boy – was sitting on the deck, and Hornblower was about to address him when his attention was suddenly distracted.

'Sir! Sir!'

It was an English seaman he did not recognize, in a striped shirt of white and red, his pigtail shaking from side to side as he gesticulated with the violence of his emotion.

'Sir! I was fightin' against the Frogs. Your men saw me. Me an' these other lads here.'

He motioned behind him to an anxious little group of seamen who had heretofore hung back, but now came forward, some of them bursting into speech, all of them nodding their heads in agreement.

'Mutineers?' asked Hornblower. In the heat of battle he had forgotten about the mutiny.

'I'm no mutineer, sir. I did what I had to or they'd 'a killed me. Ain't that so, mates?'

'Stand back, there!' blared Brown; there was blood on the blade of his cutlass.

A vivid prophetic picture suddenly leaped into Hornblower's mind's eye – the court martial, the semicircle of judges in glittering full dress, the tormented prisoners, tongue-tied, watching, only half understanding, the proceedings which would determine their lives or deaths, and he himself giving his evidence, trying conscientiously to remember every word spoken on both sides; one word remembered might make the difference between the lash and the rope.

'Arrest those men!' he snapped. 'Put them under confinement.'

'Sir! Sir!'

'None o' that!' growled Brown.

Remorseless hands dragged the protesting men away.

'Where are the other mutineers?' demanded Hornblower.

'Down below, sir, I fancies,' said Brown. 'Some o' the Frenchies is down there, too.'

Odd how a beaten crew so often scuttled below. Hornblower honestly believed that he would rather face the fighting madness of the victors on deck than surrender ignominiously in the dark confines of the 'tween-decks.

A loud hail from the *Porta Coeli* came to his ears.

'Sir Horatio!' hailed Freeman's voice. 'We'll be all aground if we don't get way on the ships soon. I request permission to cast off and make sail.'

'Wait!' replied Hornblower.

He looked round him; the three ships locked together, prisoners under guard here, there, and everywhere.

Below decks, both in the *Bonne Celestine* and in the *Flame*, there were enemies still unsecured, probably many more in total than he had men under his orders. A shattering crash below him, followed by screams and cries; the *Flame* shook under a violent blow. Hornblower remembered the sound of a cannon shot striking on his inattentive ears a second before; he looked round. The two surviving gunboats were resting on their oars a couple of cables' lengths away, their bows pointing at the group of ships. Hornblower could guess they were in shoal water, almost immune from attack. A jet of smoke from one of the gunboats, and another frightful crash below, and more screams. Those twenty-four-pounder balls were probably smashing through the whole frail length of the brig, whose timbers could resist their impact hardly better than paper. Hornblower plunged into the urgency of the business before him like a man into a raging torrent which he had to swim.

'Get those hatches battened down, Brown!' he ordered. 'Put a sentry over each. Mr Gibbons!'

'Sir?'

'Secure your hatches. Get ready to make sail.'

'Aye aye, sir.'

'What topmen are there here? Man the halliards. Who can take the wheel? Wheel none of you? Mr Gibbons! Have you a quartermaster to spare? Send one here immediately. Mr Freeman! You can cast off and make sail. Rendezvous at the other prize.'

Another shot from those accursed gunboats crashed into the *Flame*'s stern below him. Thank God the wind was off shore and he could get clear of them. The *Porta Coeli* had set her boom-mainsail again and had got clear of the *Bonne Celestine*; Gibbons was supervising the setting of the latter's lug-mainsail while half a dozen hands boomed her off from the *Flame*.

'Hoist away!' ordered Hornblower as the vessels separated. 'Hard a-starboard, quartermaster.'

A sound overside attracted his attention. Men – mutineers or Frenchmen – were scrambling out through the shot-holes and hurling themselves into the sea, swimming towards the gunboats. Hornblower saw the white hair of Nathaniel Sweet trailing on the surface of the water as he struck out, twenty feet away from him. Of all the mutineers he was the one who most certainly must not be allowed to escape. For the sake of England, for the sake of the service, he must die. The seaman acting as sentry at the after hatchway did not look as if he were a capable marksman.

'Give me your musket,' said Hornblower, snatching it.

He looked at priming and flint as he hurried back to the taffrail. He trained the weapon on the white head, and pulled the trigger. The smoke blew back into his face, obscuring his view only for a moment. The long white hair was visible for a second at the surface when he looked again, and then it sank, slowly, out of sight. Sweet was dead. Maybe there was an old widow who would bewail him, but it was better that Sweet was dead. Hornblower turned back to the business of navigating the *Flame* back to the rendezvous.

8

This fellow Lebrun was an infernal nuisance, demanding a private interview in this fashion. Hornblower had quite enough to do as it was; the gaping shot-holes in *Flame*'s side had to be patched sufficiently well to enable her to recross the Channel; the exiguous crew of the *Porta Coeli* – not all of them seamen by any means – had to be distributed through no fewer than four vessels (the two brigs, the Indiaman, and the *chasse-marée*), while at the same time an adequate guard must be maintained over more than a hundred prisoners of one nationality or another; the mutineers must be supervised so that nothing could happen to prejudice their trial; worst of all, there was a long report to be made out. Some people would think this last an easy task, seeing that there was a long string of successes to report, two prizes taken, the *Flame* recaptured, most of the mutineers in irons below decks and their ringleader slain by Hornblower's own hand. But there was the physical labour of writing it out, and Hornblower was very weary. Moreover, the composition of it would be difficult, for Hornblower could foresee having to steer a ticklish course between the Scylla of open boastfulness and the Charybdis of mock-modesty – how often had his lip wrinkled in distaste when reading the literary efforts of other officers! And the killing of Nathaniel Sweet by the terrible Commodore Hornblower, although it would look well in a naval history, and although, from the point of view of the discipline of the service, it was the best way in which the affair could have ended, might not appear so well in Barbara's eyes. He himself did not relish the memory of that white head sinking beneath the waves, and he felt that Barbara, with her attention forcibly called to the fact that he had shed blood, had taken a human life, with his own hands (those hands which she said she loved, which she had sometimes kissed), might feel a repulsion, a distaste.

Hornblower shook himself free from a clinging tangle of thoughts and memories, of Barbara and Nathaniel Sweet, to find himself still staring abstractedly at the young seaman who had brought to him Freeman's message regarding Lebrun's request.

'My compliments to Mr Freeman, and he can send this fellow in to me,' he said.

'Aye aye, sir,' said the seaman, his knuckles to his forehead, turning away with intense relief. The Commodore had been looking through and through him for three minutes at least – three hours, it seemed like, to the seaman.

An armed guard brought Lebrun into the cabin, and Hornblower looked him keenly over. He was one of the half-dozen prisoners taken when the *Porta Coeli* came into Le Havre, one of the deputation which had mounted her deck to welcome her under the impression that she was the *Flame* coming in to surrender.

'*Monsieur* speaks French?' said Lebrun.

'A little.'

'More than a little, if all the tales about Captain Hornblower are true,' replied Lebrun.

'What is your business?' snapped Hornblower, cutting short this continental floweriness. Lebrun was a youngish man, of olive complexion, with glistening white teeth, who conveyed a general impression of oiliness.

'I am *adjoint* to Baron Momas, Mayor of Le Havre.'

'Yes?' Hornblower tried to show no sign of interest, but he knew that under the Imperial régime the mayor of a large town like Le Havre was a most important person, and that his *adjoint* – his assistant, or deputy – was a very important permanent official.

'The firm of Momas Frères is one you must have heard of. It has traded with the Americas for generations – the history of its rise is identical with the history of the development of Le Havre itself.'

'Yes?'

'Similarly, the war and the blockade have had a most disastrous effect upon the fortunes both of the firm of Momas and upon the city of Le Havre.'

'Yes?'

'The *Caryatide*, the vessel that you so ingeniously captured two days ago, monsieur, might have restored the fortunes of us all – a single vessel running the blockade, as you will readily understand, is worth ten vessels arriving in peacetime.'

'Yes?'

'M. le Baron and the city of Le Havre will be desperate, I have no doubt, as the result of her capture before her cargo could be taken out.'

'Yes?'

The two men eyed each other, like duellists during a pause, Hornblower determined to betray none of the curiosity and interest that he felt, and Lebrun hesitating before finally committing himself.

'I take it, monsieur, that anything further I have to say will be treated as entirely confidential.'

'I promise nothing. In fact, I can only say that it will be my duty to report anything you say to the Government of His Majesty of Great Britain.'

'They will be discreet for their own sake, I expect,' ruminated Lebrun.

'His Majesty's ministers can make their own decisions,' said Hornblower.

'You are aware, *monsieur*,' said Lebrun, obviously taking the plunge, 'that Bonaparte has been defeated in a great battle at Leipzig?'

'Yes.'

'The Russians are on the Rhine.'

'That is so.'

'The Russians are on the Rhine!' repeated Lebrun, marvelling. The whole world, pro-Bonaparte or anti-Bonaparte, was marvelling that the massive Empire should have receded half across Europe in those few short months.

'And Wellington is marching on Toulouse,' added Hornblower – there was no harm in reminding Lebrun of the British threat in the south.

'That is so. The Empire cannot much longer endure.'

'I am glad to hear your opinion in the matter.'

'And when the Empire falls there will be peace, and when peace comes trade will recommence.'

'Without a doubt,' said Hornblower, still a little mystified.

'Profits will be enormous during the first few months.

All Europe has for years been deprived of foreign produce. At this moment genuine coffee commands a price of over a hundred francs a pound.'

Now Lebrun was showing his hand, more involuntarily than voluntarily. There was a look of avarice in his face which told Hornblower much.

'All this is obvious, *monsieur*,' said Hornblower, noncommittally.

'A firm which was prepared for the moment of peace, with its warehouses gorged with colonial produce ready to distribute, would greatly benefit. It would be far ahead of its competitors. There would be millions to be made. Millions.' Lebrun was obviously dreaming of the possibility of finding some of those millions in his own pocket.

'I have a great deal of business to attend to, monsieur,' said Hornblower. 'Have the goodness to come to the point.'

'His Majesty of Great Britain might well allow his friends to make those preparations in advance,' said Lebrun, the words coming slowly; well they might, for they could take him to the guillotine if Bonaparte ever heard of them. Lebrun was offering to betray the Empire in exchange for commercial advantages.

'His Majesty would first need undeniable proof that his friends *were* his friends,' said Hornblower.

'A *quid pro quo*,' said Lebrun, thereby for the first time during the conversation putting Hornblower at a loss – the Frenchman's pronunciation of Latin being quite unlike anything he was accustomed to, so that he had to grope about in his mind wondering what unaccustomed word Lebrun was using before at length he understood.

'You may tell me the nature of your offer, *monsieur,*' said Hornblower with solemn dignity, 'but I can make no promises of any sort in return. His Majesty's Government will probably refuse to bind themselves in any way whatsoever.'

It was curious how he found himself aping the ministerial manner and diction – it might have been his solemn brother-in-law, Wellesley, speaking. Maybe high politics had that effect on everyone; it was useful in this particular case, because it helped him to conceal his eagerness.

'A *quid pro quo,*' said Lebrun, again, thoughtfully. 'Supposing the city of Le Havre declared itself against the Empire, declared itself for Louis XVIII?'

The possibility had occurred to Hornblower, but he had put it aside as being potentially too good to be true.

'Supposing it did?' he said cautiously.

'It might be the example for which the Empire is waiting. It might be infectious. Bonaparte could not survive such a blow.'

'He has survived many blows.'

'But none of this sort. And if Le Havre declared for the King the city would be in alliance with Great Britain. The blockade could not continue to apply. Or if it did a licence to import could be granted to the house of Momas Frères, could it not?'

'Possibly. Remember, I make no promises.'

'And when Louis XVIII was restored to the throne of his fathers he would look with kindness upon those who first declared for him,' said Lebrun. 'The *adjoint* to Baron Momas might expect to find a great career open to him.'

'No doubt of that,' agreed Hornblower. 'But – you have spoken of your own sentiments. Can you be sure of those of M. le Baron? And whatever may be M. le Baron's sentiments, how can he be sure that the city would follow him should he declare himself?'

'I can answer for the Baron, I assure you, sir. I know – I have certain knowledge of his thoughts.'

Probably Lebrun had been spying on his master on behalf of the Imperial Government, and had no objection to applying his knowledge in another and more profitable cause.

'But the city? The other authorities?'

'The day you took me prisoner, sir,' said Lebrun, 'there arrived from Paris some sample proclamations and advance notice of some Imperial decrees. The proclamations were to be printed – my last official act was to give the order – and next Monday the proclamations were to be posted and the decrees made public.'

'Yes?'

'They are the most drastic in the drastic history of the Empire. Conscription – the last of the class of 1815 is to be called, and the classes all the way back to that of 1802 are to be revised. Boys of seventeen, cripples, invalids, fathers of families, even those who have purchased exemption; they are all to be called.'

'France must have grown used to conscription.'

'France has grown weary of it, rather, sir. I have official knowledge of the number of deserters and the severity of the measures directed against them. But it's not merely the conscription, sir. The other decrees are more drastic still. The taxes! The direct imposts, the indirect imposts, the *droits réunis*, and the others! Those of us who survive the war will be left beggars.'

'And you think publication of these decrees will rouse

sufficient discontent to cause rebellion?'

'Perhaps not. But it would constitute an admirable starting-point for a determined leader.'

Lebrun was shrewd enough – this last remark was acute and might be true.

'But the other authorities in the town? The military governor? The Prefect of the Department?'

'Some of them would be safe. I know their sentiments as well as I know Baron Momas'. The others – a dozen well-timed arrests, carried out simultaneously, an appeal to the troops in the barracks, the arrival of British forces (*your* forces, sir), a heartening proclamation to the people, the declaration of a state of siege, the closing of the gates, and it would be all over. Le Havre is well fortified, as you know, sir. Only an army and a battering train could retake it, and Bonaparte has neither to spare. The news would spread like wildfire through the Empire, however Bonaparte tried to stop it.'

This man Lebrun had ideas and vision, whatever might be thought of his morals. That was a neat thumbnail sketch he had drawn of a typical *coup d'état*. If the attempt were successful the results would be profound. Even if it were to fail, loyalty throughout the Empire would be shaken. Treason was infectious, as Lebrun had said. Rats in a sinking ship were notoriously quick in following an example in leaving it. There would be little enough to risk losing in supporting Lebrun's notions, and the gains might be immense.

'*Monsieur*,' said Hornblower, 'so far I have been patient. But in all this time you have made me no concrete proposal. Words – nebulous ideas – hopes – wishes, that is all, and I am a busy man, as I told you.

Please be specific. And speedy, if that is not too much trouble to you.'

'I shall be specific, then. Set me on shore – as an excuse I could be sent to arrange a cartel for the exchange of prisoners. Let me be able to assure M. le Baron of your instant support. In the three days before next Monday I can complete the arrangements. Meanwhile, you remain close in the vicinity with all the force you can muster. The moment we secure the citadel we shall send up the white flag, and the moment you see that you enter the harbour and overawe any possible dissentients. In return for this – a licence to Momas Frères to import colonial produce, and your word of honour as a gentleman that you will inform King Louis that it was I, Hercule Lebrun, who first suggested the scheme to you.'

'Ha – h'm,' said Hornblower. He hardly ever made use of that sound now, after his wife had teased him about it, but it escaped from him at this moment of crisis. He had to think. He had to have time to think. The long conversation in the French which he was not accustomed to using had been exhausting. He lifted his voice in a bellow to the sentry outside the door.

'Pass the word for the armed guard to take this prisoner away.'

'Sir!' protested Lebrun.

'I will give you my decision in an hour,' said Hornblower. 'Meanwhile for appearance's sake you must be treated harshly.'

'Sir! Remember to be secret! Remember not to utter a word! For God's sake –!'

Lebrun had a very proper sense of the necessity for

secrecy in planning a rebellion against such a potentate as Bonaparte. Hornblower took that into consideration as he went up on deck, there to pace up and down, thrusting the minor administrative problems out of his mind as he debated this, the greatest problem of all.

9

The tricolour was still flying over the citadel – the fortress of Ste Adresse – of Le Havre; Hornblower could see it through his glass as he stood on the deck of the *Flame*, which was creeping along under easy sail, just out of range of the shore batteries. He had decided, inevitably, to assist Lebrun in his scheme. He was telling himself again, at that very moment, and for the thousandth time, that there was much to gain whatever the result, and little enough to lose. Only Lebrun's life, and perhaps Hornblower's reputation. Heaven only knew what Whitehall and Downing Street would say when they heard of what he had been doing. No one had decided yet what to do about the government of France when Bonaparte should fall; certainly there was no unanimity of opinion regarding the restoration of the Bourbons. The Government could refuse to honour the promises he had made regarding import licences; they could come out with a bold announcement that they had no intention of recognizing Louis XVIII's pretensions; they could rap him over the knuckles very sharply indeed for most of his actions since recapture of the *Flame*.

He had used his powers to pardon forty mutineers, all the seamen and boys, in fact, that were in the crew of the latter vessel. He could plead sheer necessity as a defence for that decision; to keep the mutineers as well as the prisoners under guard, and to provide prize-crews for the two prizes, would have called for the services of every man at his disposal. He would hardly have had enough to handle the vessels, and certainly he could have attempted nothing further. As it was, he had relieved himself of all these difficulties by a few simple decisions. Every Frenchman had been sent on shore in the *Bonne Celestine* under flag of truce, with Lebrun ostensibly to arrange for their exchange; the Indiaman had been manned by a minimum crew and sent with dispatches to Pellew and the Mid-Channel Squadron, and he had been able to retain the two brigs, each at least sufficiently manned, under his own command. That had been a convenient way of getting rid of Chadwick, too – he had been entrusted with the dispatches and the command of the Indiaman. Chadwick had been pale, as a result of two weeks' confinement in the Black Hole, and two weeks' imminent danger of hanging. There had been no evident pleasure in his red-rimmed eyes when he realized that his rescuer had been young Hornblower, once his junior in the gunroom of the *Indefatigable* and now his immeasurable superior. Chadwick had snarled a little on receiving his orders – only a little. He had weighed the dispatches in his hand, presumably wondering what was said in them about himself, but discretion or long habit had their way, and he said, 'Aye aye, sir,' and turned away.

By now those dispatches should have passed through Pellew's hands, and, their contents noted, might even be on their way to Whitehall. The wind had been fair for the Indiaman to have fetched the Mid-Channel Squadron off the Start – fair, too, for the reinforcements Hornblower had asked for to make their way to him. Pellew would send them, he knew. It was fifteen years since they had last met; nearly twenty years since Pellew had promoted him to a lieutenancy in the *Indefatigable*. Now Pellew was an admiral and a commander-in-chief, and he was commodore, but Pellew would be the loyal friend and the helpful colleague he had always been.

Hornblower glanced out to seaward, where, dim on the horizon, the *Porta Coeli* patrolled in the mist. She would halt the reinforcements before they could be sighted from the shore, for there was no reason why the authorities in Le Havre should be given the least chance to think that anything unusual portended, although it was not a vital matter. England had always flaunted her naval might in sight of the enemy, making the hostile coast her sea frontier – the *Flame*, here, wearing the White Ensign under the noses of the citizens of Le Havre, was no unusual sight to them. That was why he did not hesitate to stay here, with the tricolour on the citadel within range of his telescope.

'Keep a sharp lookout for any signal from the *Porta Coeli*,' he said sharply to the midshipman of the watch.

'Aye aye, sir.'

Porta Coeli, the Gate of Heaven; the Silly Porter was what the men called her. Hornblower had a vague memory of reading about the action which resulted in the strange name appearing in the Navy List. The first *Porta Coeli* had been a Spanish privateer – half pirate, probably – captured off Havannah. She had put up so fierce a resistance that the action had been commemorated by naming an English ship after her. The *Tonnant*, the *Temeraire*, most of the foreign names in the Navy List came there as a result of similar actions – if the war were to go on long enough there would be more ships in the Navy with foreign names than with English ones, and among the rival navies the converse might eventually become true. The French Navy boasted a *Swiftsure*; maybe the Americans would have a *Macedonian* on their Navy List in future years. He had not heard yet of a French *Sutherland*; Hornblower felt a sudden twinge of strange regret. He snapped his telescope shut and turned abruptly on his heel, walking fast as though to shake off the memories that assailed him. He did not like to think about surrendering the *Sutherland*, even though the court martial had so honourably acquitted him; and, strangely enough, the passage of time made his feelings of shame about the incident more acute instead of less. And his regrets about the *Sutherland* brought with them, inevitably, memories of Maria, now nearly three years in her grave. Memories of poverty and despair, of pinchbeck shoebuckles; of the pity and sympathy he had felt for Maria – a poor substitute for love, and yet the memory of it hurt intensely. The past was coming to life again in his mind, a resurrection as horrible as any other resurrection would be. He remembered Maria, snoring softly in her sleep beside him, and he remembered the sour smell of her hair; Maria, tactless and stupid, of whom he had been fond as one is fond of a child, although not nearly as fond as he was now of Richard. He was almost shaking with the memory when it abruptly faded out and was replaced by the memory of Marie de Graçay – why the Devil was he thinking about *her*? The unreserved love that she gave him, her warmth and tenderness, the quickness of perception with which she understood his moods; it was insane that he should find himself hungering at this day for Marie de Graçay, and yet he was, even though it was hardly a week since he had left the arms of a loyal and understanding wife. He tried to think about Barbara, and yet the mental images he conjured up were instantly thrust again into the background by pictures of Marie. It would be better even to think about surrendering the *Sutherland*. Hornblower walked the deck of the Flame with ghosts at his side in the chill, bleak winter day. Men saw his face and shrank from crossing his path with greater care even than usual. Yet most of them thought Hornblower was only planning some further deviltry against the French.

It was later afternoon before the expected interruption came.

'Signal from *Porta Coeli*, sir! Eighteen – fifty-one – ten. That's friendly ships in sight, bearing nor'west.'

'Very good. Ask their numbers.'

This must be the reinforcements sent by Pellew. The signal hands bent on the flags and hauled away at the halliards; it was several minutes before the midshipman noted the reply and translated it by reference to the list.

'*Nonsuch*, seventy-four, Captain Bush, sir.'

'Bush, by God!'

The exclamation leaped uncontrolled from Hornblower's lips; the devils that surrounded him were chased away as though by holy water at the thought of his old staunch matter-of-fact friend being only just over the horizon. Of course Pellew would send Bush if he were available, knowing the friendship that had so long existed between him and Hornblower.

'*Camilla*, thirty-six, Captain Howard, sir.'

He knew nothing about Howard whatever. He looked at the list – a captain of less than two years' seniority. Presumably Pellew had selected him as junior to Bush.

'Very good. Reply – "Commodore to –"'

'*Porta*'s still signalling, begging your pardon, sir. "*Nonsuch* to Commodore. Have – on board – three hundred – marines – above – complement."'

Good for Pellew. He had stripped his squadron to give Hornblower a landing force that could make itself felt. Three hundred marines, and the *Nonsuch*'s detachment as well, and a body of seamen. He could march five hundred men into Le Havre should the opportunity arise.

'Very good. Make "Commodore to *Nonsuch* and *Camilla*. Delighted to have you under my command."'

Hornblower looked again over at Le Havre. He looked up at the sky, he gauged the strength of the wind, remembered the state of the tide, calculated the approach of night. Over there Lebrun must be bringing his plans to fruition, tonight if at all. He must be ready to strike his blow.

'Make "Commodore to all vessels. Join me here after dark. Night signal two lanterns horizontally at fore-yardarms".'

'– foreyardarms. Aye aye, sir,' echoed the midshipman, scribbling on his slate.

It was good to see Bush again, to shake his hand in welcome as he hoisted himself in the darkness on to the *Flame*'s deck. It was good to sit in the stuffy little cabin with Bush and Howard and Freeman as he told them about his plans for the morrow. It was wonderful to be planning action after that day of horrible introspection. Bush looked at him closely with his deep-set eyes.

'You've been busy, sir, since you came to sea again.'

'Of course,' said Hornblower.

The last few days and nights had been a turmoil; even after the recapture of the *Flame* the business of reorganization, the sessions with Lebrun, the writing of the dispatches had all been exhausting.

'Too busy, if you'll pardon me, sir,' went on Bush. 'It was too soon for you to resume duty.'

'Nonsense,' protested Hornblower. 'I had almost a year's leave.'

'Sick leave, sir. After typhus. And since then –'

'Since then,' interjected Howard, a handsome, dark, young-looking man, 'cutting-out action. A battle. Three prizes taken. Two vessels sunk. An invasion planned. A midnight council of war.'

Hornblower felt suddenly irritated.

'Are you gentlemen trying to tell me,' he demanded, glowering round at them, 'that I'm unfit for service?'

They quailed before his anger.

'No, sir,' said Bush.

'Then be so good as to keep your opinions to yourselves.'

It was hard luck on Bush, who, after all, was only making a kindly inquiry about his friend's health. Hornblower knew it, and he knew how desperately unfair it was to make Bush pay for the miseries Hornblower had suffered that day. Yet he could not resist the temptation for the moment. He swept his glance round them again, forcing them to drop their gaze to the deck, and he had no sooner done it, no sooner obtained for himself this pitiful bit of self-gratification, than he regretted it and sought to make amends.

'Gentlemen,' he said, 'I spoke in haste. We must all have the most complete confidence in each other when we go into action tomorrow. Will you forgive me?'

They mumbled back at him, Bush profoundly embarrassed at receiving an apology from a man who, in his opinion, was free to say what he liked to anyone.

'You all understand what I want done tomorrow – if tomorrow is the day?' Hornblower went on.

They nodded, turning their eyes to the chart spread out in front of them.

'No questions?'

'No, sir.'

'I know this is only the sketchiest plan. There will be contingencies, emergencies. No one can possibly foresee what will happen. But of one thing I am certain, and that is that the ships of this squadron will be commanded in a way that will bring credit to the service. Captain Bush and Mr Freeman have acted with bravery and decision under my own eyes too often, and I know Captain Howard too well by reputation for me to have any doubt about that. When we attack Havre, gentlemen, we shall be turning a page, we shall be writing the end of a chapter in the history of tyranny.'

They were pleased with what he said, and they could have no doubt regarding his sincerity, because he spoke from his heart. They smiled as he met their eyes. Maria, when she was alive, had sometimes made use of a strange expression about polite phrases uttered in order to get the recipient into a good humour. She referred to them as 'a little bit of sugar for the bird'. That was what this final speech of his had been, a little bit of sugar for the bird – and yet he had meant every word of it. No, not quite – he was still almost ignorant of Howard's achievements. To that extent the speech was formal. But it had served its purpose.

'Then we have finished with business, gentlemen. What can I offer you by way of entertainment? Captain Bush can remember games of whist played on the nights before going into action. But he is by no means an enthusiastic whist player.'

That was understating the case – Bush was the most reluctant whist player in the world, and he grinned sheepishly in acknowledgement of Hornblower's gentle gibe; but it was pathetic to see him pleased at Hornblower's remembering this about him.

'You should have a night's rest, sir,' he said, speaking, as the senior, for the other two, who looked to him for guidance.

'I should get back to my ship, sir,' echoed Howard.

'So should I, sir,' said Freeman.

'I don't want to see you go,' protested Hornblower.

Freeman caught sight of the playing-cards on the shelf against the bulkhead.

'I'll tell your fortunes before we leave,' he volunteered. 'Perhaps I can remember what my gipsy grandmother taught me, sir.'

So there really was gipsy blood in Freeman's veins; Hornblower had often wondered about it, noticing his swarthy skin and dark eyes. Hornblower was a little surprised at the carelessness with which Freeman admitted it.

'Tell Sir Horatio's,' said Bush.

Freeman was shuffling the pack with expert fingers; he laid it on the table, and took Hornblower's hand and placed it on the pack.

'Cut three times, sir.'

Hornblower went through the mumbo-jumbo tolerantly, cutting and cutting again as Freeman shuffled. Finally Freeman caught up the pack and began to deal it face upward on the table.

'On this side is the past,' he announced, scanning the complicated pattern, 'on that side is the future. Here in the past there is much to read. I see money, gold. I see danger. Danger, danger, danger. I see prison – prison twice, sir. I see a dark woman. And a fair woman. You have journeyed over sea.'

He poured out his patter professionally enough, reeling it off without stopping to take breath. He made a neat résumé of Hornblower's career, and Hornblower listened with some amusement and a good deal of admiration for Freeman's glibness. What Freeman was saying could be said by anyone with an ordinary knowledge of Hornblower's past. Hornblower's eyebrows came together in momentary irritation at the brief allusion to the dead Maria, but he smiled again when Freeman passed rapidly on, telling of Hornblower's experiences in the Baltic, translating the phrases of ordinary speech into the gipsy clichés with a deftness that could not but amuse.

'And there's an illness, sir,' he concluded, 'a very serious illness, ending only a short time back.'

'Amazing!' said Hornblower, in mock admiration. The glow of anticipated action always brought out his best qualities; he was cordial and human towards this junior officer in a way that would be impossible to him at any other time.

'Amazing's the word, sir,' said Bush.

Hornblower was astonished to see that Bush was actually impressed; the fact that he was taken in by Freeman's adroit use of his knowledge of the past would go far towards explaining the success of the charlatans of this world.

'What about the future, Freeman?' asked Howard. It was a relief to see that Howard was only tolerantly interested.

'The future,' said Freeman, drumming with his fingers on the table as he turned to the other half of the arrangement. 'The future is always more mysterious. I see a crown. A golden crown.'

He rearranged the pattern.

'A crown it is, sir, try it any way you will.'

'Horatio the First, King of the Cannibal Isles,' laughed Hornblower. The clearest proof of his present mellowness was this joke about his name – a sore subject usually with him.

'And here there is more danger. Danger and a fair woman. The two go together. Danger because of a fair woman – danger with a fair woman. There's all kinds of danger here, sir. I'd advise you to beware of fair women.'

'No need to read cards to give that advice,' said Hornblower.

'Sometimes the cards speak truth,' replied Freeman, looking up at him with a peculiar intensity in his glittering eyes.

'A crown, a fair woman, danger,' repeated Hornblower. 'What else?'

'That's all that I can read, sir,' said Freeman, sweeping the cards together.

Howard was looking at the big silver watch that he pulled from his pocket.

'If Freeman could have told us whether or no we will see a white flag over the citadel tomorrow,' he said, 'it might help us to decide to prolong this pleasant evening. As it is, sir, I have my orders to give.'

Hornblower was genuinely sorry to see them go. He stood on the deck of the *Flame* and watched their gigs creep away in the black winter night, while the pipe of the bosun's mate was calling the hands for the middle watch. It was piercing cold, especially after the warm stuffiness of the cabin, and he felt suddenly even more lonely than usual, maybe as a result. Here in the *Flame* he had only two watchkeeping officers, borrowed from the *Porta Coeli*; tomorrow he would borrow another from the *Nonsuch* or the *Camilla*. Tomorrow? That was today. And today perhaps Lebrun's attempt to gain control of Le Havre might be successful. Today he might be dead.

10

It was as misty as might be expected of that season and place when day broke, or rather when the grey light crept almost unnoticed into one's consciousness. The *Porta Coeli* was dimly visible, an almost unnoticeable denser nucleus in the fog. Hailing her at the top of his lungs, Hornblower received the faint reply that *Nonsuch* was in sight astern of her, and a few seconds later the additional information that *Camilla* was in sight of *Nonsuch*. He had his squadron in hand, then, and there was nothing to do but wait, and to ponder for the hundredth time over the question as to how the hands, barefooted with the icy water surging round their feet, could possibly bear their morning duty of washing down the decks. But they were laughing and skylarking as they did it; the British seaman was of tough material. Presumably the lower deck guessed that there was something in the wind, that this concentration of force portended fresh action, and they found the prospect exhilarating. Partly, Hornblower knew, it was because they felt assured of success in the unknown enterprise before them. It must be amazingly pleasant to be able to put one's trust in a man and have no further doubts. Hornblower watched the men at work with envy as well as pity.

He himself was in a fever of anxiety, turning over in his mind the arrangements he had finally made with

Lebrun before sending him ashore. They were simple enough; absurdly simple, it seemed to him now. The whole plan seemed a feeble thing with which to overturn an Empire that dominated Europe. Yet a conspiracy should be simple – the more elaborate the machinery the greater the chance of its breaking down. That was one reason why he had insisted on daylight for his part of the business. He had dreaded the possible mishaps if he had plunged ashore in darkness into an unknown town with his little army. Daylight doubled the chances of success while it doubled at least the possible loss in case of failure.

Hornblower looked at his watch – for the last ten minutes he had been fighting down the urge to look at it.

'Mr Crawley,' he said, to the master's mate who was his new first lieutenant in the *Flame*. 'Beat to quarters and clear the brig for action.'

The wind was a light air from the east, as he had expected. Fetching into Le Havre would be a ticklish business, and he was glad that he had resolved to lead in the small and hardy *Flame* so as to show the way to the ponderous old *Nonsuch*.

'Ship cleared for action, sir,' reported Crawley.

'Very good.'

Hornblower looked at his watch – it was fully a quarter-hour yet before he should move in. A hail to the *Porta Coeli* astern brought him the information that all the other vessels had cleared for action, and he smiled to himself. Freeman and Bush and Howard had no more been able to wait the time out than he had been.

'Remember, Mr Crawley,' he said, 'if I am killed as

we go in, the *Flame* is to be laid alongside the quay. Captain Bush is to be informed as soon as possible, but the Flame is to go on.'

'Aye aye, sir,' said Crawley. 'I'll remember.'

Damn his eyes, he need not be so infernally ordinary about it. From the tone of Crawley's voice one might almost assume that he expected Hornblower to be killed. Hornblower turned away from him and walked the deck briskly to shake off the penetrating cold. He looked along at the men at their stations.

'Skylark, you men,' he ordered. 'Let's see how you can jump.'

There was no use going into action with men chilled to numbness. The men at the guns and waiting at the sheets began to caper at their posts.

'Jump, you men, jump!'

Hornblower leaped grotesquely up and down to set them an example; he wanted them thoroughly warmed up. He flapped his arms against his sides as he leaped, the epaulettes of the full-dress uniform he was wearing pounded on his shoulders.

'Higher than that! Higher!'

His legs were beginning to ache, and his breath came with difficulty, but he would not stop before the men did, although he soon came to regret the impulse which had made him start.

'Still!' he shouted at last, the monosyllable taking almost the last breath from his body. He stood panting, the men grinning.

'Horny for ever!' yelled an unidentifiable voice forward, and a ragged cheer came from the men.

'Silence!'

Brown was beside him with his pistols, a twinkle in his eye.

'Take that grin off your face!' snapped Hornblower.

There would be another Hornblower legend growing up in the Navy, similar to the one about the hornpipe danced on the deck of the *Lydia* during the pursuit of the *Natividad*. Hornblower pulled out his watch, and when he had replaced it took up his speaking-trumpet.

'Mr Freeman! I am going about on the other tack. Hail the squadron to tack in succession. Mr Crawley!'

'Sir!'

'Two hands at the lead, if you please.'

One man might be killed, and Hornblower wanted no possible cessation in the calling of soundings.

'Headsail sheets! Mains'l sheets!'

The *Flame* went about on the starboard tack, making about three knots under fore and aft sail in the light breeze. Hornblower saw the shadowy *Porta Coeli* follow the *Flame*'s example. Behind her, and invisible, was the old *Nonsuch* – Hornblower had still to set eyes on her since her arrival. He had not seen her, for that matter, since he quitted her to catch the typhus in Riga. Good old Bush. It gave Hornblower some comfort to think that he would be supported today by the *Nonsuch*'s thundering broadsides and Bush's stolid loyalty.

The leadsmen were already chanting the depths as the *Flame* felt her way up the fairway towards Le Havre. Hornblower wondered what was going on in the city, and then petulantly told himself that he would know soon enough. It seemed to him as if he could remember every single word of the long discussion he had had with Lebrun, when between them they had settled the details of Lebrun's hare-brained scheme. They had taken into account the possibility of fog – any seaman would be a fool who did not do so in the Bay of the Seine in winter.

'Buoy on the starboard bow, sir,' reported Crawley.

That would mark the middle ground – it was the only buoy the French had left on the approaches to Le Havre. Hornblower watched it pass close alongside and then astern; the flowing tide was heeling it a little and piling up against the seaward side of it. They were nearing the entrance.

'Listen to me, you men,' said Hornblower, loudly. 'Not a shot is to be fired without my orders. The man who fires a gun, for no matter what reason, unless I tell him to, I will not merely flog. I'll hang him. Before sunset today he'll be at the yardarm. D'you hear me?'

Hornblower had every intention of executing his threat – at least at that moment – and as he looked round him his expression showed it. A few muttered Aye aye, sir's showed him he had been understood.

'*Qui va là?*' screamed a voice through the fog from close overside; Hornblower could just see the French boat which habitually rowed guard over the entrance in thick weather. The guard-boat, as Hornblower and Lebrun had agreed, would not be easily diverted from its duty.

'Dispatches for M. le Baron Momas,' hailed Hornblower in return.

The confident voice, the fluent French, the use of Momas' name, might all gain time for the squadron to enter.

'What ship?'

It was inconceivable that the seamen in the guard-boat did not recognize the *Flame* – the question must be a merely rhetorical one asked while the puzzled officer in command collected his thoughts.

'British brig *Flame*,' called Hornblower; he had the helm put over at that moment to make the turn past the point.

'Heave-to, or I will fire into you!'

'If you fire, you will have the responsibility,' replied Hornblower. 'We bear dispatches for Baron Momas.'

It was a fair wind now for the quay. The turn had brought the guard-boat close alongside; Hornblower could see the officer standing up in the bows beside the bow-gun, a seaman at his shoulder with a glowing linstock in his hand. Hornblower's own full-dress uniform must be visible and cause some delay, too, for men expecting to fight would not be expected to wear full dress. He saw the officer give a violent start, having caught sight of the *Porta Coeli* looming up in the mist astern of the *Flame*. He saw the order given, saw the spark thrust on the touchhole. The three-pounder roared, and the shot crashed into the *Flame*'s side. That would give the alarm to the batteries at the point and above the quay.

'We do not fire back,' he hailed – maybe he could gain a little more time, and maybe that time would be of use, although he doubted it.

Here inside the harbour the mist was not so thick. He could see the shadowy shape of the quay rapidly defining itself. In the next few seconds he would know if this were a trap or not, if the batteries should open in a tempest of flame. One part of his mind raced through the data, while another part was working out how to approach the quay. He could not believe that Lebrun was playing a double game, but if it were so only he and the *Flame* would be lost – the other vessels would have a chance to get clear.

'Luff!' he said to the helmsman. There were a few busy seconds as he applied himself to the business of bringing the *Flame* alongside the quay as speedily as possible and yet without damaging her too severely. She came alongside with a creak and a clatter, the fenders groaning as if in agony. Hornblower sprang onto the bulwark and from there to the quay, sword, cocked hat, epaulettes and all. He could not spare time to look round, but he had no doubt that the *Porta Coeli* had anchored, ready to give assistance where necessary, and that the *Nonsuch* in her turn was nearing the quay, her marines drawn up ready for instant landing. He strode up the quay, his heart pounding. There was the first battery, the guns glaring through the embrasures. He could see movement behind the guns, and more men running to the battery from the guardhouse in the rear. Now he had reached the edge of the moat, his left hand held up in a gesture to restrain the men at the guns.

'Where is your officer?' he shouted.

There was a momentary delay, and then a young man in blue and red artillery uniform sprang upon the parapet.

'What do you want?' he asked.

'Tell your men not to fire,' said Hornblower. 'Have you not received your new orders?'

The full dress, the confident bearing, the extraordinary circumstances puzzled the young artillery officer.

'New orders?' he asked feebly.

Hornblower simulated exasperation.

'Get your men away from those guns,' he said. 'Otherwise there may be a deplorable accident.'

'But, *monsieur* –' The artillery lieutenant pointed down to the quay, and Hornblower now could spare the time to glance back, following the gesture. What he saw made his pounding heart pound harder yet for sheer pleasure. There was the *Nonsuch* against the quay, there was the *Camilla* just coming alongside; but more important yet, there was a big solid block of red coats forming up on the quay. One section with an officer at its head was already heading towards them at a quick step, muskets sloped.

'Send a messenger instantly to the other battery,' said Hornblower, 'to make sure the officer in command there understands.'

'But, *monsieur* –'

Hornblower stamped his foot with impatience. He could hear the rhythmic tread of the marines behind him, and he gesticulated to them with his hand behind his back. They marched along past him.

'Eyes left!' ordered the subaltern in command, with a smart salute to the French officer. The courtesy took what little wind was left out of the sails of the Frenchman, so that his new protest died on his lips. The marine detachment wheeled to its left round the flank of the battery on the very verge of its dry ditch. Hornblower did not dare take his eyes from the young Frenchman on the parapet, but he sensed what was going on in the rear of the battery. The sally-port there was open, and the marines marched in, still in column of fours, still with their muskets sloped. Now they were in among the guns, pushing the gunners away from their pieces, knocking the smouldering linstocks out of their hands. The young officer was wringing his hands with anxiety.

'All's well that ends well, *monsieur,*' said Hornblower. 'There might have been a most unpleasant incident.'

Now he could spare a moment to look round. Another marine detachment was off at the quickstep, marching for the other battery. Other parties, seamen and marines, were heading for the other strategic points he had listed in his orders. Brown was coming panting up the slope to be at his side.

The clatter of a horse's hoofs made him turn back again; a mounted French officer was galloping towards them, and reined up amid a shower of flying gravel.

'What is all this?' he demanded. 'What is happening?'

'The news apparently has been delayed in reaching you, monsieur,' said Hornblower. 'The greatest news France has known for twenty years.'

'What is it?'

'Bonaparte rules no more,' said Hornblower. 'Long live the King!'

Those were magic words; words like those of some old-time spell or incantation. No one in the length and breadth of the Empire had dared to say '*Vive le Roi!*' since 1792. The mounted officer's jaw dropped for a moment.

'It is false!' he cried, recovering himself. 'The Emperor reigns.'

He looked about him, gathering his reins into his hands, about to ride off.

'Stop him, Brown!' said Hornblower.

Brown took a stride forward, seized the officer's leg in his huge hands, and with a single heave threw him out of the saddle, Hornblower grabbing the bridle in time to prevent the horse from bolting. Brown ran round and extricated the fallen officer's feet from the stirrups.

'I have need of your horse, sir,' said Hornblower.

He got his foot into the stirrup and swung himself awkwardly up into the saddle. The excited brute plunged and almost threw him, but he squirmed back into the saddle, tugged the horse's head round, and then let him go in a wild gallop towards the other battery. His cocked hat flew from his head, his sword and his epaulettes jerked and pounded as he struggled to keep his seat. He tore past the other marine detachment, and heard them cheer him, and then he managed to rein in the frantic horse on the edge of the ditch. Struck with a new idea, he trotted round to the rear of the battery to the main gate.

'Open,' he shouted, 'in the name of the King!'

That was the word of power. There was a clatter of bolts and the upper half of the huge oaken door opened and a couple of startled faces looked out at him. Behind them he saw a musket levelled at him – someone who was a fanatical Bonapartist, probably, or someone too stolid to be taken in by appearances.

'Take that imbecile's musket away from him!' ordered Hornblower. The pressing need of the moment gave an edge to his tone, so that he was obeyed on the instant. 'Now, open the gate.'

He could hear the marines marching up towards him.

'Open the gate!' he roared.

They opened it, and Hornblower walked his horse forward into the battery.

There were twelve vast twenty-four-pounders mounted inside, pointing out through the embrasures down into the harbour. At the back stood the furnace for heating shot with a pyramid of balls beside it. If the two batteries had opened fire nothing hostile could have endured long on the water, and not merely the water but the quay and the waterfront could have been swept clean. And those batteries, with their parapets five feet thick and eight feet high, and their dry ditches, ten feet deep, cut square in the solid rock, could never have been stormed without regular siege methods. The bewildered gunners stared at him, and at the red-coated marines who came marching in behind him. A callow subaltern approached him.

'I do not understand this, sir,' he said. 'Who are you, and why did you say what you did?'

The subaltern could not bring himself to utter the word 'King'; it was a word that was taboo – he was like some old maid posing a delicate question to a doctor. Hornblower smiled at him, using all his self-control to conceal his exultation, for it would never do to triumph too openly.

'This is the beginning of a new age for France,' he said.

The sound of music came to his ears. Hornblower dismounted and left his horse free, and ran up the steps cut in the back of the parapet, the subaltern following. Standing on the top of the parapet with the vast arms of the semaphore over their heads, the whole panorama of the port was open to them; the squadron lying against the quay, the detachments of the landing party, red-coated or white-shirted, on the march hither and thither, and, on the quay itself, the marine band striding up towards the town, the drums thundering and the bugles braying, the red coats and the white cross-belts and the glittering instruments making a brave spectacle. That had been Hornblower's crowning idea; nothing would be more likely to convince a wavering garrison that he came in peace than a band calmly playing selections as it marched in.

The harbour defences were secured now; he had carried out his part of the scheme. Whatever had happened to Lebrun, the squadron was not in serious danger; if the main garrison had refused to be seduced, and turned against him, he could spike the batteries' guns, blow up the magazines, and warp his ships out almost at leisure, taking with him whatever prisoners and booty he could lay his hands on. The awkward moment had been when the guard-boat had fired its gun – firing is infectious. But the fact of only one shot being fired, the delay, the mist, had made the inexperienced officer in command at the batteries wait for orders, giving him time to use his personal influence. It was evident already that part of Lebrun's scheme, at least, had been successful. Lebrun had not made up his mind, at the time of his leaving the *Flame*, whether it would be a banquet or a council of war to which he would summon the senior officers, but whichever it was he had clearly succeeded in depriving the harbour defences of all direction. Apparently, too, Lebrun's story that a blockade runner was expected to arrive during the night, and his request that the harbour defences should hold their fire until certain as to the identity of any ship entering the port, had had their effect as well – Lebrun had told Hornblower of his intention of making much of the fact that the *Flame*, on her way in to surrender, had actually been attacked so as to give the English the opportunity to recapture her.

'I will have no more muddles of that sort,' Lebrun had said, with a grin. 'Order, counter-order, disorder.'

One way and another he had certainly contrived to create such disorder and such an atmosphere of uncertainty in the batteries as to give Hornblower every chance – the man was a born intriguer; but Hornblower still did not know whether the rest of his *coup d'état* had succeeded. This was no time for delay; there were too many examples in history of promising enterprises brought to naught after a good beginning solely because someone did not push on at the psychological moment.

'Where is my horse?' said Hornblower, leaving the subaltern's desire for information unsatisfied except by the vague statement that a new age was beginning for France.

He climbed down from the parapet again, to find that an intelligent marine was holding the horse's head. The red-coats were making a ludicrous attempt to fraternize with the puzzled French recruits. Hornblower climbed up into the saddle, and trotted out into the open. He wanted to make a bold push, but at the same time he felt nervous about involving his landing party in the narrow streets of the town without some assurance of a friendly reception there. Here came Howard, riding gracefully; apparently he, too, had been able to procure himself a horse.

'Any orders, sir?' Howard asked. Two midshipmen and Brown were running beside him, the midshipmen presumably to act as messengers.

'Not yet,' answered Hornblower, fuming inwardly with anxiety while trying to appear calm.

'Your hat, sir,' said the admirable Brown, who had picked the thing up while on his way from the other battery.

Here came a horseman at a gallop, a white band on his arm, a white handkerchief fluttering in his hand. He reined in when he saw Hornblower's gold lace.

'You are Monsieur – Monsieur –' he began.

'Hornblower.' No Frenchman had ever been able to pronounce that name.

'From Baron Momas, sir. The citadel is secure. He is about to descend into the main square.'

'The soldiers in the barracks?'

'They are tranquil.'

'The main guard at the gate?'

'I do not know, sir.'

'Howard, take your reserve. March for the gate as hard as you can. This man will go with you to explain to the guard. If they will not come over, let them desert. They can march out into the open country – it will not matter. No bloodshed if you can help it, but make sure of the gate.'

'Aye aye, sir.'

Hornblower explained to the Frenchman what he had said.

'Brown, come with me. I shall be in the main square if needed, Howard.'

It was not much of a procession Howard was able to form, two score marines and seamen, but the band blared out as best it could as Hornblower marched triumphantly up the street. The people on the route looked at them, curious or sullen or merely indifferent, but there was no sign of active resentment. In the Place de l'Hôtel de Ville there was far more bustle and life. Numerous men sat their horses there; a detachment of police, drawn up in line, gave an appearance of respectability to the proceedings. But what caught the eye was the multitude of white emblems. There were white cockades in the hats of the gendarmes, and the mounted officials wore white scarves or armbands. White flags – bed sheets, apparently – hung from most of the windows. For the first time in more than twenty years the Bourbon white was being flaunted on the soil of France. A fat man on foot, a white sash round his belly where (Hornblower guessed) yesterday he had worn the tricolour, hurried towards him as he rode in. Hornblower signalled frantically to the band to stop, and scrambled down from the saddle, handing the reins to Brown as he advanced towards the man he guessed to be Momas.

'Our friend!' said Momas, his arms outspread. 'Our ally!'

Hornblower allowed himself to be embraced – even at that moment he wondered at what the leathernecks behind him would think about the sight of a commodore being kissed by a fat Frenchman – and then saluted the rest of the Mayor's staff as they came to greet him. Lebrun was at their head, grinning.

'A great moment, sir,' said the Mayor.

'A great moment indeed, Monsieur le Baron.'

The Mayor waved his hand towards the flagstaff that stood outside the Mairie.

'The ceremony is about to take place,' he said.

Lebrun was at his side with a paper, and Momas took it and mounted the steps at the foot of the flagstaff. He inflated his lungs and began to read at the top of his voice. It was curious how the French love of legal forms and appearances showed itself even here, at this moment of treason; the proclamation was studded with archaisms and seemed interminable in its prolixity. It mentioned the misdeeds of the usurper, Napoleon Bonaparte, it denounced all his pretensions to sovereignty, it disclaimed all allegiance to him. Instead it declared that all Frenchmen voluntarily recognized the unbroken reign of His Most Christian Majesty, Louis XVIII, King of France and Navarre. At those resounding words the men at the foot of the flagstaff hauled busily at the halliards, and the white standard of the Bourbons soared up the mast. It was time for a gesture on the part of the British. Hornblower turned to his men.

'Three cheers for the King!' he yelled.

He waved his cocked hat over his head.

'Hip – hip – hip –' he called.

'Hooray!' yelled the marines.

The cheer rang hollowly round the square; probably not one marine in ten had any idea as to which king he was cheering, but that did not matter.

'Hip – hip – hip –'

'Hooray!'

'Hip – hip – hip –'

'Hooray!'

Hornblower replaced his hat and stiffly saluted the white flag. Now it was time, and high time, to start organizing the defence of the town against Bonaparte's wrath.

II

'Your Excellency,' said Lebrun, sidling into the room where Hornblower sat at his desk, 'a fishermen's deputation has asked for an audience.'

'Yes?' said Hornblower. With Lebrun he was careful not to commit himself prematurely.

'I have endeavoured to discover what it is they seek, Your Excellency.'

Anyone could be quite sure that Lebrun would try to find things out. And so far Hornblower had carefully left Lebrun under the not unnatural illusion that he liked being addressed as 'Your Excellency' in every other sentence, and would be more malleable in consequence.

'Yes?'

'It is a question of one of their vessels being taken as a prize.'

'Yes?'

'It carried one of your certificates to the effect that the vessel was sailing from the free port of Le Havre, and yet an English ship of war took possession of her.'

'Indeed?'

What Lebrun did not know was that lying on the desk before him Hornblower had the report of the captain of the English brig which had made the capture. The captain was convinced that the vessel, before he took her, had just slipped out from Honfleur, across the estuary, having sold her catch there. Honfleur, being still under Bonaparte's rule, and under blockade in consequence, would pay three times as much for fish as could be obtained in liberated Le Havre. It was a question of trading with the enemy, and the Prize Court could be relied upon to adjudicate on the matter.

'We wish to retain the goodwill of the people, Your Excellency, especially of the maritime population. Could you not assure the deputation that the boat will be returned to its owners?'

Hornblower wondered how much the fishing-boat owners of the city had paid Lebrun to exert his influence on their behalf. Lebrun must be making the fortune he craved as much as he craved power.

'Bring the deputation in,' said Hornblower; he had a few seconds in which to compose his speech to them – that was always as well, because his French was deficient enough to make circumlocutions necessary when a word or a grammatical construction evaded him.

The deputation, three grey-haired Norman fishermen with an intense air of respectability and in their Sunday best, came in as near smiles as was possible to their solemn natures; Lebrun must have assured them in the anteroom of the certainty of their request being granted. They were quite taken aback when Hornblower addressed them on the subjects of trading with the enemy and its consequences. Hornblower pointed out that Le Havre was at war with Bonaparte, war to the death. Heads would fall in hundreds if Bonaparte should emerge victorious from this war and recapture Le Havre. The scenes of horror that had been witnessed when Toulon fell twenty years before would be reproduced a thousandfold in Le Havre. A united effort was still necessary to pull the tyrant down.

Let them attend to that, and make no further attempt to increase their personal fortunes. Hornblower wound up by announcing not merely his intention of allowing the fishing-boat to come under the adjudication of the British Prize Court, but also his fixed determination, in the case of any repetition of the offence, to send officers and crew before a court martial whose sentence undoubtedly would be death.

Lebrun ushered the deputation out again. For a moment Hornblower wondered how Lebrun would explain the failure, but he had no time to wonder for more than a moment. The demands upon the time and energy of the Governor of Le Havre were enormous; Hornblower sighed as he looked at the papers stacked on his desk. There was so much to do; Saxton, the engineer officer just arrived from England, was clamouring to build a new battery, a demi-lune or a redan in his barbarous sapper vocabulary – to cover the defences of the Rouen Gate. All very well, but he would have to exact forced labour from the citizens to construct it. There was a mass of papers from Whitehall, mostly reports of spies regarding Bonaparte's strength and movements; he had skimmed through them, but one or two of them needed closer reading. There was the question of unloading the food ships which Whitehall had sent him – Le Havre should undoubtedly be well stocked with food in case of a close siege, but it was left to him to plan the warehousing of a thousand barrels of salt beef. There was the question of policing the streets. Old personal scores had been wiped out, Hornblower guessed, in the one or two murders of prominent Bonapartists – he even suspected Lebrun of having a hand in one of them – and there had already been some attempt at reprisal by secret assassination. He could run no risk, now that the city was under control, of allowing it to be divided against itself. The court martial was in progress of those mutineers of the *Flame* whom he had not pardoned. In every case the sentence would be death, inevitably, and there was food for thought in that. He was Commodore of the British Squadron as well as Governor of Le Havre, and there was all the manifold business of the squadron to be attended to. He must decide about –

Hornblower was already walking up and down. This vast room in the Hôtel de Ville was far better adapted for walking in than was any quarterdeck. He had had two weeks now to adapt himself to the absence of fresh air and wide horizons; his head was bent on his breast and his hands were clasped behind him as he paced, forming the decisions that were demanded of him. This was the reward of success; confinement in an office, chained to a desk; parcelling out his time among a dozen heads of departments and innumerable persons seeking favours. He might as well be a harassed City merchant instead of a naval officer, with the exception that as a naval officer he had the additional labour and responsibility of sending long daily reports to Whitehall. It may have been a great honour to be entrusted with the governorship of Le Havre, to head the attack upon Bonaparte, but it was onerous.

Here came another interruption; an elderly officer in a dark-green uniform waving a paper in his hand. This was – what was his name again? – Hau, a captain in the 60th Rifles. Nobody knew quite what his nationality was by this time; maybe he did not know himself. The 60th, since it had lost its title of Royal Americans, had become rather a depository for aliens in the service of the Crown. He apparently, before the French Revolution, had been a Court official of one of the innumerable little states on the French side of the Rhine. His master had been an exile for twenty years, his master's subjects had been Frenchmen for twenty years, and he himself had been for twenty years employed in odd duties by the British Government.

'The Foreign Office bag is in, sir,' said Hau, 'and this dispatch was marked "urgent".'

Hornblower took his mind from the problem of nominating a new *juge de paix* (to take the place of the recent incumbent, who had apparently escaped to Bonapartist territory) to deal with the new problem.

'They're sending us a prince,' said Hornblower, having read the letter.

'Which one, sir?' asked Hau, with keen and immediate interest.

'The Duc d'Angoulême.'

'Eventual heir of the Bourbon line,' said Hau, judiciously. 'Eldest son of the Comte d'Artois, Louis' brother. By his mother he descends from the House of Savoy. And he married Marie Thérèse, the Prisoner of the Temple, daughter of the martyred Louis XVI. A good choice. He must be aged about forty now.'

Hornblower wondered vaguely what use a royal prince would be to him. It might sometimes be a convenience to have a figurehead, but he could foresee – Hornblower was labouring under all the burden of disillusionment – that the Duke's presence would much more often involve him in additional and unprofitable labours.

'He will arrive tomorrow if the wind is fair,' said Hau.

'And it is,' said Hornblower, looking out of the window at the flagstaff, where fluttered, side by side, the Union flag of England and the white flag of the Bourbons.

'He must be received with all the solemnity the occasion demands,' said Hau, dropping unconsciously into French through a fairly obvious association of ideas. 'A Bourbon prince setting foot on French soil for the first time in twenty years. At the quay he must be greeted by all the authorities. A royal salute. A procession to the church. Te Deum to be sung there. A procession to the Hôtel de Ville, and there a grand reception.'

'That is all your business,' said Hornblower.

The bitter cold of winter still persisted unbroken. Down on the quay, where Hornblower waited while the frigate bearing the Duke was being warped in, a cutting north-easterly wind was blowing, which pierced through the heavy cloak he was wearing. Hornblower was sorry for the seamen and the troops drawn up in line, and for the other seamen who manned the yards of the men-of-war in the harbour. He himself had only just come down from the Hôtel de Ville, staying there until the last moment when a messenger brought him the information that the Duke was about to land, but the dignitaries and minor officials grouped behind him had been assembled some time. It seemed to Hornblower that where he stood he could hear teeth chattering in unison.

He watched with professional interest the warping in

of the frigate; he heard the clanking of the windlass and the sharp orders of the officers. Slowly she drew up to the quay. The sideboys and the bosun's mates came running up the gangway, followed by the officers in full dress. The marine guard of honour formed up. A brow was thrown from the gangway to the quay, and here came the Duke, a tall, stiff man in a Hussar uniform, a blue ribbon across his chest. In the ship the pipes of the bosun's mates twittered in a long call, the marines presented arms, the officers saluted.

'Step forward to greet His Royal Highness, sir,' prompted Hau at Hornblower's elbow.

There was a magic mid-point in the brow over which the Duke was walking; as he passed it he crossed from the British ship to the soil of France. Down came the French royal standard from the frigate's masthead. The pipes died away in one last ecstatic wail. The massed bands burst out in a triumphal march, the salutes began to roar, seamen and soldiers of the guard of honour presented arms after the fashion of two services and two nations. Hornblower found himself stepping forward, laying his cocked hat across his breast in the gesture he had painfully rehearsed under Hau's guidance that morning, and bowing to the representative of His Most Christian Majesty.

'Sir 'Oratio,' said the Duke cordially – for all his lifetime in exile apparently he still had a Frenchman's difficulty in dealing with aspirates. He looked round him. 'France, beautiful France.'

Anything less beautiful than the waterfront of Le Havre with a nor'easter blowing Hornblower could not imagine, but perhaps the Duke meant it, and, anyway, the words would sound well to posterity. Probably the Duke had been coached beforehand to say them, by the grave and uniformed dignitaries who followed him down the brow. One of these the Duke indicated as Monsieur – Hornblower did not catch the name – the *chevalier d'honneur*, and this gentleman in turn presented the equerry and the military secretary.

Out of the tail of his eye Hornblower saw the massed dignitaries behind him straightening themselves up from their concerted bow, their hats still across their stomachs.

'Cover yourselves, gentlemen, I beg of you,' said the Duke, and the grey hairs and the bald heads disappeared as the dignitaries gratefully shielded themselves from the wintry wind.

The Duke's teeth, too, apparently were chattering with cold. Hornblower darted a glance at Hau and at Lebrun, who were, with imperturbable politeness, elbowing each other to be nearest him and the Duke, and decided on the spot to cut down the further presentations to a bare minimum, ignoring the elaborate programme with which Hau and Lebrun had provided him. There would be no use in having a Bourbon prince sent him if he let him die of pneumonia. He had to present Momas, of course – the Baron's name would go down through history; and Bush, the senior naval officer – one of each country to mark the alliance between them, which was convenient, for Bush loved a lord, and royalty he adored. The Duke would be an important name on the list in Bush's memory headed by the Tsar of All the Russias. Hornblower turned and beckoned for the horses to be led up; the equerry hastened to hold the stirrup, and the Duke swung himself into the saddle, a born horseman like all his family. Hornblower mounted the quiet horse he had reserved for himself, and the others followed his example, a few of the civilians a little hampered by their unaccustomed swords. It was only a scant quarter of a mile to the church of Our Lady, and Lebrun had seen to it that every yard of it proclaimed a welcome to the Bourbons – there were white banners in every window, and a triumphal arch in fleurs-de-lis over the approach to the west portal of the church. But the cheers of the people in the street sounded thin in the cutting wind, and the procession could not have been very inspiring, with everybody hunched forward in self-protection.

The church offered them grateful shelter – like the figurative shelter she had to offer to all sinners, thought Hornblower, in a moment before he was engulfed in affairs again. He took his seat behind the Duke; in the tail of his eye he could see Lebrun, who was intentionally stationed there for Hornblower's benefit. By watching him Hornblower could see what had to be done, when to stand and when to kneel, for this was the first time he had ever been in a Catholic church or attended a Catholic ceremony. He was a little sorry that the activity of his mind prevented him from observing everything as closely as he would have liked. The vestments, the age-old ceremonial, might have appealed to him, but he was distracted by thoughts about what sort of pressure Lebrun had put on the officiating priests to get them to risk Bonaparte's wrath in this fashion, and by his wonderings about how much this scion of the Bourbons would wish to take a real part in the campaign, and about what was the exact significance of the reports which had begun to dribble in to the effect that at last Imperial troops were moving on Le Havre.

The incense and the warmth and his fatigue and the inconsequence of his thoughts made him drowsy; he was on the point of nodding off when he was roused by Lebrun's rising to his feet. He hastened to do the same, and the procession filed out of the church again.

From Notre Dame they rode up the Rue de Paris, scourged by the wind, and all round the grand square before dismounting again outside the Hôtel de Ville. The cheers of the people seemed thin and spiritless, and the wave of the hand or the lifting of the hat with which the Duke acknowledged them seemed wooden and mechanical. His Royal Highness possessed much of that stoical power to endure hardship in public without flinching which royalty must always display, but seemingly it had been acquired at the cost of making him silent and reserved. Hornblower wondered whether anything could be made of him, for under the Duke's nominal leadership Frenchmen would soon be shedding the blood of Frenchmen, or would be the moment Hornblower could be sure that he could trust the Bourbon partisans in action against the Bonapartists.

Hornblower watched him down the length of the great hall in the Hôtel de Ville – freezing cold, too, despite the fires which blazed at either end – as he greeted in turn the local dignitaries and their wives who were led up to him. The mechanical smile, the apt but formal phrase of greeting, the carefully graded courtesies, from the inclination of the head to the slight bow; all these indicated the care taken in his schooling. And clustered behind him and at his side were his advisers, the émigré nobles he had brought with him, Momas and Lebrun representing France since the revolution, Hau watching over British interests. No wonder the man acted like a wooden puppet, with all these people pulling the strings.

Hornblower saw the red noses and, above their gloves, the red elbows of the women shivering in the extreme *décolleté* of their Court gowns. Tradesmen's wives, petty officials' wives, badly dressed in clothes hurriedly run up that very day at the news that they were invited to the reception; some of the fat ones panted in corsets pulled tight, and some of the more slender ones tried to display the languorous uncorseted grace which had been fashionable ten years ago. They seethed with excitement at the prospect of meeting royalty. Their husbands caught some of the infection, and bustled about from group to group, but Hornblower knew of the anxiety that gnawed at them, the fear lest the monstrous power of Bonaparte should not be destroyed, lest a few days should find them stripped of their petty fortunes or their prospects of pensions, penniless exiles or victims of the guillotine. One reason why the Duke had come was to force these people to declare themselves openly for the Bourbon cause, and doubtless private hints from Lebrun had much to do with their appearance here. The doubts and the heartaches were concealed – history later would only tell of the brilliant reception which signalled the arrival of a Bourbon prince on French soil. The Young Pretender's reception at Holyrood must have been full of similar undercurrents, Hornblower realized suddenly, whatever popular legend made of it nowadays. But, on the other hand, the Pretender's reception had not been graced by the scarlet of the marines and the blue and gold of the Navy.

Someone was twitching at his sleeve; there seemed to be warning in the touch, and Hornblower turned slowly to find Brown, soberly dressed in his best clothes, at his elbow.

'Colonel Dobbs sent me in to you, sir,' said Brown.

He spoke quietly, without looking directly at his captain, and without moving his lips more than was absolutely necessary. He neither wanted to call the attention of the company to his presence nor to give anyone an opportunity of hearing what he said.

'Well?' asked Hornblower.

'Dispatch come in, sir, and Colonel Dobbs says he'd like you to see it, sir.'

'I'll come in a moment,' said Hornblower.

'Aye aye, sir.'

Brown sidled away; despite his bulk and height, he could be very unobtrusive when he wished. Hornblower waited long enough to make it appear unlikely that his own departure was connected with Brown's message, and then made his way out past the sentries at the door. He strode up the stairs two at a time to his office, where the red-coated marine colonel stood waiting for him.

'They're on their way at last, sir,' said Dobbs, handing over the message for Hornblower to read.

It was a long, narrow strip of paper, yet narrow as it was, it had been longitudinally folded as well as crossways; such a peculiar letter that Hornblower looked a question at Dobbs before reading it.

'It was folded up in a button on the messenger's coat, sir,' explained Dobbs. 'From an agent in Paris.'

Plenty of people in high position, Hornblower knew, were betraying their Imperial master, selling military and political secrets either for present gain or for future advancement. This letter must have been sent by some-one of that sort.

'The messenger left Paris yesterday,' said Dobbs. 'He rode post to Honfleur, and crossed the river after dark today.'

The message was written by someone who knew his business.

'This morning,' it said, 'siege artillery left the artillery park at Sablons by river, going downstream. It included the 107th Regiment of Artillery. The guns were 24-pounders and I believe there were 24 of them. Three companies of sappers and a company of miners were attached. It is said that General Quiot will command. I do not know what other forces he will have.'

There was no signature, and the handwriting was disguised.

'Is this genuine?' asked Hornblower.

'Yes, sir. Harrison says so. And it agrees with those other reports we've been receiving from Rouen.'

So Bonaparte, locked in a death struggle in eastern France with the Russians and the Prussians and the Austrians, fighting for his life in the south against Wellington, had yet contrived to scrape together a force to counter the new menace in the north. There could be no doubt against whom the siege artillery was destined to be used. Down the Seine from Paris his only enemies were the rebels in Le Havre; the presence of sappers and miners was a clear proof that a siege was intended, and that the guns were not merely intended to strengthen some land fortification. And Quiot had some two divisions mustering in Rouen.

The Seine offered Bonaparte every convenience for striking a blow at Le Havre. By water the heavy guns could be moved far more quickly than by road, especially by winter roads; even the troops, packed into barges, would travel faster than on their own feet. Night and day those barges would be towed downstream – by now they must already be nearing Rouen. It could be no more than a matter of a few days before Quiot closed in on the city. Hornblower went back in his mind to the last siege he had witnessed, that of Riga. He remembered the relentless way the approaches crept forward, the steady advance with gabion and fascine; within a few days it would be his responsibility to counter that deadly menace.

He felt a sudden gust of resentment against London for having left him so poorly supported; during the two weeks that Le Havre had been in British hands much might have been done. He had written as strongly as he dared on the inadvisability of an inactive policy – those were the very words he had used, he remembered – but England, with her whole army engaged under Wellington in the south, her life-blood drained by twenty years of warfare, had little enough to spare for him. The rebellion he had instigated had been forced to remain a rebellion on the defensive, and as such only a minor military factor in the tremendous crisis. Politically and morally the effect of his action had been enormous, so they assured him, flatteringly, but the means were utterly wanting to reap any military harvest. Bonaparte, whose Empire was supposed to be tottering, who was fighting for his life on the snow-covered fields of Champagne, could still find two divisions and a siege-train to recapture Le Havre. Was it possible that man could ever be beaten?

Hornblower had forgotten the presence of the marine colonel; he looked past him into vacancy. It was time for the rebellion to cease the defensive, and to take the offensive, however limited its means, however powerful the enemy. Something must be done, something must be dared. He could not bear the thought of cowering behind the fortifications of Le Havre, like a rabbit in its burrow, waiting for Quiot and his sappers to come and ferret him out.

'Let me see that map again,' he said to Dobbs. 'How are the tides now? You don't know? Then find out, man, immediately. And I want a report on the roads between here and Rouen. Brown! Go and get Captain Bush out of the reception.'

He was still making plans and giving provisional orders, when Hau came into the room.

'The reception is ending, sir,' said Hau. 'His Royal Highness is about to retire.'

Hornblower cast one more look at the map of the lower Seine spread before him; his brain was seething, with calculations regarding tides and road distances.

'Oh, very well,' he said. 'I'll come for five minutes.'

He was smiling as he walked in – many eyes turned towards him and noticed it. It was a little ironical that the good people at the reception should feel reassured just because Hornblower had received news of the developing threat to their city.

12

The murky winter day was giving place to murky night. There was little of the grey winter afternoon left as Hornblower stood on the quay watching the boats make ready. It was already dark enough and misty enough for the preparations to be invisible to anyone outside the town, whatever point of vantage he might have chosen for himself. So it was safe for the seamen and the marines to begin to man the boats; it was only an hour before the flood tide should begin, and no moment of the tide ought to be wasted.

This was another of the penalties of success; that he should have to stand here and watch others set off on an expedition that he would have loved to head. But the Governor of Le Havre, the Commodore, could not possibly risk his life and liberty with a petty sortie; the force he was sending out crammed into half a dozen ships' longboats, was so small that he was hardly justified in putting a post captain in command.

Bush came stumping up to him, the thump of his wooden leg on the cobbles alternating with the flatter sound of his one shoe.

'No further orders, sir?' asked Bush.

'No, none. I only have to wish you the best of good fortune now,' said Hornblower.

He put out his hand, and Bush took it – amazing how Bush's hand remained hard and horny as if he still had to haul on braces and halliards. Bush's frank blue eyes looked into his.

'Thank you, sir,' said Bush, and then, after a moment's hesitation. 'Don't you go worrying about us, sir.'

'I won't worry with you in command, Bush.'

There was some truth in that. In all these years of close association Bush had learned his methods, and could be relied upon to execute a plan intelligently. Bush knew as well as he did now the value of surprise, the importance of striking swiftly and suddenly and unexpectedly, the necessity for close cooperation between all parts of the force.

The *Nonsuch*'s longboat was against the quay, and a detachment of marines was marching down into it. They sat stiff and awkward on the thwarts, their muskets pointing skywards between their knees, while the seamen held the boat off.

'All ready, sir?' piped up a voice from the sternsheets.

'Goodbye, Bush,' said Hornblower.

'Goodbye, sir.'

Bush's powerful arms swung him down into the longboat with no difficulty despite his wooden leg.

'Shove off.'

The boat pushed out from the quay; two other boats left the quay as well. There was still just enough light to see the rest of the flotilla pull away from the sides of the ships moored in the harbour. The sound of the orders came to Hornblower's ears across the water.

'Give way.'

Bush's boat swung round and headed the procession out into the river, and the night swallowed it. Yet Hornblower stood looking after them into the blackness for some time before he turned away. There could be no doubt at all, having regard to the state of the roads, and the reports of the spies, that Quiot would bring his siege-train as far as Caudebec by water – barges would carry his vast twenty-four-pounders fifty miles in a day, while over those muddy surfaces they would hardly move fifty miles in a week. At Caudebec there was an *estacade* with facilities for dealing with large cargoes. Quiot's advanced guards at Lillebonne and Bolbec would cover the unloading – so he would think. There was a good chance that boats, coming up the river in the darkness swiftly with the tide, might arrive unobserved at the *estacade*. The landing party could burn and destroy to their hearts' content in that case. Most likely Bonaparte's troops, which had conquered the land world, would not think of the possibility of an amphibious expedition striking by water round their flank; and even if they did think of it there was more than a chance that the expedition, moving rapidly on the tide, would break through the defence in the darkness as far as the barges. But though it was easy enough to form these comforting conclusions, it was not so easy to see them go off in the darkness like this. Hornblower turned away from the quay and began to walk up the dark Rue de Paris to the Hôtel de Ville. Half a dozen dimly perceived figures detached themselves from street corners and walked along a few yards in front and behind him; these were the bodyguards that Hau and Lebrun had detailed for him. They had both of them raised hands and eyes in horror at the thought that he should go about the town unescorted – on foot to make it worse – and when he had refused utterly to have a military guard permanently about him they had made this other arrangement. Hornblower aroused himself by walking as fast as his long thin legs would carry him. The exercise was pleasurable, and it made him smile to himself to hear the pattering of feet as his escort strove to keep pace with him; it was curious that nearly all of them were short-legged men.

In his bedroom there was a privacy to be obtained which he could not hope for elsewhere. He dismissed Brown as soon as the latter had lighted the candles in the stick on the night table at the bedhead, and with a grateful sigh he stretched himself out on the bed, careless of his uniform. He rose again to get his boat-cloak and spread it over himself, for the room was dank and cold despite the fire in the grate. Then at last he could take the newspaper from the top of the pile at the bedhead, and set himself to read seriously the marked passages at which previously he had merely glanced – Barbara had sent him those newspapers; her letter, read and reread, was in his pocket, but all through the day he had not found leisure for the papers.

If the Press was, as it claimed to be, the voice of the people, then the British public most strongly approved of him and his recent actions. It was strangely difficult for Hornblower to recapture the mood of only a few weeks back; the manifold distractions of his duties as Governor of Le Havre made the events preceding the capture of the city very blurred and indistinct in his memory. But here was *The Times* running over with praise for his handling of the situation in the Bay of the Seine. The measure he had taken to make it impossible for the mutineers to take the *Flame* in to the French authorities were described as 'a masterpiece of the ingenuity and skill which we have come to expect of this brilliant officer'. The pontifical manner of the article left Hornblower with the impression that it would have been more appropriate if the 'we' had been spelt with a capital W.

Here was the *Morning Chronicle* expatiating on his capture of the *Flame* across the decks of the *Bonne Celestine*. There was only one example in history of a similar feat – Nelson's capture of the *San Josef* at Cape St Vincent. Hornblower's eyebrows rose as he read. The comparison was quite absurd. There had been nothing else for him to do; he had had only to fight the *Bonne Celestine*'s crew, for hardly a man in the *Flame*'s company had raised a hand to prevent the vessel's recapture. And it was nonsense to compare him with Nelson. Nelson had been brilliant, a man of lightning thought, the inspiration of all who came in contact with him. He himself was only a fortunate plodder by comparison. Extraordinary good fortune was the root of all his success; good fortune, and long thought, and the devotion of his subordinates. It was perfectly horrible that he should be compared with Nelson; horrible and indecent. As Hornblower read on he felt a disquieting sensation in his stomach, exactly as he felt during his first hours at sea after a spell on land, when the ship he was in slid down a wave. Now that this comparison with Nelson had been made the public and the service would judge his future actions by the same standard, and would turn and rend him in their disappointment should be fail. He had climbed high, and as a natural result there was a precipice at his feet. Hornblower remembered how he had felt as a king's letter-boy, when he had first climbed to the maintruck of the *Indefatigable*. The climbing had not been so difficult, not even the futtock-shrouds, but when at the masthead he had looked down he felt dizzy and nauseated, appalled at the distance below him – just as he felt now.

He flung the *Morning Chronicle* aside and took up the *Anti Gallican*. The writer here gloated over the fate of the mutineers. He exulted over the death of Nathaniel Sweet, laying special stress on the fact that he had died at Hornblower's own hands. He went on to hope that Sweet's accessories in the horrible crime of mutiny would shortly meet the fate they deserved, and he hoped that the happy issue of Hornblower's recapture of the *Flame* would not be allowed to serve as an excuse for mercy or sentimental considerations. Hornblower, with twenty sentences of death awaiting his signature, felt his nausea renewed. This writer in the *Anti Gallican* did not know what death was. Before Hornblower's eyes floated once more the memory of Sweet's white hair in the water as the smoke from the musket-shot drifted away. That old man – Chadwick had sworn to disrate him and then flog him. Hornblower decided for the twentieth time that he would have mutinied, too, if confronted with the certainty of a flogging. This writer knew nothing of the sickening crack of the cat-o'-nine-tails as it fell on a naked back. He could never have heard the yell of agony of a grown man under torment.

A later number of *The Times* discussed the capture of Le Havre. There were the words he had been dreading to read, but in Latin, as one might expect of *The Times*. *Initium finis* – the beginning of the end. *The Times* expected

Bonaparte's dominion, which had endured all these years, to melt away in the next few days. The crossing of the Rhine, the fall of Le Havre, the declaration of Bordeaux in favour of the Bourbons, made the writer certain that Bonaparte would be dethroned immediately. Yet Bonaparte with a solid army was still striking back at his enemies today. The last reports told of his victories over the Prussians and the Austrians; Wellington in the south was making only the slowest progress against Soult. No one could foresee an immediate end to the war save this inky scribbler safe in some dusty office in Printing House Square.

But there was a morbid fascination about reading these newspapers. Hornblower put down this copy and reached for another, knowing as he did so that it would only disgust him or frighten him. It was as hard to resist as opium was to an addict. Hornblower read on and on through the marked passages, which dealt mainly with his own achievements, in much the same way that an old maid, by chance alone in her house on a wintry night, might go on reading one of Monk Lewis' terrifying novels, too frightened to stop, and yet knowing that every word she read would only make the stopping more frightening still.

He had hardly finished the pile of newspapers when he noticed the bed jar slightly under him and the candle-flames flicker for a moment. He paid almost no attention to the phenomenon – it might have been a heavy gun being fired, although he had not heard the explosion – but a few seconds later he heard the bedroom door stealthily opened. He looked up to see Brown peering round the corner at him to see if he were asleep.

'What do you want?' he snapped. His ill temper was so obvious that even Brown hesitated to speak.

'Out with it,' snarled Hornblower. 'Why am I being disturbed contrary to my orders?'

Howard and Dobbs made their appearance behind Brown; it was to their credit that they were willing not merely to take the responsibility but to receive the first impact of the wrath of the Commodore.

'There's been an explosion, sir,' said Howard. 'We saw the flash of it in the sky, east by north of here – I took the bearing. That could be at Caudebec.'

'We felt the jar, sir,' said Dobbs. 'But there was no sound – too far away. A big explosion to shake us here and yet be unheard.'

That meant, almost for certain, that Bush had been successful. He must have captured the French powder-barges and blown them up. A thousand rounds for each of twenty-four twenty-four-pounders – the minimum for a siege; eight pounds of powder for each round. That would be eight times twenty-four thousand. That would be nearly two hundred thousand pounds. That would be almost a hundred tons. A hundred tons of gunpowder would make a fair explosion. Having computed his calculation, Hornblower refocused his eyes on Dobbs and Howard; until then he had looked at them without seeing them. Brown had tactfully slipped out from this council of his betters.

'Well?' said Hornblower.

'We thought you would like to know about it, sir,' said Dobbs, lamely.

'Quite right,' said Hornblower, and held up his newspaper between them again. Then he pulled it down again just long enough to say, 'Thank you.'

From behind his newspaper Hornblower heard his two staff officers creep out of the room and shut the door gently behind them. He was pleased with his performance; that final 'thank you' had been a masterly touch, conveying the impression that, even though he was loftily above such trifles as the mere destruction of a siege-train, he could yet remember his manners before his inferiors. Yet it was only a moment before he was sneering at himself for relishing such a petty triumph. He felt a sudden self-contempt, which even when it passed left him depressed and unhappy. The unhappiness had a special quality; Hornblower, laying aside his newspaper to look up at the play of shadows on the bedtester, suddenly realized he was lonely. He wanted company. He wanted friendship. Much more than that, he wanted comforting, he wanted affection, he wanted just what he could not have as governor of this bleak, beleaguered city. He bore all the vast weight of responsibility, and he had no one to share his fears and hopes. Hornblower pulled himself up on the verge of an abyss of self-pity, his self-contempt greatly increased by the discovery. He had always been too self-analytical and too conscious of his own faults to be sorry for himself. His present loneliness was of his own making. He need not have been so gratuitously reserved with Dobbs and Howard; a sensible man would have shared their pleasure, would have sent for a bottle of champagne to celebrate the success, would have passed a pleasant hour or two with them – and would certainly have increased their pleasure and their loyalty by hinting that the success was largely due to their contributions to the plan, even though it was not true. For the ephemeral and extremely doubtful pleasure of showing himself to be what he was not, a man untouched by human emotions, he was now having to pay the present price of loneliness. Well, decided Hornblower, swallowing a decidedly bitter truth, it served him right.

He pulled out his watch; half an hour since the explosion, and the ebb tide had been running here at the river's mouth for a full hour longer than that. It must have turned some time ago at Caudebec; it was to be hoped that Bush and his flotilla were running down with it, exulting in their victory. Fully twenty-five miles by road, thirty at least by river, from their nearest enemies at Le Havre, the soldiers of the French siege-train must have thought themselves perfectly secure with an army of nearly twenty thousand men to protect them from an enemy who so far had shown no sign of taking the offensive. Yet in less than six hours, even in darkness, well-manned boats with the racing Seine tide behind them could span the interval that infantry would take two days – the daylight hours of two days – to cross. Boats could strike and escape again in the course of a single night up the broad and bridgeless river; and the fact that the river was broad and bridgeless would encourage Quiot's army to look upon the Seine as a protection to their flank and so to forget its potentialities as a highway for their enemies. Quiot had until recently commanded a division in the Imperial Guard, and never, in its ten victorious years, had the Imperial Guard taken part in an amphibious campaign.

Hornblower realized that he had been through all this train of thought before, many times over. He snuffed the guttered candles, looked at his watch again, and stretched his legs restlessly under his cloak. His hand fluttered tentatively towards the tumbled newspapers and was withdrawn immediately. Rather the unpalatable company of his own thoughts than that of *The Times* and the *Morning Chronicle*. Rather than either – humble pie, especially as it would be made a little more appetizing by the knowledge that he would be doing his duty. He flung the cloak off his legs and rose to his feet. He went to some trouble to pull his coat into position, and he combed his hair with some care before sauntering out of his bedroom. The sentry at the door came to attention with a jerk – Hornblower guessed that he had been sleeping on his feet – while Hornblower crossed the hall to the room beyond. He opened the door into warm stuffiness. A single shaded candle hardly illuminated the room enough for him to see. Dobbs was asleep in a chair at a table, his head resting on his folded forearms; beyond the table lay Howard on a cot. The shadow there was so dense that Hornblower could not see his face, but he could hear his low, measured snores.

So nobody wanted his company after all. Hornblower withdrew and shut the door quietly. Brown presumably was asleep in some cubbyhole of his own; Hornblower toyed with the idea of sending for him and having him make him a cup of coffee, but decided against it out of pure humanity. He climbed back onto his own bed and dragged the cloak over him. A whistling draught decided him to draw the curtains round the bed, and he did so after extinguishing the candles. It occurred to him that he would have been much more comfortable had he undressed and got into the bed, but he could not face the effort – it suddenly became plain to him that he was very weary. His eyelids closed before the solid darkness within the curtains, and he slept, fully dressed.

13

The fact that he had not taken off his clothes told Brown and Dobbs and Howard at dawn that Hornblower had not been as composed and self-confident as he had tried to appear, but not one of them was foolish enough to comment on the fact. Brown merely opened the curtain and made his report.

'Day just breaking, sir. Cold morning with a bit o' fog. The last o' the ebb, sir, and no news as yet of Captain Bush an' the flotilla.'

'Right,' said Hornblower, getting stiffly to his feet. He yawned and felt his bristling cheeks. He wished he knew how Bush had succeeded. He wished he did not feel so unwashed and unclean. He wanted his breakfast, but he wanted news of Bush even more. He was still deadly tired despite his hours of unbroken sleep. Then he fought down his weariness in a direct personal struggle like that of Christian with Apollyon.

'Get me a bath, Brown. Make it ready while I shave.'

'Aye aye, sir.'

Hornblower stripped off his clothes and proceeded to shave himself at the wash-hand-stand in the corner of the room. He kept his eyes from his naked body reflected in the mirror, from his skinny, hairy legs and slightly protuberant belly, as resolutely as he kept his mind from his fatigue and from his anxiety about Bush. Brown and a marine private came in carrying the bath and put it on the floor near him; Hornblower, shaving carefully round the corners of his lips, heard the hot water being poured into it from buckets. It took a little while to compound the mixture in the right proportion so as to get the temperature suitable; Hornblower stepped into it and sank down with a sigh of satisfaction – an immense amount of water poured over the sides, displaced by his body, but he did not care. He thought about soaping himself, but flinched from the effort and the physical contortions necessary, and instead he lay back and allowed himself to soak and relax. He closed his eyes.

'Sir!'

Howard's voice caused him to reopen them.

'Two boats are in sight coming down the estuary, sir. Only two.'

Bush had taken seven boats with him to Caudebec. Hornblower could only wait for Howard to finish his report.

'One of 'em's *Camilla*'s launch, sir. I can recognize her through the glass. I don't think the other is from *Nonsuch*, but I can't be sure.'

'Very good, Captain. I'll join you in a moment.'

Ruin and destruction; five boats lost out of seven – and Bush lost too, seemingly. The destruction of the French siege-train – if it were destroyed – would be well worth the loss of the whole flotilla, to someone who could coldly balance profit and loss. But Bush gone! Hornblower could not bear the thought of it. He sprang from his bath and looked round for a towel. He saw none, and with exasperation tore a sheet from the bed on which to dry himself. Only when he was dry and seeking his clean shirt did he find the towels by the dressing table where they should have been. He dressed hurriedly, and at every moment his fears and his sorrow on account of Bush increased – the first shock had not been nearly as severe as this growing realization of his bereavement. He came out into the anteroom.

'One boat's coming into the quay, sir. I'll have the officer reporting here in fifteen minutes,' said Howard.

Brown was across the room at the far door. Now, if ever, Hornblower had the opportunity – his unaccountable brain recognized it at this moment – to show himself a man of iron. All he had to do was to say 'My breakfast, Brown' and sit down and eat it. But he could not pose, faced as he was by the possibility of Bush's death. It was all very well to do those things when it was merely a battle that lay before him, but this was the loss of his dearest friend. Brown must have read the expression on his face, for he withdrew without making any suggestion about breakfast. Hornblower stood undecided.

'I have the court-martial verdicts here for confirmation, sir,' said Howard, calling his attention to a mass of papers.

Hornblower sat down and picked one up, looked at it unseeing, and put it down again.

'I'll deal with that later on,' he said.

'Cider's begun coming into the city from the country in great quantity, sir, now that the farmers have found it's a good market,' said Dobbs. 'Drunkenness among the men's increasing. Can we –?'

'I'll leave it to your judgement,' said Hornblower. 'Now. What is it you want to do?'

'I would submit, sir, that –'

The discussion lasted a few minutes. It led naturally

to the vexed question of an established rate of exchange for British and French currency. But it could not dull the gnawing anxiety about Bush.

'Where the hell's that officer?' said Howard, petulantly pushing back his chair and going out of the room. He was back almost immediately.

'Mr Livingstone, sir,' he said. 'Third of *Camilla*.'

A middle-aged lieutenant, steady and reliable enough to outward appearance; Hornblower looked him over carefully as he came into the room.

'Make your report, please.'

'We went up the river without incident, sir. *Flame*'s boat went aground but was refloated directly. We could see the lights of Caudebec before we were challenged from the bank – we were just rounding the bend, then. Cap'n Bush's longboat was leading, sir.'

'Where was your boat?'

'Last in the line, sir. We went on without replying, as our orders said. I could see two barges anchored in midstream, an' clusters of others against the bank. I put the tiller over and ran beside the one farthest downstream, as my orders said, sir. There was a lot of musketry fire higher up, but only a few Frenchies where we were, an' we chased 'em away. On the bank where we were there were two twenty-four-pounders on travelling carriages. I had 'em spiked, and then we levered them off the bank into the river. One fell onto the barge underneath an' went through it, sir. It sank alongside my launch, deck just level with the water; just before the turn of the tide, that was. Don't know what she carried, sir, but I think she was light, judging by the height she rode out of the water when I boarded her. Her hatches were open.'

'Yes?'

'Then I led my party along the bank as ordered, sir. There was a lot of shot there, just landed from the next barge. The barge was only half unloaded. So I left a party to scuttle the barge and roll the shot into the river, an' went on myself with about fifteen men, sir. *Flame*'s boat's crew was there, an' the party they were fighting against ran away when we came on their flank. There were guns on shore and guns still in the barges, sir. We spiked 'em all, threw the ones that had been landed into the river, and scuttled the barges. There was no powder, sir. My orders were to blow the trunnions off the guns if I could, but I couldn't.'

'I understand.'

Guns spiked and pitched into the slime at the bottom of a rapid tidal river would be out of action for some time, even though it would have been better to blow off their trunnions and disable them permanently. And the shot at the bottom of the river would be difficult to recover. Hornblower could picture so well in his mind the fierce and bloody little struggle in the dark on the river bank.

'Just then we heard drums beating, sir, and a whole lot of soldiers came bearing down on us. A battalion of infantry, I should think it was – I think we had only been engaged up to then with the gunners an' sappers. My orders were to withdraw if opposed in force, so we ran back to the boats. We'd just shoved off and the soldiers were firing at us from the banks when the explosion came.'

Livingstone paused. His unshaven face was grey with fatigue, and when he mentioned the explosion his expression changed to one of helplessness.

'It was the powder-barges higher up the river, sir. I don't know who set them off. Maybe it was a shot from the shore. Maybe Cap'n Bush, sir –'

'You had not been in touch with Captain Bush since the attack began?'

'No, sir. He was at the other end of the line to me, and the barges were in two groups against the bank. I attacked one, an' Cap'n Bush attacked the other.'

'I understand. Go on about the explosion.'

'It was a big one, sir. It threw us all down. A big wave came an' swamped us, filled us to the gunnels, sir. I think we touched the bottom of the river, sir, after that wave went by. A bit of flying wreckage hit *Flame*'s boat. Gibbons, master's mate, was killed an' the boat smashed. We picked up the survivors while we bailed out. Nobody was firing at us from the bank any more, so I waited. It was just the top of the tide, sir. Presently two boats came down to us, *Camilla*'s second launch and the fishing-boat that the marines manned. We waited, but we could not see anything of *Nonsuch*'s boats. Mr Hake of the marines told me that Cap'n Bush an' the other three boats were all alongside the powder-barges when the explosion happened. Perhaps a shot went into the cargo, sir. Then they began to open fire on us from the bank again, and as senior officer I gave the order to retire.'

'Most likely you did right, Mr Livingstone. And then?'

'At the next bend they opened fire on us with field-pieces, sir. Their practice was bad in the dark, sir, but they hit and sank our second launch with almost their last shot, and we lost several more men – the current was running fast by then.'

That was clearly the end of Livingstone's story, but Hornblower could not dismiss him without one more word.

'But Captain Bush, Mr Livingstone? Can't you tell me any more about him?'

'No, sir. I'm sorry, sir. We didn't pick up a single survivor from the *Nonsuch*'s boats. Not one.'

'Oh, very well then, Mr Livingstone. You had better go and get some rest. I think you did very well.'

'Let me have your report in writing and list of casualties before the end of the day, Mr Livingstone,' interposed Dobbs – as Assistant Adjutant General he lived in an atmosphere of reports and lists of casualties.

'Aye aye, sir.'

Livingstone withdrew, and the door had hardly closed upon him before Hornblower regretted having let him go with such chary words of commendation. The operation had been brilliantly successful. Deprived of his siege-train and munitions, Quiot would not be able to besiege Le Havre, and it would probably be a long time before Bonaparte's War Ministry in Paris could scrape together another train. But the loss of Bush coloured all Hornblower's thoughts. He found himself wishing that he had never conceived the plan – he would rather have stood a siege here in Le Havre and have Bush alive at his side. It was hard to think of a world without Bush in it, of a future where he would never, never see Bush again. People would think the loss of a captain and a hundred and fifty men a small price to pay for robbing Quiot of all his offensive power, but people did not understand.

Dobbs and Howard were sitting glum and silent when

he glanced at them; they respected his sorrow. But the sight of their deferential gloom roused Hornblower's contrariness. If they expected him to be upset and unable to work, he would show them how mistaken they were.

'I'll see those court martial reports now, Captain Howard, if you please.'

The busy day's work began; it was possible to think clearly, to make decisions, to work as if nothing had happened, despite the feeling of being drained dry by unhappiness. Not merely that; it was even possible to think of new plans.

'Go and find Hau,' he said to Howard. 'Tell him I'd like to see the Duke for a moment.'

'Aye aye, sir,' Howard rose to his feet. He allowed himself a grin and a twinkle as he pompously reworded Hornblower's language.

'Sir Horatio solicits the favour of a short audience with His Royal Highness if His Royal Highness will be so kind as to condescend to receive him.'

'That's right,' said Hornblower, smiling in spite of himself. It was even possible to smile.

The Duke received him standing, warming the royal back before a cheerful fire.

'I do not know,' began Hornblower, 'if Your Royal Highness is acquainted with the circumstances which first brought me to the waters on this part of the coast.'

'Tell me about them,' said the Duke. Maybe it was not etiquette for royalty to admit ignorance on any subject. The Duke's attitude did not seem to convey a feeling of much interest in any case.

'There was a mutiny in one of His Majesty's – one of His Britannic Majesty's – ships of war.'

'Indeed?'

'I was sent to deal with it, and I succeeded in capturing the vessel and most of the mutineers, Your Royal Highness.'

'Excellent, excellent.'

'Some twenty of them were tried, convicted, and have now been sentenced to death.'

'Excellent.'

'I would be glad not to carry those sentences out, Your Royal Highness.'

'Indeed?' His Royal Highness was not apparently greatly interested – a yawn seemed to be hesitating only just inside the royal lips.

'As far as my service is concerned, it is impossible for me to pardon the men without the gravest prejudice to discipline, Your Royal Highness.'

'Quite so. Quite so.'

'But if Your Royal Highness were to intervene on behalf of the men, I might then be able to pardon them without prejudice to discipline, being in a position where I can deny Your Royal Highness nothing.'

'And why should I intervene, Sir 'Oratio?'

Hornblower sidestepped the question for the moment.

'Your Royal Highness could take the stand that it would be unfitting that the opening days of the return of the Dynasty to France should be marred by the shedding of the blood of Englishmen, however guilty. It would then be possible for me to pardon them, with a great show of reluctance. Men tempted to mutiny in the future would not have their temptation greatly increased by the hope of a similar event saving them from the consequences of their actions – the world will never again be so fortunate as to see a return of Your Royal Highness' family to its legitimate position.'

This last was a clumsy compliment, clumsily worded and susceptible to misunderstanding, but luckily the Duke took it in the spirit in which it was ostensibly meant. Nevertheless, he hardly seemed enthusiastic; he went back to his original point with Bourbon stubbornness.

'But why should I do this, Sir 'Oratio?'

'In the name of common humanity, Your Royal Highness. There are twenty lives to be saved, the lives of useful men.'

'Useful men? Mutineers? Presumably Jacobins, revolutionaries, equalitarians – even Socialists!'

'They are men who lie in irons today and expect to be hanged tomorrow, Your Royal Highness.'

'As I have no doubt whatever, they deserve, Sir 'Oratio. It would be a fine beginning to the Regency with which His Most Christian Majesty has entrusted me if my first public act should be to solicit the lives of a parcel of revolutionaries. His Most Christian Majesty has not spent the past twenty-one years combating the spirit of revolution for that. The eyes of the world are upon me.'

'I have never yet known the world offended by an act of clemency, Your Royal Highness.'

'You have strange ideas of clemency, sir. It appears to me as if this remarkable suggestion of yours has some purpose other than is apparent. Perhaps you are a Liberal yourself, one of these dangerous men who consider themselves thinkers. It would be a good stroke of policy for you to induce my family to brand itself by its first act as willing to condone revolution.'

The monstrous imputation took Hornblower completely aback.

'Sir!' he spluttered. 'Your Royal Highness –'

Even if he had been speaking in English, words would have failed him. In French he was utterly helpless. It was not merely the insult, but it was the revelation of the Bourbon narrow-mindedness and suspicious cunning that helped to strike him dumb.

'I do not see fit to accede to your request, sir,' said the Duke, his hand on the bellrope.

Outside the audience chamber Hornblower strode past courtiers and sentries, his cheeks burning. He was blind with fury – it was very rarely that he was as angry as this; nearly always his tendency to look at both sides of a question kept him equable and easy-going; weak, he phrased it to himself in moments of self-contempt. He stamped into his office, flung himself into his chair and sprang up from it again a second later, walked round the room and sat down again. Dobbs and Howard looked with astonishment at the thundercloud on his brow, and after their first glance bent their gaze studiously upon the papers before them. Hornblower tore open his neck-cloth. He ripped open the buttons of his waistcoat, and the dangerous pressure within began to subside. His mind was in a maelstrom of activity, but over the waves of thought, like a beam of sunshine through a squall at sea, came a gleam of amusement at his own fury. With no softening of his resolution his mischievous sense of humour began to assert itself; it only took a few minutes for him to decide on his next action.

'I want those French fellows brought in here who came with the Duke,' he announced. 'The equerry, and the *chevalier d'honneur*, and the almoner. Colonel Dobbs, I'll trouble you to make ready to write from my dictation.'

The émigré advisers of the Duke filed into the room a little puzzled and apprehensive; Hornblower received them still sitting, in fact almost lounging back in his chair.

'Good morning, gentlemen,' he said, cheerfully. 'I have asked you to come to hear the letter I am about to dictate to the Prime Minister. I think you understand English well enough to get the gist of the letter. Are you ready, Colonel?

> *To the Right Honourable Lord Liverpool.*
>
> *My Lord, I find I am compelled to send back to England His Royal Highness the Duke d'Angoulême.*

'Sir!' said the astonished equerry, breaking in, but Hornblower waved him impatiently to silence.

'Go on, Colonel, please.

> *I regret to have to inform Your Lordship that His Royal Highness has not displayed the helpful spirit the British nation is entitled to look for in an ally.*

The equerry and the *chevalier d'honneur* and the almoner were on their feet by now. Howard was goggling at him across the room; Dobbs' face was invisible as he bent over his pen, but the back of his neck was a warm purple which clashed with the scarlet of his tunic.

'Please go on, Colonel.

During the few days in which I have had the honour of working with His Royal Highness, it has been made plain to me that His Royal Highness has neither the tact nor the administrative ability desirable in one in so high a station.

'Sir!' said the equerry. 'You cannot send that letter.'

He spoke first in French and then in English; the *chevalier d'honneur* and the almoner made bilingual noises of agreement.

'No?' said Hornblower.

'And you cannot send His Royal Highness back to England. You cannot! You cannot!'

'No?' said Hornblower again, leaning back in his chair.

The protests died away on the lips of the three Frenchmen. They knew as well as Hornblower, as soon as they were forced to realize the unpalatable truth, who it was that held the power in Le Havre. It was the man who had under his command the only disciplined and reliable military force, the man who had only to give the word to abandon the city to the wrath of Bonaparte, the man at whose word the ships came in and went out again.

'Don't tell me,' said Hornblower with elaborate concern, 'that His Royal Highness would physically oppose an order from me consigning him on board a ship? Have you gentlemen ever witnessed a deserter being brought in? The frogmarch is a most undignified method of progression. Painful, too, I am informed.'

'But that letter,' said the equerry, 'would discredit His Royal Highness in the eyes of the world. It would be a most serious blow to the cause of the Family. It might endanger the succession.'

'I was aware of that when I invited you gentlemen to hear me dictate it.'

'You would never send it,' said the equerry with a momentary doubt regarding Hornblower's strength of will.

'I can only assure you gentlemen that I both can and will.'

Eyes met eyes across the room, and the equerry's doubt vanished. Hornblower's mind was entirely made up.

'Perhaps, sir,' said the equerry, clearing his throat and looking sidelong at his colleagues for their approval 'there has been some misunderstanding. If His Royal Highness has refused some request of Your Excellency's, as I gather has been the case, it must have been because His Royal Highness did not know how much importance Your Excellency attached to the matter. If Your Excellency would allow us to make further representations to His Royal Highness –'

Hornblower was looking at Howard, who very intelligently recognized his cue.

'Yes, sir,' said Howard. 'I'm sure His Royal Highness will understand.'

Dobbs looked up from his paper and made corroborative sounds. But it took several minutes before Hornblower could be persuaded to postpone putting his decision into instant effect. It was only with the greatest reluctance that he yielded to the pleadings of his own staff and the Duke's. After the equerry had led his colleagues from the room to seek the Duke, Hornblower sat back with a real relaxation replacing the one he had simulated. He was tingling and glowing both with the after-effects of excitement and with his diplomatic victory.

'His Royal Highness will see reason,' said Dobbs.

'No doubt about it,' agreed Howard, judiciously.

Hornblower thought of the twenty seamen chained in the hold of the *Nonsuch*, expecting to be hanged tomorrow.

'An idea has struck me, sir,' said Howard. 'I can send a flag of truce out to the French forces. A *parlementaire* – a mounted officer with a white flag and a trumpeter. He can carry a letter from you to General Quiot, asking for news about Captain Bush. If Quiot knows anything at all I'm sure he'll have the courtesy to inform you, sir.'

Bush! In the excitement of the last hour Hornblower had forgotten about Bush. His pleasurable excitement escaped from him like grain from a ripped sack. Depression closed in upon him again. The others saw the change that came over him; as an example of the affection for him which he had inspired in this short time of contact it is worthy of mention that they would rather have seen the black thundercloud of rage on his brow than this wounded unhappiness.

14

It was the day that the *parlementaire* returned; Hornblower would always remember it for that reason. Quiot's courteous letter left no ground for hope whatever; the gruesome details which it included told the whole story. A few rags and tatters of men had been found and had been buried, but nothing that could be identified as any individual. Bush was dead; that burly body of his had been torn into shreds by the explosion. Hornblower was angry with himself for allowing the fact that Bush's grave would never be marked, that his remains were utterly destroyed, to increase his sadness. If Bush had been given a choice, he presumably would have chosen to die at sea, struck down by a shot in the moment of victory at the climax of a ship-to-ship action; he would have wished to have been buried in his hammock, round-shot at his feet and head, with seamen weeping as the grating tilted and the hammock slid from under the flag into the sea and the ship rocked on the waves, hove-to with backed topsails. It was a horrid irony that he should have met his end in a minor skirmish on a river bank, blown into bloody unidentifiable rags.

And yet what did it matter how he died? One moment he had been alive and the next dead, and in that he had been fortunate. It was a far greater irony that he should have been killed now, after surviving twenty years of desperate warfare. Peace was only just over the horizon, with the allied armies closing in on Paris, with France fast bleeding to death, with the allied Governments already assembling to decide on the peace terms. Had Bush survived this one last skirmish, he would have been able to enjoy the blessings of peace for many years, secure in his captain's rank, in his pension, in the devotion of his sisters. Bush would have enjoyed all that, if only because he knew that all sensible men enjoyed peace and security. The thought of that only increased Hornblower's feeling of bitter personal loss. He had never thought he could mourn for anyone as he mourned for Bush.

The *parlementaire* had only just returned with Quiot's letter; Dobbs was still eagerly questioning him about what he had been able to observe of the condition of the French forces, when Howard came rapidly in.

'*Gazelle*, sloop of war, just entering the harbour, sir. She is wearing the Bourbon flag at the main and makes this signal, sir. "Have on board Duchess of Angoulême."'

'She has?' said Hornblower. His spirit climbed wearily out of its miserable lethargy. 'Tell the Duke. Let Hau know and tell him to arrange about salutes. I must meet her on the quay along with the Duke. Brown! Brown! My dress coat and my sword.'

It was a watery day with a promise of early spring. The *Gazelle* came warping against the quay, and the salutes rolled round the harbour just as they had done when His Royal Highness arrived. The Duke and his entourage stood in almost military formation on the quay; upon the deck of the *Gazelle* was gathered a group of women in cloaks awaiting the casting of the brow across to the quay. Bourbon court etiquette seemed to dictate a rigid absence of any appearance of excitement; Hornblower, standing with his staff a little to the rear and to the side of the Duke's party, noted how the women on deck and the men on the quay made no signal of welcome to each other. Except for one woman, who was standing by the mizzen-mast waving a handkerchief. It was something of a comfort to see that there was at least one person who refused to be bound by stoical etiquette; Hornblower supposed that it must be some serving-woman or lady's maid who had caught sight of her lover in the ranks on the quay.

Over the brow came the Duchess and her suite; the Duke took the regulation steps forward to greet her. She went down in the regulation curtsy, and he lifted her up with the regulation condescension, and they put cheek to cheek in the regulation embrace. Now Hornblower had to come forward to be presented, and now he was bowing to kiss the gloved hand laid upon his levelled forearm.

'Sir 'Oratio! Sir 'Oratio!' said the Duchess.

Hornblower looked up to meet the blue Bourbon eyes. The Duchess was a beautiful woman of some thirty years of age. She had something urgent to say, obviously. As if tongue-tied, she was unable to say it, the rules of etiquette making no allowance for this situation. Finally she made a frantic gesture, and looked round her to call Hornblower's attention to someone behind her. A woman stood there, standing alone, separated a little from the group of ladies-in-waiting and *dames d'honneur*. It was Barbara – Hornblower had to look twice before he could believe his eyes. She stepped towards him, smiling. Hornblower took two strides towards her – in the midst of them he thought briefly of the necessity of not turning his back upon royalty, but threw discretion to the winds – and she was in his arms. There was a tumult of thoughts in his mind as she put her lips, icy cold from the sea air, against his. It was sensible enough that she had come, he supposed, although he had always strongly disapproved of captains and admirals who had their wives with them on active service. As the Duchess had come it would be quite desirable to have Barbara here as well. All this in a flash, before more human feelings became apparent. A warning cough from Hau behind him told him that he was holding up the proceedings, and he hastily took his hands from Barbara's shoulders and stepped back a little sheepishly. The carriages were waiting.

'You go with the royal pair, sir,' whispered Hau, hoarsely.

The carriages requisitioned in Le Havre were not striking examples of coach-building, but they served. The Duke and Duchess were seated, and Hornblower handed Barbara in and took his seat beside her, his back and hers to the horses. With a clatter of hoofs and a generous squeaking they set off up the Rue de Paris.

'Was that not a pleasant surprise, Sir 'Oratio?' asked the Duchess.

'Your Royal Highness was far too kind,' said Hornblower.

The Duchess leaned forward and put her hand on Barbara's knee.

'You have a most beautiful and most accomplished wife,' she said.

The Duke beside her uncrossed his knees and

coughed uncomfortably, for the Duchess was acting with a condescension a trifle excessive in a king's daughter, a future queen of France.

'I trust you had a comfortable voyage,' said the Duke, addressing himself to his wife; a mischievous curiosity prompted Hornblower to wonder if there was ever a moment when he did not use a tone of such rigid formality towards her.

'We will pass over the memory of it,' said the Duchess with a laugh.

She was a high-spirited and lovely creature, and running over with excitement at this new adventure. Hornblower watched her curiously. Her infancy had been passed as a princess in the most splendid Court of Europe; her childhood as a prisoner of the revolutionaries. Her father and mother, the king and queen, had died under the guillotine; her brother had died in prison. She herself had been exchanged for a parcel of captive generals, and married to her cousin, had wandered through Europe as the wife of the heir to a penniless but haughty Pretender. Her experiences had left her human – or was it that the formalities of shabby-genteel royalty had not succeeded in dehumanizing her? She was the only living child of Marie Antoinette, whose charm and vivacity and indiscretion had been proverbial. That might explain it.

Here they were, climbing out of the carriage at the Hôtel de Ville; a naval cocked hat was a clumsy thing to keep under the arm while handing ladies out. There was to be a reception later, but time must be allowed for the Duchess' trunks to be swayed up out of the *Gazelle*'s hold, and for the Duchess to change her dress.

Hornblower found himself leading Barbara to the wing which constituted his headquarters. In the lobby orderlies and sentries came to attention; in the main office Dobbs and Howard gaped at the spectacle of the Governor ushering in a lady. They scrambled to their feet and Hornblower made the presentations. They bowed and scraped to her; they knew of her, of course – everyone had heard about Lady Barbara Hornblower, the Duke of Wellington's sister.

Glancing automatically at his desk, Hornblower caught sight of Quiot's letter lying there where he had left it, with its beautiful handwriting and elaborate signature and paraph. It reminded him once more that Bush was dead. *That* sorrow was real, acute, actual; Barbara's coming had been so unexpected that it was not real to him yet. That fantastic mind of his refused to dwell on the central point that Barbara was once more with him, but flew off at ridiculous tangents. It liked its details well-ordered, and insisted on them; it would not let him sink into simple uxorious happiness, but rather chose to work on the practical details – never thought of until that time – of the arrangement of the life of an officer on active service, who, while locked in a death grapple with an Emperor, yet had a wife to think about. Many-sided Hornblower may have been, but the mainspring of his life was his professional duty. For more than twenty years, for all his adult life, he had been accustomed to sacrifice himself for that, to such an extent and for so long that the sacrifice now was automatic and usually ungrudging. He was so set on his struggle with Bonaparte and had been plunged so deep into it during the last months that he was inclined to resent distractions.

'This way, dear,' he said, at length, a little hoarsely – he was about to clear his throat when he checked himself. The need for throat-clearing was a sure symptom of nervousness and shyness. Barbara had lightly teased him out of it years ago, and he would not clear his throat now, not in front of Barbara, not in front of himself.

They crossed the little ante-room and Hornblower threw open the door into the bedroom, standing aside for Barbara to pass through, and then he entered after her and shut the door. Barbara was standing in the centre of the floor, her back to the foot of the big bed. There was a smile on one side of her mouth; one eyebrow was raised above the other. She raised one hand to unfasten the clasp of her cloak, but let it drop again, its work uncompleted. She did not know whether to laugh or to cry over this incalculable husband of hers; but she was a Wellesley, and pride forbade her to weep. She stiffened herself just one second before Hornblower came forward to her one second too late.

'Dear,' he said, and took her cold hands.

She smiled at him in return, but there could have been more tenderness in her smile, light and playful though it was.

'You are pleased to see me?' she asked; she kept her tone light, and kept her anxiety out of it.

'Of course. Of course, dear.' Hornblower tried to make himself human, fighting down the instinctive impulse to withdraw into himself that was roused when his telepathic sensitivity warned him of danger. 'I can hardly believe yet that you *are* here, dear.'

That was the truth, heartfelt, and to say it was a relief,

easing some of his tension. He took her into his arms and they kissed; tears were stinging her eyes when their lips parted again.

'Castlereagh decided the Duchess should come here, just before he left for Allied Headquarters,' she explained. 'So I asked if I could come too.'

'I'm glad you did,' said Hornblower.

'Castlereagh calls her the only man in the whole Bourbon family.'

'I shouldn't be surprised if that were true.'

They were warming to each other now; two proud people, learning anew the sacrifice each had to make to admit to the other their mutual need of each other. They kissed again, and Hornblower felt her body relaxing under his hands. Then came a knocking at the door, and they drew apart. It was Brown, supervising the work of a half-dozen seamen dragging in Barbara's trunks. Hebe, Barbara's little Negro maid, hovered on the threshold before coming in with the baggage. Barbara walked over to the mirror and began to take off her hat and cloak before it.

'Little Richard,' she said, in a conversational tone, 'is very well and happy. He talks unceasingly, and he still digs. His particular corner of the shrubbery looks as if an army of badgers had been at work. In that trunk I have some drawings of his that I kept for you – although one can hardly say they display any noticeable artistic ability.'

'I'd be astonished if they did,' said Hornblower, sitting down.

'Easy with that there portmanteau,' said Brown to one of the seamen. 'That's no barrel o' beef you're handling. Handsomely, now. Where shall we put Her Ladyship's trunk, sir?'

'Leave it against the wall there, Brown, if you please,' said Barbara. 'Here are the keys, Hebe.'

It seemed quite fantastic and unnatural to be sitting here watching Barbara at the mirror, watching Hebe unpack the baggage, here in a city of which he was military governor. Hornblower's masculine narrow-mindedness was disquieted by the situation. Twenty years of life at sea had made his lines of thought a little rigid. There should be a time and a place for everything.

A little squeal came from Hebe, instantly suppressed; Hornblower, looking round, caught a rapid interchange of glances between Brown and the seaman – the latter, seemingly, had no such views about time and place and had taken a sly pinch at Hebe. Brown could be trusted to deal with the seaman; it was not a matter in which it was consonant with the diginity of a commodore and a governor to interfere. And Brown had hardly taken his working party away when a succession of knocks at the door heralded a procession of callers. An equerry came in, bearing the royal command that at dinner tonight the company should be in full dress with powder. Hornblower stamped with rage at that; he had not floured his head more than three times in his life, and he felt ridiculous when he did. Immediately afterwards came Hau, his mind beset with the same problems, in a different guise, as were disturbing Hornblower. Under what authority should he issue rations to Lady Barbara and Lady Barbara's maid? Where should the latter be quartered? Hornblower drove him forth with orders to read the regulations for himself and discover his own legal formulas; Barbara, coolly straightening her ostrich feathers, told him that Hebe would sleep in the dressing room opening from this bedroom. Next came Dobbs; he had read through the dispatches brought by *Gazelle*, and there were some which Hornblower should see. Moreover, there were certain papers which needed the Governor's attention. A packet was sailing tonight. And the night orders certainly needed the Governor's signature. And –'

'All right, I'll come,' said Hornblower. 'Forgive me, my dear.'

'Boney's been beaten again,' said Dobbs, gleefully, the moment they were out of the bedroom. 'The Prussians have taken Soissons and cut up two of Boney's army corps. But that's not all.'

By now they were in the office and Dobbs produced another dispatch for Hornblower's perusal.

'London's going to put some force at our disposal at last, sir,' explained Dobbs. 'The militia have begun to volunteer for foreign service – now that the war's nearly over – and we can have as many battalions as we want. This should be answered by tonight's packet, sir.'

Hornblower tried to shake from his mind thoughts about hair powder, about Hebe's amorous proclivities, to deal with this new problem regarding the launching of a campaign up the Seine valley against Paris. What did he know about the military capacity of the militia? He would have to have a general to command them, who would certainly be senior in rank to himself. What was the law regarding seniority as between a governor appointed by letters-patent and officers commanding troops? He ought to know, but it was not easy to remember the wording. He read the dispatch through once without comprehending a word of it and had to apply himself to it again seriously from the beginning. He put aside the temptation that momentarily assailed him, to throw the dispatch down and tell Dobbs to act according to his own judgement; mastering himself, he began soberly to dictate his reply. As he warmed to his work he had to restrain himself so as to give Dobbs' flying pen a chance to keep up with him.

When it was all done, and he had dashed off his signature on a dozen documents, he went back to the bedroom. Barbara was before the mirror, looking herself over in a white brocade gown, feathers in her hair and jewels at her throat and ears; Hebe was standing by her with the train ready to attach. Hornblower stopped short at sight of Barbara, lovely and dignified, but it was not only her distinguished appearance that checked him. It was also the sudden realization that he could not have Brown in to help him dress, not here. He could not exchange his trousers for breeches and stockings with Barbara and Hebe and Brown all present. He made his apologies, for Brown, aware by his usual sixth sense that Hornblower had finished his office work, was already tapping at the door. They gathered up whatever they thought they might need and went into the dressing room – even here women's perfumes were instantly noticeable – and Hornblower began hurriedly to dress. The breeches and stockings, the gold-embroidered sword-belt. Brown had already, as might have been expected, found a woman in the town who could starch neckcloths admirably, stiff enough to retain their curves when folded, and yet soft enough not to snap in the bending. Brown hung a dressing gown over Hornblower's shoulders, and Hornblower sat with his head lowered while Brown plied the flour-dredger and comb. When he straightened up and looked in the mirror he felt a sneaking pleasure at the result. He had allowed what was left of his curls to grow long lately, simply because he had been too busy to have his hair cropped, and Brown had combed the snow-white mop to the best advantage so that no trace of bare scalp was visible. The powdered hair set off his weatherbeaten face and brown eyes admirably: The cheeks were a little hollow and the eyes a little melancholy, but it was by no means the face of an old man, so that the white hair made a most effective contrast, giving him the youthful appearance and calling that attention to his personality which presumably the fashion had in mind when it began. The blue and gold of the uniform, the white of neckcloth and powder, the ribbon of the Bath and the glittering star set him off as a very personable figure. He could wish he had more calf inside the stockings; that was the only fault he could find with his appearance. He made sure that his belt and sword were properly adjusted, put his hat under his arm, picked up his gloves, and went back into the bedroom, remembering in the nick of time to pound on the door before he turned the handle.

Barbara was ready; stately, almost like a statue, in her white brocade. The likeness to a statue was something more than what a casual simile implied; Hornblower remembered a statue of Diana that he had seen somewhere – was it Diana? – with the end of her robe caught up over her left arm exactly the way

Barbara was carrying her train. Her powdered hair made her face seem a little cold in its expression, for the style did not suit her colouring and features. A glance at it reminded Hornblower of Diana again. She smiled when she saw him.

'The handsomest man in the British Navy,' she said.

He gave her a clumsy bow in return.

'I only wish I were worthy of my lady,' he said.

She took his arm and stood beside him in front of the mirror. Because of her height her feathers overtopped him; she flicked open her fan with an effective gesture.

'How do you think we look?' she asked.

'As I said,' repeated Hornblower, 'I only wish I were worthy of you.'

Brown and Hebe were gaping at them behind them, as he could see in the mirror, and Barbara's reflection smiled at him.

'We must go,' she said, with a pressure upon his arm. 'It would never do to keep Monseigneur waiting.'

They had to walk from one end of the Hôtel de Ville to the other, through corridors and ante-rooms filled with a multitude dressed in every type of uniform – it was a curious chance that had made this not very distinguished building a seat of government, the palace of a regent, the headquarters of an invading army, and the flagship of a squadron, too, for that matter, all at the same time. People saluted and drew aside respectfully against the walls as they went by – Hornblower had a clear notion of what it felt like to be royalty as he acknowledged the compliments on either side. There was noticeable an obsequiousness and a subservience very unlike the disciplined respect he was accustomed to receive in a ship. Barbara sailed along beside him; the glances that Hornblower stole at her sidelong showed her to him as struggling conscientiously against the artificiality of her smile.

A silly wave of feeling came over him; he wished he were some simple-minded fellow who could rejoice naturally and artlessly in the unexpected arrival of his wife, who could take lusty pleasure of her without self-consciousness. He knew himself to be absurdly sensitive to minute influences, even influences that did not exist except in his own ridiculous imagination but which were none the less powerful. His mind was like a bad ship's compass, not sufficiently deadbeat, wavering uncertainly and swinging to every little variation of course, swinging more widely in response to the correction, until at the hands of a poor helmsman the ship would find herself chasing her tail or taken all aback. He felt as if he were chasing his tail at the present moment; it made no difference to the complexity of his relations with his wife to know that it was all his fault, that her emotions towards him would be simple and straightforward did they not reflect his own tangled feelings – on the contrary, thinking about that made confusion worse confounded.

He tried to fling off his melancholy, to cling to some simple fact or other to steady himself, and with frightful clarity one of the central facts in his consciousness made its appearance in his mind, horribly real – like the memory of a man he had once seen hanged, writhing with handkerchief-covered face at the end of a rope. He had not yet told Barbara about it.

'Dear,' he said, 'you didn't know. Bush is dead.'

He felt Barbara's hand twitch on his arm, but her face still looked like that of a smiling statue.

'He was killed, four days back,' babbled on Hornblower with the madness of those whom the gods wish to destroy.

It was an insane thing to say to a woman about to walk into a royal reception, on the very point of setting her foot across the threshold, but Hornblower was sublimely unconscious of his offence. Yet he had at that last moment the perspicacity to realize – what he had not realized before – that this was one of the great moments of Barbara's life; that when she had been dressing, when she had smiled at him in the mirror, her heart had been singing with anticipation. It had not occurred to his stupidity that she could enjoy this sort of function, that it could give her pleasure to sail into a glittering room on the arm of Sir Horatio Hornblower, the man of the hour. He had been taking it for granted that she would extend to these ceremonies the same sort of strained tolerance that he felt.

'Their Excellencies the Governor and Milady Barbara 'Ornblor,' blared the major-domo at the door.

Every eye turned towards them as they entered. The last thing that Hornblower was conscious of, before he plunged into the imbecilities of a social function, was that he had somehow spoiled his wife's evening, and there was some angry resentment in his heart; against her, not against himself.

15

The militia had arrived, pouring, still green with seasickness, from the close-packed transports. They were something better than a rabble in their scarlet uniforms; they could form line and column, and could march off smartly enough behind the regimental bands, even though they could not help gaping at the strangeness of this foreign town. But they drank themselves into madness or stupor at every opportunity, they insulted the women either innocently or criminally, they were guilty of theft and of wanton damage and of all the other crimes of imperfectly disciplined troops. The officers – one battalion was commanded by an earl, another by a baronet – were not sufficiently experienced to keep their men in hand. Hornblower, facing the indignant protests of the Mayor and the civil authorities, was glad when the horse-transports came in bringing the two regiments of yeomanry that had been promised him. They provided the cavalry he needed for an advanced guard, so that now he could send his little army out in its push towards Rouen, towards Paris itself.

He was at breakfast with Barbara when the news arrived; Barbara in a grey-blue informal garment with the silver coffee-pot before her, pouring his coffee, and being helped by him to bacon and eggs – a domesticity that was still unreal to him. He had been hard at work for three hours before he had come in to breakfast, and he was still too set in his ways to make the change easily from a military atmosphere to one of connubial intimacy.

'Thank you, dear,' said Barbara, accepting the plate from him.

A thump at the door.

'Come in!' yelled Hornblower.

It was Dobbs, one of the few people privileged to knock at that door when Sir Horatio was at breakfast with his wife.

'Dispatch from the army, sir. The Frogs have gone.'

'Gone?'

'Up-stick and away, sir. Quiot marched for Paris last night. There's not a French soldier in Rouen.'

The report that Hornblower took from Dobbs' hand merely repeated in more formal language what Dobbs had said. Bonaparte must be desperate for troops to defend his capital; by recalling Quiot he had left all Normandy exposed to the invader.

'We must follow him up,' said Hornblower to himself, and then to Dobbs 'Tell Howard – no, I'll come myself. Excuse me, my dear.'

'Is there not even time,' said Barbara to him, sternly, 'to drink your coffee and eat your breakfast?'

The struggle on Hornblower's face was so apparent that she laughed outright at him.

'Drake,' she went on, 'had time to finish the game and beat the Spaniards too. I was taught that in the schoolroom.'

'You're quite right, my dear,' said Hornblower. 'Dobbs, I'll be with you in ten minutes.'

Hornblower applied himself to bacon and eggs.

Maybe it would be good for discipline, in the best sense of the term, if it became known that the legendary Hornblower, the man of so many exploits, was human enough to listen sometimes to his wife's protests.

'This is victory,' he said, looking at Barbara across the table. 'This is the end.'

He knew it in his soul now; he had arrived at this conclusion by no mere intellectual process. The tyrant of Europe, the man who had bathed the world in blood, was about to fall. Barbara met his eyes, and their emotion admitted of no words. The world which had been at war since their childhood was about to know peace, and peace had something of the unknown about it.

'Peace,' said Barbara.

Hornblower felt a little unsteady. It was impossible for him to analyse his feelings, for he had no data from which to begin his deductions. He had joined the Navy as a boy, and he had known war ever since; he could know nothing of the Hornblower, the purely hypothetical Hornblower, who would have existed had there been no war. Twenty-one years of frightful strain, of peril and hardship, had made a very different man of him from what he would have become otherwise. Hornblower was no born fighting man; he was a talented and sensitive individual whom chance had forced into fighting, and his talents had brought him success as a fighter just as they would have brought him success in other walks of life, but he had had to pay a higher price. His morbid sensitiveness, his touchy pride, the quirks and weaknesses of his character might well be the result of the strains and sorrows he had had to endure. There was a coldness between him and his wife at the moment (a coldness masked by camaraderie; the passion to which both of them had given free rein had done nothing to dispel it) which might in large part be attributed to the defects of his character – a small part of it was Barbara's fault, but most of it was his.

Hornblower wiped his mouth and stood up.

'I really should go, dear,' he said. 'Please forgive me.'

'Of course you must go if you have your duty to do,' she answered, and held up her lips to him.

He kissed her and hurried from the room. Even with the kiss on his lips he knew that it was a mistake for a man to have his wife with him on active service; it was liable to soften him, to say nothing of the practical inconveniences, like the occasion two nights ago when an urgent message had to be brought in to him when he was in bed with Barbara.

In the office he read the reconnaissance report again. It stated unequivocally that no contact could be made with any Imperial troops whatever, and that prominent citizens of Rouen, escaping from the town, assured the outposts that not a Bonapartist soldier remained there. Rouen was his for the taking, and obviously the tendency to desert Bonaparte and join the Bourbons was becoming more and more marked. Every day the number of people who came into Le Havre by road or by boat to make their submission to the Duke grew larger and larger.

'*Vive le Roi!*' was what they called out as they neared the sentries. 'Long live the King!'

That was the password which marked the Bourbonist – no Bonapartist, no Jacobin, no republican would soil his lips with those words. And the number of deserters and refractory conscripts who came pouring in was growing enormous. The ranks of Bonaparte's army were leaking like a sieve, and Bonaparte would find it difficult to replace the missing ones, when his conscripts were taking to the woods or fleeing to English protection to avoid service. It might be thought possible that a Bourbonist army could be built up from this material, but the attempt was a failure from the start. Those runaways objected not merely to fighting for Bonaparte, but to fighting at all. The Royalist army which Angoulême had been sent here to organize still numbered less than a thousand men, and of these thousand more than half were officers, old émigrés sent here after serving in the armies of the enemies of France.

But Rouen awaited a conqueror, nevertheless. His militia brigade could tramp the miry roads to the city, and he and Angoulême could get into carriages and drive after them. He would have to make the entrance as spectacular as possible; the capital of Normandy was no mean city, and beyond it lay Paris, quivering and sensitive. A fresh idea struck him. In eastern France the allied monarchs were riding every few days into some new captured town. It was in his power to escort Angoulême into Rouen in more spectacular fashion, demonstrating at the same time the long arm of England's sea power, and rubbing in the lesson that it was England's naval strength which had turned the balance of the war. The wind was westerly; he was a little vague about the state of the tide, but he could wait until it should serve.

'Captain Howard,' he said, looking up, 'warn *Flame* and *Porta Coeli* to be ready to get under way. I shall take the Duke and Duchess up to Rouen by water. And their whole suite – yes, I'll take Lady Barbara too. Warn the captains to make preparations for their reception and accommodation. Send me Hau to settle the details. Colonel Dobbs, would you be interested in a little yachting trip?'

It seemed indeed like a yachting trip next morning, when they gathered on the quarterdeck of the *Porta Coeli*, a group of men in brilliant uniforms and women in gay dresses. *Porta Coeli* had already warped away from the quay, from which they rowed out to her, and Freeman, at a nod from Hornblower, had only to bellow the orders for sail to be set and the anchor hove in for them to start up the broad estuary. The sun was shining with the full promise of spring, the wavelets gleamed and danced. Down below decks, Hornblower could guess from the sounds, there was trouble and toil, while they were still trying to rig accommodation for the royal party, but here by the taffrail all was laughter and expectancy. And it was heavenly to tread a deck again, to feel the wind on his cheeks, to look aft and see *Flame* under all fore-and-aft sail in her station astern, to have the white ensign overhead and his broad pendant hoisted, even though the Bourbon white and gold flew beside it.

He met Barbara's eye and smiled at her; the Duke and Duchess condescended to step to his side and engage him in conversation. The fairway led close by the northern shore of the estuary; they passed Harfleur, and the battery there exchanged salutes with them. They were bowling up the channel at a full eight knots, faster than if they had gone in carriages, but of course when the river began to narrow and to wind it might be a different story. The southern shore came northward to meet them, the flat green shore becoming more and more defined, until in a flash, as it seemed, they were out of the estuary and between the banks of the river, leaving Quilleboeuf behind and opening up the long reach that led to Caudebec, the left bank green pastureland studded with fat farms, the right bank lofty and wooded. Over went the helm, the sheets were hauled in. But with the wind tending to funnel up the valley it was still well over their quarter, and with the racing tide behind them they fairly tore along the river. Luncheon was announced, and the party trooped below, the women squealing at the lowness of the decks and the difficulty of the companion. Bulkheads had been ripped out and replaced to make ample room for royalty – Hornblower guessed that half the crew would be sleeping on deck in consequence of the presence of the Duke and Duchess. The royal servants, assisted by the wardroom stewards – the former as embarrassed by their surroundings as the latter by the company on whom they had to wait – began to serve the food, but luncheon had hardly begun when Freeman came in to whisper to Hornblower as he sat between the Duchess and the *dame d'honneur*.

'Caudebec in sight, sir,' whispered Freeman; Hornblower had left orders to be told when this happened.

With an apology to the Duchess and a bow to the Duke, Hornblower slipped unobtrusively out of the room; the etiquette of royalty even covered events on shipboard, and sailors could come and go with little ceremony if the management of the vessel demanded it. Caudebec was in sight at the top of the reach, and they were approaching it fast, so that it was only a matter of minutes before there was no need for the glass that Hornblower trained on the little town. The damage caused by the explosion which had cost Bush's life was very obvious. Every house had been cut off short six or eight feet from the ground; the massive church had withstood the shock save that most of its roof had been stripped off and its windows blown in. The long wooden quay was in ruins, and a few stumps of blackened wrecks showed above water-level beside it. A single cannon – a twenty-four-pounder on a travelling carriage – stood on the river bank above the quay, all that remained of Quiot's siege-train. A few people were to be seen; they stood staring at the two men-o'-war brigs sailing along the river past them.

'A nasty sight, sir,' said Freeman beside him.

'Yes,' said Hornblower.

This was where Bush died; Hornblower stood silent in tribute to his friend. When the war was over he would erect a little monument on the river bank there above the quay. He could wish that the ruined town would never be rebuilt; that would be the most striking monument to his friend's memory – that or a pyramid of skulls.

'Mains'l sheets! Jib sheets!' roared Freeman.

They had come to the head of the reach, and were beginning the long turn to starboard. Jibing a big brig in a narrow river was no child's play. The flattened sails roared like thunder as they caught the backlash of the wind from the heights. The brig's way carried her forward, and she rounded to, slowly, round the bend. Letting out the mainsail sheet gave them the needed push and steerage way; the farther she came round the flatter the sails were hauled, until at last she was close-hauled on a course almost opposite to the one by which she had approached Caudebec, sailing close-hauled up the new reach which presented itself to their gaze.

Here was Hau beside him now.

'Monseigneur wishes to know,' he said, 'whether your business on deck is very urgent. His Royal Highness has a toast to propose, and wishes that you could join in it.'

'I'll come,' said Hornblower.

He took a last glance aft at Caudebec, vanishing round the bend, and hurried below. The big extemporized cabin was particoloured with sunlight coming in through the open ports. Angoulême caught sight of him as he entered, and rose to his feet, crouching under the low deck-beams.

'To His Royal Highness the Prince Regent!' he said, lifting his glass. The toast was drunk, and everyone looked to Hornblower for the proper response.

'His Most Christian Majesty!' said Hornblower, and when the ceremony was completed raised his glass again. 'His Most Christian Majesty's Regent in Normandy, Monseigneur His Royal Highness the Duke d'Angoulême!'

The toast was drunk amid a roar of acclamation. There was something dramatic and painful about being down here below decks drinking toasts while an Empire was falling in ruins outside. The *Porta Coeli* was sailing as close to the wind as she could lie, so Hornblower guessed from the feel of the vessel under his feet and the sound of her passage through the water. Freeman on deck would have difficulty in weathering the next bend – he had noticed before he came down that the reach they had entered trended a little into the wind. Hornblower heard Freeman roar a fresh order on deck, and was consumed with restlessness. Down here it was like being with a nursery party of children, enjoying themselves while the adults attended to the management of the world. He made his apologetic bow again and slipped out to go on deck.

It was as he thought; The *Porta Coeli* was as close-hauled as she would lie, almost closer. Her sails were shivering and her motion sluggish, and the bend in the river that would give her relief was a full half-mile farther ahead. Freeman looked up at the flapping sails and shook his head.

'You'll have to club-haul her, Mr Freeman,' said Hornblower. To tack in that narrow channel, even with the tide behind them, would be too tricky an operation altogether.

'Aye aye, sir,' said Freeman.

He stood for a second judging his distances; the hands at the sheets, in no doubt about the delicacy of the ensuing manoeuvres, waiting keyed up for the rapid succession of orders that would follow. Filling the sails for a moment gave them plenty of way again, although it brought them perilously close to the leeward shore. Then in came the sheets, over went the helm, and the *Porta Coeli* snatched a few yards into the wind, losing most of her way in the process. Then out went the sheets, up came the helm a trifle, and she gathered way again, close-hauled yet edging down perceptibly towards the lee shore.

'Well done,' said Hornblower. He wanted to add a word of advice to the effect that it would be as well not to leave it so late next time, but he glanced at Freeman sizing up the distances and decided it was unnecessary. Freeman wanted none of the brig's way lost this time. The moment the sails flapped he threw them back, put his helm over, and this time gained the full width of the river into the wind. Looking aft, Hornblower saw that the *Flame* was following her consort's example. The lee shore seemed to come to meet them; it seemed a very short time before the manoeuvre would have to be repeated, and Hornblower was relieved to see that the bend was appreciably nearer.

It was at that moment that the Duke's head appeared above the coaming as he climbed the little companion, and the royal party began to swarm on deck again. Freeman looked with despair at Hornblower, who took the necessary decision. He fixed the nearest courtier – the equerry, it happened to be – with a look that cut short the laughing speech he was addressing to the lady at his side.

'It is not convenient for His Royal Highness and his suite to be on deck at present,' Hornblower said loudly.

The gay chatter stopped as if cut off with a knife; Hornblower looked at the crestfallen faces and was reminded of children again, spoiled children deprived of some minor pleasure.

'The management of the ship calls for too much attention,' went on Hornblower, to make his point quite clear. Freeman was already bellowing at the hands at the sheets.

'Very well, Sir 'Oratio,' said the Duke. 'Come, ladies. Come, gentlemen.'

He beat as dignified a retreat as possible, but the last

courtier down the companion was sadly hustled by the rush of the hands across the deck.

'Up helm!' said Freeman to the steersman, and then, in the breathing space while they gathered way close-hauled, 'Shall I batten down, sir?'

The outrageous suggestion was made with a grin.

'No,' snapped Hornblower, in no mood for joking.

On the next tack *Porta Coeli* succeeded in weathering the point. Round she came and round; Freeman jibbed her neatly, and once more with the wind on her quarter the brig was running free up the next reach, wooded hills on one side, fat meadowland on the other. Hornblower thought for a moment of sending a message down that the royal party could come on deck for the next quarter of an hour, but thought better of it. Let 'em stay below, Barbara and all. He took his glass and laboriously climbed the mainshrouds; from the main-crosstrees his view over the countryside was greatly extended. It was oddly pleasant to sit up here and look over this green and lovely land of France like some sight-seeing traveller. The peasants were at work in the fields, hardly looking up as the two beautiful vessels sailed past them. There was no sign of war or desolation here; Normandy beyond Caudebec was untouched as yet by invading armies. Then, for one moment, as the brig neared the next bend and preparations were being made for jibing her round, Hornblower caught a glimpse of Rouen far away across the country, cathedral towers and steeples. It gave him a queer thrill, but immediately the wooded heights as the brig came round cut off his view, and he snapped his glass shut and descended again.

'Not much of the tide left, sir,' said Freeman.

'No. We'll anchor in the next reach, if you please, Mr Freeman. Anchor bow and stern, and make a signal to *Flame* to the same effect.'

'Aye aye, sir.'

Natural phenomena, like nightfall and tides, were far more satisfactory things to deal with than human beings and their whims, than princes – and wives. The two brigs anchored in the stream to ride out the ebb tide and the hours of darkness to follow. Hornblower took the natural precautions against attack and surprise, rigging the boarding-nettings and keeping a couple of boats rowing guard during the night, but he knew there was little to fear from that exhausted and apathetic countryside. If there had been any of the army left within striking distance, if Bonaparte had been operating west of Paris instead of east, it would be a different story. But save for Bonaparte and the armed forces which he compelled to fight for him there was no resistance left in France; she lay helpless, the inert prize of the first conqueror to arrive.

The party on board the *Porta Coeli* went on being gay. It was a nuisance that the Duke and Duchess and their suite continually discovered that servants or pieces of baggage needed in *Porta Coeli* were in *Flame*, and vice versa, so that there was a continual need for boats between the two vessels, but presumably that was only to be expected from these people. They made surprisingly little complaint about the crowding in the sleeping accommodations. Barbara went off philosophically to bed in Freeman's cabin along with four other women – Freeman's cabin would be uncomfortable quarters for two. The royal servants slung hammocks for themselves under the amused tuition of the hands with no demur at all; it seemed as if during twenty years of exile, of wandering through Europe, they had learned in adversity some lessons which they had not forgotten as yet. No one seemed likely to sleep – but in the prevailing excitement and pleasurable anticipation they would probably not have slept even in downy beds in palaces.

Certainly Hornblower, after trying to compose himself for an hour or two in the hammock slung for him on deck (he had not slept in a hammock since the time when he refitted the *Lydia* at the island of Coiba), gave up the attempt, and lay looking up at the night sky, save when a couple of sharp showers drove him to cover himself over, head and all, with the tarpaulin provided for him. Staying awake did at least keep him assured that the westerly wind was still blowing, as might be expected at that time of year. If it had dropped or changed he was prepared to push on for Rouen in the ships' boats. There was no need; dawn and an increase in the westerly breeze came together, along with more rain, and two hours after the first daylight the flood set in and Hornblower could give the word to up anchor.

At the next bend Rouen's cathedral towers were plain to the sight; at the one after that only a comparatively narrow neck of land separated them from the city, although there was still a long and beautiful curve of the river to navigate. It was still early afternoon when they rounded the last bend and saw the whole city stretched before them, the island with its bridges, its wharves cluttered with river boats, the market hall across the quay, and the soaring Gothic towers which had looked down upon the burning of Joan of Arc. It was a tricky business anchoring there just below the town with the last of the flood still running; Hornblower had to take advantage of a minor bend in the stream to throw all aback and anchor by the stern, two cables' lengths farther from the city than he would have chosen in other circumstances. He scanned the city through his glass for signs of a deputation coming to greet them, and the Duke stood beside him, inclined to chafe at any delay.

'I'll have a boat, if you please, Mr Freeman,' Hornblower said at length. 'Will you pass the word for my coxswain?'

Crowds were already gathering on the quays to stare at the English ships, at the White Ensign and at the Bourbon lilies; it was twenty years since either had been seen there. There was quite a mass of people assembled when Brown laid the boat alongside the quay just below the bridge. Hornblower walked up the steps, eyed by the crowd. They were apathetic and silent, not like any French crowd he had seen or heard before. He caught sight of a man in uniform, a sergeant of *douaniers*.

'I wish to visit the Mayor,' he said.

'Yes, sir,' said the *douanier* respectfully.

'Call a carriage for me,' said Hornblower.

There was a little hesitation; the *douanier* looked about him doubtfully, but soon voices from the crowd began to make suggestions, and it was not long before a rattling hackney coach made its appearance. Hornblower climbed in, and they clattered off. The Mayor received him on the threshold of the Hôtel de Ville, having hastened there to meet him from his desk as soon as he heard of his arrival.

'Where is the reception for His Royal Highness?'

demanded Hornblower. 'Why have no salutes been fired? Why are the church bells not ringing?'

'*Monsieur* – Your Excellency –' The Mayor knew not quite what Hornblower's uniform and ribbon implied and wanted to be on the safe side. 'We did not know – we were not certain –'

'You saw the royal standard,' said Hornblower. 'You knew that His Royal Highness was on his way here from Le Havre.'

'There had been rumours, yes,' said the Mayor reluctantly. 'But –'

What the Mayor wanted to say was that he hoped the Duke would arrive not only with overpowering force but also would make an unassuming entrance so that nobody would have to commit themselves too definitely on the Bourbon side according him a welcome. And that was exactly what Hornblower had come to force him to do.

'His Royal Highness,' said Hornblower, 'is seriously annoyed. If you wish to regain his favour, and that of His Majesty the King who will follow him, you will make all the amends in your power. A deputation – you, all your councillors, all the notables, the Prefect and the Sub-Prefect if they are still here, every person of position, in fact, must be on hand two hours from now to welcome Monseigneur when he lands.'

'*Monsieur* –'

'Note will be taken of who is present. And of who is absent,' said Hornblower. 'The church bells can begin to ring immediately.'

The Mayor tried to meet Hornblower's eyes. He was still in fear of Bonaparte, still terrified in case some reversal of fortune should leave him at Bonaparte's mercy, called to account for his actions in receiving the Bourbon. And, on the other hand, Hornblower knew well enough that if he could persuade the city to offer an open welcome, Rouen would think twice about changing sides again. He was determined upon winning allies for his cause.

'Two hours,' said Hornblower, 'will be ample for all preparations to be made for the deputation to assemble, for the streets to be decorated, for quarters to be prepared for His Royal Highness and his suite.'

'*Monsieur*, you do not understand all that this implies,' protested the Mayor. 'It means –'

'It means that you are having to decide whether to enjoy the King's favour or not,' said Hornblower. 'That is the choice before you.'

Hornblower ignored the point that the Mayor was also having to decide whether or not to risk the guillotine at Bonaparte's hands.

'A wise man,' said Hornblower, meaningfully, 'will not hesitate a moment.'

So hesitant was the Mayor that Hornblower began to fear that he would have to use threats. He could threaten dire vengeance tomorrow or the next day when the advancing army should arrive; more effectively, he could threaten to knock the town to pieces immediately with his ships' guns, but that was not a threat he wanted to put into execution at all; it would be far from establishing the impression he wished to convey of a people receiving its rulers with acclamation after years of suffering under a tyrant.

'Time presses,' said Hornblower, looking at his watch.

'Very well,' said the Mayor, taking the decision which

might mean life or death to him. 'I'll do it. What does Your Excellency suggest?'

It took only a matter of minutes to settle the details; Hornblower had learned from Hau much about arranging the public appearances of royalty. Then he took his leave, and drove back again to the quay through the silent crowds, to where the boat lay with Brown growing anxious about him. They had hardly pushed off into the stream when Brown cocked his ear. A church carillon had begun its chimes, and within a minute another had joined in. On the deck of the *Porta Coeli* the Duke listened to what Hornblower had to tell him. The city was making ready to welcome him.

And when they landed on the quay there was the assembly of notables, as promised; there were the carriages and the horses; there were the white banners in the streets. And there were the apathetic crowds, numbed with disaster. But it meant that Rouen was quiet during their stay there, the reception could at least have an appearance of gaiety, so that Barbara and Hornblower went to bed each night worn out.

Hornblower turned his head on the pillow as the thumping on the door penetrated at last into his consciousness.

'Come in!' he roared; Barbara beside him moved fretfully as he reached out, still half asleep, and pulled open the curtains.

It was Dobbs, slippered and in his shirtsleeves, his braces hanging by his thighs, his hair in a mop. He held a candle in one hand and a dispatch in the other.

'It's over!' he said. 'Boney's abdicated! Blücher's in Paris!'

So there it was. Victory; the end of twenty years of war. Hornblower sat up and blinked at the candle.

'The Duke must be told,' he said. He was gathering his thoughts. 'Is the King still in England? What does that dispatch say?'

He got himself out of bed in his nightshirt, while Barbara sat up with her hair in disorder.

'All right, Dobbs,' said Hornblower. 'I'll be with you in five minutes. Send to wake the Duke and warn him that I am about to come to him.'

He reached for his trousers as Dobbs left him, and balancing on one leg, he met Barbara's sleepy gaze.

'It's peace,' he said. 'No more war.'

Even when roused out in this fashion Hornblower dressed, as he did all that came his way, extraordinarily quickly. He was tucking his nightshirt into his trousers – the long skirts of the warm and bulky garment packed the latter uncomfortably full – before Barbara replied.

'We knew it would come,' she said, a little fretfully. During recent events Barbara had had small time to sleep.

'The Duke must be told immediately, all the same,' said Hornblower, thrusting his feet into his shoes. 'I expect he'll start for Paris at dawn.'

'At dawn? What time is it now?'

'Six bells, I should fancy – three o'clock.'

'Oh!' said Barbara, sinking back on her pillow.

Hornblower pulled on his coat and stopped to kiss her, but she kissed him back only perfunctorily.

The Duke kept him waiting fifteen minutes in the drawing room of the residence of the departed Prefect where he had been installed. He heard the news with his council round him, and with royal stoicism showed no sign of emotion.

'What about the usurper?' was his first question after hearing what Hornblower had to say.

'His future is partially decided, Your Royal Highness. He has been promised a minor sovereignty,' said Hornblower. It sounded absurd to him as he said it.

'And His Majesty, my uncle?'

'The dispatch does not say, Your Royal Highness. Doubtless His Majesty will leave England now. Perhaps he is already on his way.'

'We must be at the Tuileries to receive him.'

16

Hornblower sat in his sitting room in the Hôtel Meurice in Paris rereading the crackling parchment document that had arrived for him the previous day. The wording of it might be called as gratifying as the purport of it, to one who cared for such things.

As the grandeur and stability of the British Empire depend chiefly upon knowledge and experience in maritime affairs, We esteem those worthy of the highest honours who, acting under Our influence, exert themselves in maintaining Our dominion over the sea. It is for this reason that We have determined to advance to the degree of Peerage Our trusty and well beloved Sir Horatio Hornblower, Knight of the Most Honourable Order of the Bath, who, being descended from an ancient family in Kent, and educated from his youth in the sea service, hath through several posts arrived to high station and command in Our navy, by the strength of his own abilities, and a merit distinguished by Us, in the many important services, which he has performed with remarkable fidelity, courage and success. In the late vigorous wars, which raged so many years in Europe; wars fruitful of naval combats and expeditions; there was scarce any action of consequence wherein he did not bear a principal part, nor were any dangers or difficulties too great, but he surmounted them by his exquisite conduct, and a good fortune that never failed him.

It is just, therefore, that We should distinguish with higher titles a subject who has so eminently served Us and his country, both as monuments of his own merit, and to influence others into a love and pursuit of virtue.

So now he was a Peer of the Realm, a Baron of the United Kingdom, Lord Hornblower of Smallbridge, County of Kent. There were only two or three other examples in history of a naval officer being raised to the peerage before attaining flag rank. Lord Hornblower of Smallbridge; of course he had decided to retain his own name in his title. There might be something grotesque about the name of Hornblower, and yet he was fond of it, and he had no desire to lose it in the almost anonymity of Lord Smallbridge or Lord Something-else. Pellew, he had heard, had elected to become Lord Exmouth. That might suit Pellew, but it would not suit him. His brother-in-law, when he received a step in the peerage, had actually reverted from a territorial to a personal title, becoming Marquis Wellesley instead of Earl of Mornington. Another brother-in-law, unable to use the Wellesley name in consequence of his brother's pre-emption of it, had become Wellington, apparently in an effort to retain as much of the family name as possible. He was a duke now, far above a mere baron, and yet they were all three peers together. Lords, hereditary legislators. Little Richard was now the Honourable Richard Hornblower, and some time would be Lord Hornblower in succession to his father. All the formalities regarding titles were a little amusing. Barbara, for instance; as the daughter of an earl – it was her father's rank that mattered, not the fact that one brother was now a marquis and one a duke – she had had higher precedence than as the wife of a Knight of the Bath. She had been Lady Barbara Hornblower up to yesterday. But now as a result of her husband's peerage she would be Lady Hornblower. Lord and Lady Hornblower. It sounded well. It was a great honour and distinction, the coping-stone of his professional career. Oh, to be truthful about it, it was the sheerest lot of tommy-nonsense. Robes and a coronet. Hornblower stiffened in his chair as a thought struck him. Freeman's ridiculous prophecy over the cards in the cabin of the *Flame* about a golden crown had this much confirmation now. It was an amazingly shrewd guess on the part of Freeman; it had never occurred to him himself for one moment that he might become a peer. But the rest of Freeman's prophecy had fallen to the ground. Danger and a fair woman, Freeman had foreseen. And now the danger was all over with the coming of peace, and there was no fair woman in his life, unless Barbara, with her blue eyes and light-brown hair, could be called fair.

He rose to his feet in his irritation, and perhaps was going to stamp round the room, but Barbara came in at that moment from her bedroom, ready for the Ambassador's party. She was all in unrelieved white, for the party had been planned as a culminating demonstration of loyalty to the Bourbons, and the women were to wear white regardless as to whether or not their complexions could stand it; maybe that was the most convincing proof of loyalty to the newly restored dynasty that could be offered. Hornblower picked up his hat and cloak in readiness to escort her; it was the fortieth time in forty nights, he fancied, that he had done just the same thing.

'We won't stay at Arthur's late,' said Barbara.

Arthur was her brother the Duke of Wellington, lately and strangely transferred from commanding the army fighting France to His Britannic Majesty's Embassy to His Most Christian Majesty. Hornblower looked his surprise.

'We shall go on to the Polignacs,' explained Barbara. 'To meet M. le Prince.'

'Very well, dear,' said Hornblower. He thought he kept the resignation out of his voice perfectly convincingly.

M. le Prince; that was the Prince of Condé, of a younger Bourbon line. Hornblower had begun to learn his way through the complexities of French society – the complexities of the last century transported bodily back into this. He wondered if he were the only man who thought of them as outmoded anachronisms, M. le Prince; M. le Duc – that was the Duc de Bourbon, wasn't it? Monsieur – plain Monsieur, with no honorifics at all – was the Comte d'Artois, the King's brother and heir. Monseigneur, on the other hand, was the Duc d'Angoulême, Monsieur's son, who would one of these days be Dauphin if his father survived his uncle. The very name of Dauphin was anachronistic, smacking of the Dark Ages. And the future Dauphin, as Hornblower well knew, was a man of convinced stupidity whose characteristic most easily remembered was a high-pitched mirthless laugh something like the cackling of a hen.

They had descended the stairs by now and Brown was waiting to hand them into the waiting carriage.

'The British Embassy, Brown,' said Hornblower.

'Yes, my lord.'

Brown had not stumbled over the new title once in the twenty-four hours he had borne it; Hornblower felt in his exasperation that he would have given anything for Brown to slip into 'Aye aye, sir'. But Brown was too clear-headed and quick-thinking a person to make any such blunder; it was surprising that Brown should have elected to stay on in his service. He might well have made a career for himself.

'You're not listening to a word I'm saying,' said Barbara.

'Please forgive me, dear,' said Hornblower – there was no denying the accusation.

'It's very important indeed,' said Barbara. 'Arthur is going to Vienna to represent us at the Congress. Castlereagh has to come home to manage the House.'

'Arthur will give up the Embassy?' asked Hornblower, making polite conversation. The carriage roared over the cobbles; the occasional lights revealed through the windows the bustling multi-uniformed crowd of Paris in the whirl of peace.

'Of course. *This* is much more important. All the world will be in Vienna – every court in the world will be represented.'

'I suppose so,' said Hornblower. The destinies of the world were to be decided at the Congress.

'That's what I was going to tell you about. Arthur will need a hostess there – there'll be constant entertaining, of course – and he has asked me to come and act for him.'

'My God!' Polite conversation had led straight to the brink of this abyss.

'Don't you think it's wonderful?' asked Barbara.

Hornblower was on the point of saying, 'Yes, dear,' when rebellion surged up within him. He had endured for his wife's sake uncounted martyrdoms already. And this would be one far more violent and prolonged. Barbara would be the lady of the house, hostess of the most important delegate to the most important Congress in the world. The seeds of diplomacy, Hornblower had already learned, were planted for more often in drawing rooms than in Cabinets. Barbara's drawing room would be a place of intrigue and double-dealing. She would be hostess, Wellington would be the man of the house, and he – what would he be? Something even more unnecessary than he was at present. Hornblower saw stretching before him a three months' vista of salons and balls and visits to the ballet, outside the inner circle, outside the outer circle too. No Cabinet secrets would be entrusted to him, and he did not want to have anything to do with the petty gossip and polite scandal of the great world. A fish out of water was what he would be – and not a bad metaphor, either, when applied to a naval officer in the salons of Vienna.

'You don't answer me?' said Barbara.

'I'm utterly damned if I'll do it!' said Hornblower – strange that, with all his tact and intuition, he always took a sledgehammer in his rare arguments with Barbara, to kill flies with.

'You won't do it, dear?'

In the course of that brief sentence Barbara's tone changed from disappointment at the beginning to bitter hostility at the end.

'No!' said Hornblower, in a roar.

He had kept the lid on his feelings for so long and so

tightly that the explosion was violent when it came.

'You'll deprive me of the greatest thing that has ever happened to me?' said Barbara, a hint of ice edging the words.

Hornblower fought down his feelings. It would be easier to give way – ever so easy. But no, he would not. Could not. Yet Barbara was quite right about its being a wonderful thing. To be hostess to a European Congress, to help mould the future of the world – and then, on the other hand, Hornblower had no wish whatever to be a member, and an unimportant member at that, of the Wellesley clan. He had been captain of a ship too long. He did not like politics, not even politics on a European scale. He did not want to kiss the hands of Hungarian countesses, and exchange inanities with Russian grand dukes. That had been fun in the old days when his professional reputation hinged on some such success, as it had done. But he needed more of a motive than the mere maintenance of his reputation as a beau.

Quarrels in a carriage always seemed to reach a climax just as the drive ended. The carriage had halted and porters in the Wellington livery were opening the door before Hornblower had had time either to explain or make amends. As they walked into the Embassy Hornblower's apprehensive side glances revealed that Barbara's colour was high and her eyes dangerously bright. So they remained during the whole of the reception; Hornblower looked across the room at her whenever he could, and every time she was clearly in high spirits, or laughing with the groups in conversation with her, tapping with her fan. Was she flirting? The red coats and the blue coats, the black coats and the green coats, that assembled round her bent their shoulders in obvious deference to her. Every glance Hornblower took seemed to increase his resentment.

But he fought it down, determined to make amends.

'You had better go to Vienna, dear,' he said, as they were once more in the carriage on their way to the Polignacs'. 'Arthur needs you – it's your duty.'

'And you?' Barbara's tone was still chilly.

'You don't need me. The skeleton at the feast, dear. I'll go to Smallbridge.'

'That is very kind of you,' said Barbara. Proud as she was, she resented a little having to be beholden to anyone. To ask permission was bad enough; to receive grudging permission was dreadful.

Yet here they were at the Polignacs'.

'Milord and milady Hornblower,' roared the major-domo.

They paid their respects to the Prince, received their host's and hostess's greetings. What in the world –? What –? Hornblower's head was spinning. His heart was pounding, and there was a roaring in his ears like when he had battled for his life in the waters of the Loire. The whole glittering room was seemingly banked in fog, save for a single face. Marie was looking at him across the room, a troubled smile on her lips. Marie! Hornblower swept his hand over his face, forced himself to think clearly as he had sometimes had to do when exhausted in battle. Marie! Not so many months before his marriage to Barbara he had told Marie he loved her, and he had been on the verge of sincerity when he said it. And she had told him she loved him, and he had felt her tears on his face. Marie the tender, the devoted, the sincere. Marie, who had needed him, whose memory he had betrayed to marry Barbara.

He forced himself to cross the room to her, to kiss with simple formality the hand she offered. That troubled smile was still on her lips; she had looked like that when – when – when he had selfishly taken all she had to give, like some thoughtless child claiming a sacrifice from a loving mother. How could he meet her eyes again? And yet he did. They looked each other over with mock whimsicality. Hornblower had the impression of something vivid and vital. Marie was dressed in cloth of gold. Her eyes seemed to burn into him – that was no careless metaphor. Mentally he tried to cling to Barbara, like a shipwrecked sailor to a broken mast tossing in the surf. Barbara slim and elegant; and Marie warm and opulent. Barbara in white which did not do her justice, Marie in gold. Barbara's blue eyes, sparkling, and Marie's brown eyes, warm and tender. Barbara's hair fair and almost brown; Marie's, golden and almost auburn. It did not do to think about Barbara while looking at Marie.

Here was the count, quizzically kindly, awaiting his attention – the kindliest man in all the world, whose three sons had died for France, and who had told Hornblower once that he felt towards him as towards a son. Hornblower clasped hands with him in an outpouring of affection. The introductions were not easy. It was not easy to introduce his wife and his mistress.

'Lady Hornblower – Mme la Vicomtesse de Graçay. Barbara, my dear – M. le Comte de Graçay.'

Were they sizing each other up, these two women? Were they measuring swords, his wife and his mistress, the woman whom he had publicly chosen and the one he had privately loved?

'It was M. le Comte,' said Hornblower, feverishly, 'and his daughter-in-law who helped me escape from France. They hid me until the pursuit was over.'

'I remember,' said Barbara. She turned to them and spoke in her shocking schoolroom French. 'I am eternally grateful to you for what you did for my husband.'

It was difficult. There was a puzzled look on the faces of Marie and the Count; this was nothing like the wife Hornblower had described to them four years ago when he had been a fugitive hidden in their house. They could hardly be expected to know that Maria was dead and that Hornblower had promptly married Barbara, who was as unlike her predecessor as she well could be.

'We would do as much again, madame,' said the Count. 'Fortunately there will never be any need.'

'And Lieutenant Bush?' asked Marie of Hornblower. 'I hope he is well?'

'He is dead, madame. He was killed in the last month of the war. He was a captain before he died.'

'Oh!'

It was silly to say he had been a captain. For anyone else it would not have been. A naval officer hungered and yearned so inexpressibly for that promotion that speaking of a casual acquaintance one could think his death requited by his captaincy. But not with Bush.

'I am sorry,' said the Count. He hesitated before he spoke again – now that they had emerged from the nightmare of war it was apprehensively that one asked about old friends who might have been killed. 'But Brown? That pillar of strength? He's well?'

'Perfectly well, M. le Comte. He is my confidential servant at this moment.'

'We read a little about your escape,' said Marie.

'In the usual garbled Bonaparte form,' added the Count. 'You took a ship – the – the –'

'The *Witch of Endor*, sir.'

Was all this too painful or too pleasant? Memories were crowding in on him, memories of the Château de Graçay, of the escape down the Loire, of the glorious return to England; memories of Bush; and memories – honey-sweet memories – of Marie. He met her eyes, and the kindness in them was unfathomable. God! This was unendurable.

'But we have not done what we should have done at the very first,' said the Count. 'We have not offered our felicitations, our congratulations, on the recognition your services have received from your country. You are an English lord, and I well know how much that implies. My sincerest congratulations, milord. Nothing – nothing can ever give me greater pleasure.'

'Nor me,' said Marie.

'Thank you, thank you,' said Hornblower. He bowed shyly. It was for him, too, one of the greatest pleasures in his life to see the pride and affection beaming in the old Count's face.

Hornblower became aware that Barbara standing by had lost the thread of the conversation. He offered her a hurried English translation, and she nodded and smiled to the Count – but the translation was a false move. It would have been better to have let Barbara blunder along with French; once he started interpreting for her the barrier of language was raised far higher, and he was put into the position of intermediary between his wife and his friends, tending to keep her at a distance.

'You are enjoying life in Paris, *madame*?' asked Marie.

'Very much, thank you,' said Barbara.

It seemed to Hornblower as if the two women did not like each other. He plunged into a mention of the possibility of Barbara's going to Vienna; Marie listened apparently in rapture at Barbara's good fortune. Conversation became formal and stilted; Hornblower refused to allow himself to decide that this was a result of Barbara's entry into it, and yet the conclusion formed in his inner consciousness. He wanted to chatter free and unrestrained with Marie and the Count, and somehow it could not be done with Barbara standing by. Relief actually mingled with his regret when the surge of people round them and the approach of their host meant that their group would have to break up. They exchanged addresses; they promised to call on each other, if Barbara's probable departure for Vienna left her time enough. There was a soul-searing glimpse of sadness in Marie's eyes as he bowed to her.

In the carriage again, going back to their hotel, Hornblower felt a curious little glow of virtue over the fact that he had suggested that Barbara should go to Vienna without him before they had met the Graçays. Why he should derive any comfort from that knowledge was more than he could possibly imagine, but he hugged the knowledge to him. He sat in his dressing gown talking to Barbara while Hebe went through the elaborate processes of undressing her and making her hair ready for the night.

'When you first told me about Arthur's suggestion, my dear,' he said. 'I hardly realized all that it implied. I am so delighted. You will be England's first lady. And very properly, too.'

'You do not wish to accompany me?' said Barbara.

'I think you would be happier without me,' said Hornblower with perfect honesty. Somehow he would spoil her pleasure, he knew, if he had to endure a succession of balls and ballets in Vienna.

'And you?' asked Barbara. 'You will be happy at Smallbridge, you think?'

'As happy as I ever can be without you, dear,' said Hornblower, and he meant it.

So far not a word about the Graçays had passed between them. Barbara was commendably free from the vulgar habit which had distressed him so much in his first wife of talking over the people they had just met. They were in bed together, her hands in his, before she mentioned them, and then it was suddenly, with no preliminary fencing, and very much not *à propos*.

'Your friends the Graçays are very charming,' she said.

'Are they not all that I told you about them?' said Hornblower, immensely relieved that in telling Barbara of his adventures he had made no attempt to skirt round that particular episode, even though he had not told her all – by no means all. Then a little clumsily he went on, 'The Count is one of the most delightful and sweetest-natured men who ever walked.'

'She is beautiful,' said Barbara, pursuing undeflected her own train of thought. 'Those eyes, that complexion, that hair. So often women with reddish hair and brown eyes have poor complexions.'

'Hers is perfect,' said Hornblower – it seemed the best thing to do to agree.

'Why has she not married again?' wondered Barbara. 'She must have been married very young, and she had been a widow for some years, you say?'

'Since Aspern,' he explained. 'In 1809. One son was killed at Austerlitz, one died in Spain, and her husband, Marcel, at Aspern.'

'Nearly six years ago,' said Barbara.

Hornblower tried to explain; how Marie was not of blue blood herself, how whatever fortune she had would certainly revert to the Graçays on her remarriage, how their retired life gave her small chance of meeting possible husbands.

'They will be moving much in good society now,' commented Barbara, thoughtfully. And some time afterwards, *à propos* of nothing, she added. 'Her mouth is too wide.'

Later that night, with Barbara breathing quietly beside him, Hornblower thought over what Barbara had said. He did not like to think about Marie's remarriage, which was perfectly ridiculous of him. He would almost never see her again. He might call once, before he returned to England, but that would be all. Soon he would be back in Smallbridge, in his own house, with Richard, and with English servants to wait on him. Life in future might be dull and safe, but it would be happy. Barbara would not be in Vienna for always. With his wife and his son he would lead a sane, orderly, and useful life. That was a good resolution on which to close his eyes and compose himself to sleep.

17

Two months later saw Hornblower sitting in a chaise driving along through France towards Nevers and the Château of Graçay. The Congress of Vienna was still sitting, or dancing – someone had just made the remark that the Congress danced but made no progress – and Barbara was still entertaining. Little Richard spent his mornings in the schoolroom now, and there was nothing for an active man to do in Smallbridge except feel lonely. Temptation had crept up on him like an assassin. Six weeks of mooning round the house had been enough for him; six weeks of an English winter of rain and cloud, six weeks of being hovered over by butler and housekeeper and governess, six weeks of desultory riding through the lanes and of enduring the company of his bucolic neighbours. As a captain he had been a lonely man and yet a busy one, a very different thing from being a lonely man with nothing to do. Even going round to parties in Paris had been better than this.

He had caught himself talking to Brown, harking back to old experiences, reminiscing, and that would never do. He had his dignity still to consider; no strong man could be weak enough to yearn for activity and interest. And Brown had talked eagerly about France, about the Château of Graçay, about their escape down the Loire – maybe it was Brown's fault that Hornblower's thoughts had turned more and more towards Graçay. As a fugitive he had found a welcome there, a home, friendship, and love. He thought about the Count – it may have been because his conscience troubled him, but undoubtedly at first it was the Count that he thought about rather than Marie – with his courtesy and kindliness and general loveableness. With Bush dead it was likely that the Count was the man of whom Hornblower was fondest in all the world. The spiritual tie of which Hornblower had been conscious years ago was still in existence. Under the surface of his thoughts there may have been a tumultuous undercurrent of thoughts about Marie, but it was not apparent to him. All he knew was that one morning the pressure of his restlessness had become overwhelming. He fingered in his pocket the Count's pleasant letter, received some days ago, telling him of his and his daughter-in-law's return to Graçay and repeating his invitation to come and stay. Then he had shouted to Brown to pack clothes for both of them and to have horses put to the chaise.

Two nights ago they had slept at the Sign of the Siren in Montargis; last night at the posthouse at Briare. Now here they were driving along a lonely road overlooking the Loire, which ran like a grey ocean at their right hand, wide and desolate, with forlorn willows keeping a desperate foothold waist deep in the flood. Lashing rain beat down upon the leather tilt of the chaise, thundering down upon the taut material with a noise that made conversation difficult. Hornblower had Brown beside him in the chaise; the unfortunate postilion, hat drawn down over his ears to meet the collar of his cape, riding the near-side horse in front of them. Brown sat with folded arms, the model gentleman's servant, ready to converse politely if Hornblower showed any inclination to do so, keeping a discreet silence until addressed. He had managed every detail of the journey remarkably well – not that it would be difficult to manage any journey in France for an English milord. Every posthouse keeper, however insolent in his office, was reduced to instant deference at the mention of Hornblower's rank.

Hornblower felt Brown stiffen beside him, and then peer forward through the driving rain.

'The Bec d'Allier,' said Brown, without being spoken to first.

Hornblower could see where the grey Allier joined the grey Loire at an acute angle – all this country was under moderate floods. There was something a little odd about having a coxswain who spoke French with the facility and good accent of Brown, who must have made (of course Hornblower knew he had) the best use of his months of living below stairs at Graçay when they had been escaped prisoners of war together – they and Bush. Hornblower could feel a mounting excitement in Brown, comparable with his own, and that was hard to explain in Brown's case. There was no reason for Brown to feel the same sort of homesickness for Graçay that Hornblower felt.

'Do you remember coming down here?' asked Hornblower.

'Aye, my lord, that I do,' said Brown.

It was down the Loire that they had made their historic escape from France, a long, curiously happy voyage to Nantes, to England, and to fame. Graçay could only be a few miles ahead now; Brown was leaning forward expectantly in the chaise. There it was, the grey pepper-pot turrets only just visible in the distance against the grey sky through the rain. A flag flying from the flagstaff made a tiny darker spot above the château. The Count was there. Marie was there. The postilion shook up his depressed horses into a smarter trot, and the château came nearer and nearer; the unbelievable moment was at hand. All the way from Smallbridge, from the time when Hornblower had decided to start, it had seemed as if it was quite impossible that they were going to Graçay. Hornblower had seemed to himself like a child crying for the moon, for their goal was so desirable as to seem necessarily unattainable. Yet here they were, reining up at the gates, and here the gates were opening and they were trotting forward into the so-well-remembered courtyard. Here was old Felix the butler hurrying out into the rain to welcome them, and over there by the kitchens stood a group of servingwomen, fat Jeanne the cook among them. And here, beside the chaise, at the head of the far stone steps sheltered from the rain by the projecting roof overhead, were the Count and Marie. It was a homecoming.

Hornblower scrambled down awkwardly from the chaise. He stooped to kiss Marie's hand; he went into the Count's arms and laid cheek to cheek to the manner born. The Count was patting his shoulder.

'Welcome. Welcome.'

There was no pleasure on earth comparable with this sensation of being looked for and of feeling that his arrival was causing pleasure. Here was the well-remembered drawing room with the old gilt Louis-Seize chairs. The Count's wrinkled old face was mobile with delight, and Marie was smiling. This man had broken her heart once, and she was ready to let him break it all over again – she knew he would – because she loved him. All Hornblower was conscious of was her smile, welcoming and – and – was it maternal? There was a proud sadness in that smile, like that perhaps of a mother watching her son grown up now and soon to be lost to her. It was only a fleeting feeling that Hornblower had; his powers of observation were negatived immediately by his own wave of personal feeling. He wanted to take Marie to him, to feel her rich flesh in the circle of his arms, to forget his troubles and doubts and disillusionments in the intoxication of her embrace; just as four years ago he had found oblivion there, selfishly.

'A more cheerful arrival than your last, milord,' said the Count.

Hornblower's last arrival had been as a fugitive, carrying the wounded Bush, and hunted by Bonaparte's gendarmes.

'Yes, indeed,' said Hornblower. Then he realized how formally the Count had addressed him. 'Must I be "milord" to you, sir? It seems –'

They all smiled together.

'I shall call you 'Oratio, then, if you will permit me,' said the Count. 'I feel the greatness of the honour of such intimacy.'

Hornblower looked towards Marie.

''Oratio,' she said. ''Oratio.'

She had called him that before in little broken tones when they had been alone together. Just to hear her say it again sent a wave of passionate emotion through Hornblower's body. He was filled with love – the sort of love of which he was capable. He was not conscious yet of any wickedness about his action in coming thus to torment Marie again. He had been overborne by his own wild longing – and perhaps in his excuse it could also be pleaded that his silly modesty made him incapable of realizing how much a woman could love him. Here came Felix with wine; the Count raised his glass.

'To your happy return, 'Oratio,' he said.

The simple words called up a momentary pageant in Hornblower's memory, a sort of procession of returns, like the procession of kings in Macbeth's imagination. A sailor's life was a chain of departures and homecomings. Homecomings to Maria now dead and gone, homecomings to Barbara – and now this homecoming to Marie. It was not well to think of Barbara while he was with Marie; he had thought of Marie while he was with Barbara.

'I suppose Brown has made himself comfortable, Felix?' he asked. A good master always sees after the well-being of his servant – but this question was also intended to change his own train of thought.

'Yes, milord,' said Felix. 'Brown has made himself at home.'

Felix's face was devoid of expression, his voice devoid of tone. Were they too much so? Was there some subtle implication about Brown of which Hornblower should be aware? It was curious. Yet Brown was still the model servant when Hornblower found him in his room on withdrawing there to make ready for dinner. The portmanteaux and dressing-case were unpacked, the black dress coat – London's latest fashion – was laid out with the shirt and cravat. A cheerful fire burned in the bedroom grate.

'Are you glad to be here again, Brown?'

'Very glad indeed, my lord.'

An accomplished linguist indeed was Brown – he could speak with fluency the language of the servant, the language of the lower deck, the language of the country lanes and of the London alleys, and French besides. It was faintly irritating that he never mixed them up, thought Hornblower, tying his cravat.

In the upper hall Hornblower met Marie, about to descend to dinner like himself. They both of them stood stock-still for a moment, as though each of them was the last person in the world the other expected to see. Then Hornblower bowed and offered his arm, and Marie curtsied and took it. The hand she laid on his arm was trembling, and the touch of it sent a wave of warmth against him as though he were passing by an open furnace door.

'My darling! My love!' whispered Hornblower, driven almost beyond his self-control.

The hand on his arm fluttered, but Marie continued unfaltering to walk on down the stair.

Dinner was a cheerful function, for fat Jeanne the cook had surpassed herself, and the Count was in his best form, droll and serious in turns, witty and well informed. They discussed the policy of the Bourbon Government, wondered about the decisions being reached at the Congress of Vienna, and spared a few passing thoughts for Bonaparte in Elba.

'Before we left Paris,' remarked the Count, 'there was talk that he was too dangerous a neighbour there. It was being suggested that he should be transferred to a safer place – your island of St Helena in the South Atlantic was named in that connexion.'

'Perhaps that would be better,' agreed Hornblower.

'Europe will be in a ferment as long as that man can be the centre of intrigues,' said Marie. 'Why should he be allowed to unsettle us all?'

'The Tsar is sentimental, and was his friend,' explained the Count with a shrug. 'The Emperor of Austria is, after all, his father-in-law.'

'Should they indulge their preferences at the expense of France – of civilization?' asked Marie, bitterly.

Women always seemed to be more hotly partisan than men.

'I don't think Bonaparte constitutes a very active danger,' said Hornblower, complacently.

As the Count sipped his coffee after dinner his eyes wandered longingly towards the card-table.

'Have you lost your old skill at whist, 'Oratio?' he asked. 'There are only the three of us, but I thought we might make use of a dummy. In some ways – heretical though the opinion may appear – I feel that the game with a dummy is the more scientific.'

Nobody mentioned how Bush used to play with them, but they all thought of him. They cut and shuffled and dealt, cut and shuffled and dealt. There was some truth in what the Count said about whist with a dummy being more scientific; certainly it allowed for a closer calculation of chances. The Count played with all his old verve, Marie seemingly with all her old solid skill, and Hornblower sought to display his usual scientific precision. Yet something was not quite right. Dummy whist was somehow unsettling – perhaps it was because the need for changing seats as the deal passed broke the continuity of the play. There was no question of simply losing oneself in the game, as Hornblower usually could do. He was vastly conscious of Marie, now beside him, now opposite him, and twice he made minor slips in play. At the end of the second rubber Marie folded her hands on her lap.

'I think I have played all I can this evening,' she said. 'I am sure 'Oratio is as much a master of piquet as he is of whist. Perhaps you can entertain each other with that while I go to bed.'

The Count was on his feet with his usual deferential politeness, asking if she felt quite well, and, when she assured him that she was merely tired, escorting her to the door exactly as he would have escorted a queen.

'Goodnight, 'Oratio,' said Marie.

'Goodnight, *madame*,' said Horatio, standing by the card-table.

One glance passed between them – one glance, enduring less than one-tenth of a second, but long enough for each to tell the other all.

'I trust Marie was correct in her assumption that you are a master of piquet, 'Oratio,' said the Count, returning from the door. 'She and I have played much together in default of whist. But I am taking it for granted that you wish to play? How inconsiderate of me! Please –'

Hornblower hastened to assure the Count that he would like nothing better.

'That is delightful,' said the Count, shuffling the cards with his slender white fingers. 'I am a fortunate man.'

He was fortunate at least in his play that night, taking his usual bold risks and being rewarded by unpredictable good luck in his discards. His minor *seizièmes* outranked Hornblower's major quints, a quatorze of knaves saved him when Hornblower had three aces, three kings and three queens, and twice *carte blanche* rescued him from disaster in face of Hornblower's overwhelming hands. When Hornblower was strong, the Count was lucky; and when Hornblower was weak the Count was overpoweringly strong. At the conclusion of the third *partie* Hornblower gazed helplessly across at him.

'I fear this has not been very interesting for you,' said the Count remorsefully. 'This is a discourteous way to treat a guest.'

'I would rather lose in this house,' said Hornblower, perfectly truthfully, 'than win in any other.'

The Count smiled with pleasure.

'That is too high a compliment,' he said. 'And yet I can only say in reply that with you in this house I care not whether I win or lose. I trust that I shall have the further good fortune of your making a long stay here?'

'Like the fate of Europe,' said Hornblower, 'that depends on the Congress of Vienna.'

'You know this house is yours,' said the Count, earnestly. 'Marie and I both wish you to look on it as your own.'

'You are too good, sir,' said Hornblower. 'May I ring for my candle?'

'Allow me,' said the Count, hastening to the bell-cord. 'I trust you are not overtired after your journey? Felix, milord is retiring.'

Up the oaken stairs with their carved panelling, Felix hobbling goutily ahead with the candle. A sleepy Brown was waiting for him in the sitting room of the little suite, to be dismissed at once when Hornblower announced his intention of putting himself to bed. That door there, inconspicuous in the corner, led to the hall outside Marie's suite in the turret – how well Hornblower remembered it. Generations of the Ladons, Counts of Graçay, had conducted intrigues in the château; perhaps kings and princes had passed through that door on the way to their lights-of-love.

Marie was waiting for him, weighted down with longing, heavy with love, tender and sweet. To sink into her arms was to sink into peace and happiness, illimitable peace, like that of a sunset-lit sea. The rich bosom on which he could pillow his head made him welcome; its fragrance comforted while it intoxicated. She held him, she loved him, she wept with happiness. She had no more than half his heart, she knew. He was cruel, unthinking, selfish, and yet this bony, slender body that lay in her arms was everything in the world to her. It was monstrous that he should come back to claim her like this. He had made her suffer before, and she knew her suffering in the past would be nothing compared with her suffering that lay in the future. Yet that was his way. That was how she loved him. Time went so fast; she had only this little moment before a lifetime of unhappiness to come. Oh, it was so urgent! She caught him to her madly, crying out with passion, crying out to time to stand still. It seemed to do so at that moment. Time stood still while the world whirled round her.

18

'May I speak to you, my lord?' asked Brown.

He had put the breakfast tray by the bed, and had drawn aside the window curtains. Spring sunshine was gleaming on the distant Loire. Brown had waited respectfully until Hornblower had drunk his first cup of coffee and was coming slowly back to the world.

'What is it?' asked Hornblower, blinking over at him where he stood against the wall. Brown's attitude was not a usual one. Some of the deferential bearing of the gentleman's servant had been replaced by the disciplined erectness of the old days, when a self-respecting sailor held his head up and his shoulders back whether he was being condemned to the cat or commended for gallantry.

'What is it?' asked Hornblower again, consumed with curiosity.

He had had one moment of wild misgivings, wondering if Brown were going to be such a frantic fool as to say something about his relations with Marie, but the misgiving vanished as he realized the absurdity and impossibility of such a thing. Yet Brown was acting strangely – one might almost think he was feeling shy.

'Well, sir – I mean my lord,' (that was the first time Brown had slipped over Hornblower's title since the peerage was conferred) 'I don't know rightly if it's anything Your Lordship would wish to know about. I don't want to presume, sir – my lord.'

'Oh, spit it out, man,' said Hornblower testily. 'And call me "sir" if it's any comfort to you.'

'It's this way, my lord. I'm wanting to get married.'

'Good God!' said Hornblower. He had a vague idea that Brown had been a terror for women, and the possibility of his marrying had never crossed his mind. He hastened to say what he thought would be appropriate. 'Who's the lucky woman?'

'Annette, my lord. Jeanne and Bertrand's daughter. And I am the lucky one, my lord.'

'Jeanne's daughter? Oh, of course. The pretty one with the dark hair.'

Hornblower thought about a lively French girl marrying a sturdy Englishman like Brown, and for the life of him he could see no reason against it at all. Brown would be a better husband than most – it certainly would be a lucky woman who got him.

'You're a man of sense, Brown,' he said. 'You needn't ask me about these things. I'm sure you've made a wise choice, and you have all my best wishes for your happiness and joy.'

'Thank you, my lord.'

'If Annette can cook as well as her mother,' Hornblower went on meditatively, 'you're a lucky man indeed.'

'That was another thing I wanted to say to you, my lord. She's a cook second to none, young though she is. Jeanne says so herself, and if she says so –'

'We can be sure of it,' agreed Hornblower.

'I was thinking, my lord,' went on Brown, 'not wanting to presume, that if I was to continue in your service your lordship might consider engaging Annette as cook.'

'God bless my soul,' said Hornblower.

He mentally looked down a vista a lifetime long of dinners as good as Jeanne cooked. Dinners at Smallbridge had been almost good but most decidedly plain. Smallbridge and French cooking offered a most intriguing study in contrasts. Certainly Smallbridge would be more attractive with Annette as cook. And yet what was he thinking about? What had happened to those doubts and tentative notions about never seeing Smallbridge again? Some such ideas had certainly passed through his mind when he thought about Marie, and yet here he was thinking about Smallbridge and thinking about Annette heading his kitchen. He shook himself out of his reverie.

'Of course I can give no decision on the point myself,' he said, fencing for time. 'Her Ladyship will have to be consulted, as you understand, Brown. Have you any alternative in mind?'

'Plenty, my lord, as long as you are satisfied. I've thought of starting a small hotel – I have all my prize money saved.'

'Where?'

'In London, perhaps, my lord. But maybe in Paris. Or in Rome. I have been discussing it with Felix and Bertrand and Annette.'

'My God!' said Hornblower again. Nothing like this had crossed his mind for a single moment, and yet – 'I have no doubt you would be successful, Brown.'

'Thank you, my lord.'

'Tell me, this seems to have been a lightning courtship. Is that so?'

'Not really, my lord. When I was here last Annette and I – you understand, my lord.'

'I do now,' said Hornblower.

It was fantastic that Brown, the man who hove the line that saved the *Pluto*, the man who silenced Colonel Caillard with a single blow of his fist, should be talking calmly about the possibility of opening an hotel in Rome. Actually it was no more fantastic than that he himself should have seriously debated with himself the possibility of becoming a French *seigneur*, and turning his back on England. He had done that no later than last night; love for Marie had grown during the last five days even while his passion was indulged – and Hornblower was not the sort of fool to be ignorant of how much that implied.

'When are you thinking of marrying, Brown?' he asked.

'As soon as the law of this country allows, my lord.'

'I've no idea how long that means,' said Hornblower.

'I am finding out, my lord. Will that be all you need at present?'

'No. I'll get up at once – can't stay in bed after hearing all this exciting news, Brown. I'll come through with a handsome wedding present.'

'Thank you, my lord. I'll fetch your hot water, then.'

Marie was waiting for him in her boudoir when he was dressed. She kissed him good morning, passed a hand over his smoothly shaven cheeks, and, with her arm over his shoulder, led him to her turret window to show him that the apple trees in the orchard below were showing their first blossoms. It was spring; and it was good to be in love and to be loved in this green and lovely land. He took her white hands in his, and he kissed every finger on them, with a surge of reverent passion.

As each day passed he had come to admire her the more, her sweetness of character and the unselfishness of her love. For Hornblower respect and love made a heady mixture – he felt he could kneel to her as to a saint. She was conscious of the passion that was carrying him away, as she was conscious of everything about him.

''Oratio,' she said – why should it stir him so frightfully to hear that ridiculous name of his pronounced in that fashion?

He clung to her, and she held him and comforted him as she always did. She had no thought for the future now. In the future lay tragedy for her, she knew; but this was the present, and during this present Hornblower had need of her. They came out of their paroxysm of passion smiling as they always did.

'You heard the news about Brown?' he asked.

'He is going to marry Annette. That is very proper.'

'It does not seem to be news to you?'

'I knew it before Brown did,' said Marie. There was a dimple that came and went in her cheek, and a little light of mischief could sparkle in her eyes. She was wholly and utterly desirable.

'They should make a good pair,' said Hornblower.

'Her chest of linens is all ready,' said Marie, 'and Bertrand had a *dot* for her.'

They went downstairs to tell the Count the news, and he heard it with pleasure.

'I can perform the civil ceremony myself,' he said. 'Do you remember that I am the *maire* here, 'Oratio? A position that is almost a sinecure, thanks to the efficiency of my *adjoint*, and yet I can make use of my powers should the whim ever overtake me.'

Fortunately, as regards the saving of time, Brown was able – as they found out on calling him in to ask him – to declare himself an orphan and head of his family, thus obviating the need for parental permission on which French law insisted. And King Louis XVIII and the Chamber had not yet carried out their declared intention of making a religious ceremony a necessary part of the legal marriage. There would be a religious ceremony, all the same, and the blessing of the Church would be given to the union, with the safeguards always insisted on in a mixed marriage. Annette was never to cease to try to convert Brown, and the children were to be brought up in the Catholic faith. Brown nodded as this was explained to him; religious scruples apparently weighed lightly enough on his shoulders.

The village of Smallbridge had already been scandalized by the introduction into its midst of Barbara's Negro maid; it had shaken disapproving heads over Hornblower's and Barbara's heathen habit of a daily bath; what it would say in the future about the presence of a popish female and a popish family Hornblower could hardly imagine. There he was, thinking about Smallbridge again. This was a double life in very truth. He looked uneasily across at the Count whose hospitality he was abusing. It was hard to think of guilty love in connexion with Marie – there was no guilt in her. And in himself? Could he be held guilty for something he could do nothing to resist? Was he guilty when the current whirled him away in the Loire, not a mile from where he was standing at present? He shifted his glance to Marie, and felt his passion surge up as strongly as ever, so that he started nervously when it penetrated his consciousness that the Count was addressing him in his gentle voice.

''Oratio,' said the Count, 'shall we dance at the wedding?'

They made quite a gala occasion of it, a little to the surprise of Hornblower, who had vague and incorrect ideas about the attitude of French *seigneurs* of the old régime towards their dependants. The barrels of wine were set up in the back courtyard of the château, and quite an orchestra was assembled, of fiddlers, and of pipers from the Auvergne who played instruments something like Scottish bagpipes that afflicted Hornblower's tone-deaf ear atrociously. The Count led out fat Jeanne in the dance, and the bride's father led out Marie. There was wine, there were great masses of food, there were bawdy jokes and highfalutin speeches. The countrysidc seemed to show astonishing tolerance towards this marriage of a local girl to an heretical foreigner – local peasant farmers clapped Brown on the back and their wives kissed his weatherbeaten cheeks amidst screams of mirth. But then, Brown was universally popular, and seemed to know the dances by instinct.

Hornblower, unable to tell one note of music from another, was constrained to listen intently to the rhythm, and, intently watching the actions of the others, he was able to scramble grotesquely through the movements of the dances, handed on from one apple-cheeked woman to another. At one moment he sat gorged and bloated with food at a trestle table, at another he was skipping madly over the courtyard cobbles between two buxom maidens, hand in hand with them and laughing unrestrainedly. It was extraordinary to him – even here he still had moments of self-analysis – that he could ever enjoy himself so much. Marie smiled at him from under level brows.

He was amazingly weary and yet amazingly happy when he found himself back again in the *salon* of the château, his legs stretched out in inelegant ease while Felix, transformed again into the perfect major-domo, took the orders of him and the Count.

'There is an odd rumour prevalent,' said the Count, sitting upright in his chair apparently as unwearied and as dapper as ever. 'I did not wish to disturb the fête by discussing it there. People are saying that Bonaparte has escaped from Elba and has landed in France.'

'That is indeed odd,' agreed Hornblower lazily, the import of the news taking some time to penetrate his befogged brain. 'What can he intend to do?'

'He claims the throne of France again,' said the Count, seriously.

'It is less than a year since the people abandoned him.'

'That is true. Perhaps Bonaparte will solve the problem for us that we were discussing a few nights ago. There is no doubt that the King will have him shot if he can lay hands on him, and that will be an end of all possibility of intrigue and disturbance.'

'Quite so.'

'But I wish – foolishly perhaps – that we had heard of Bonaparte's death at the same time as we heard of his landing.'

The Count appeared grave, and Hornblower felt a little disturbed. He knew his host to be an acute political observer.

'What is it you fear, sir?' asked Hornblower, gradually gathering his wits about him.

'I fear lest he gain some unexpected success. You know the power of his name, and the King – the King or his advisers – has not acted as temperately as he might have done since his restoration.'

The entrance of Marie, smiling and happy, interrupted the conversation, nor was it restarted when they resumed their seats. There were moments during the next two days when Hornblower felt some slight misgivings, even though the only news that came in was a mere confirmation of the rumour of the landing with no amplification. It was a shadow across his happiness, but so great and so intense was the latter that it took more than a slight shadow to chill it. Those lovely spring days, wandering under the orchard blossoms, and beside the rushing Loire; riding – how was it that riding was a pleasure now when always before he had detested it? – through the forest; even driving into Nevers on the one or two ceremonial calls his position demanded of him; those moments were golden, every one of them. Fear of Bonaparte's activity could not cloud them – not even fear of what would be said to him in a letter that must inevitably soon come from Vienna could do that. On the surface Barbara had nothing to complain about; she had gone to Vienna, and during her absence Hornblower was visiting old friends. But Barbara would know. Probably she would say nothing, but she would know.

And great as was Hornblower's happiness it was not untrammelled, as Brown's happiness was untrammelled – Hornblower found himself envying Brown and the public way in which Brown could claim his love.

Hornblower and Marie had to be a little furtive, a little guarded, and his conscience troubled him a little over the Count. Yet even so, he was happy, happier than he had ever been in his tormented life. For once self-analysis brought him no pangs. He had doubts neither about himself nor about Marie, and the novelty of that experience completely overlaid all his fears and misgivings about the future. He could live in peace until trouble should overtake him – if a spice to his happiness were necessary (and it was not), it was the knowledge that trouble lay ahead and that he could ignore it. All that guilt and uncertainty could do was to drive him more madly still into Marie's arms, not consciously to forget, but merely because of the added urgency they brought.

This was love, unalloyed and without reservations. There was an ecstasy in giving, and no amazement in receiving. It had come to him at last, after all these years and tribulations. Cynically it might be thought that it was merely one more example of Hornblower's yearning for the thing he could not have, but if that was the case Hornblower for once was not conscious of it. There was some line from the Prayer Book that ran in Hornblower's head during those days – 'Whose service is perfect freedom'. That described his servitude to Marie.

The Loire was still in flood; the cataract where once he had nearly drowned – the cataract which was the cause of his first meeting with Marie – was a rushing slope of green water, foam-bordered. Hornblower could hear the sound of it as he lay in Marie's arms in her room in the turret; often they walked beside it, and Hornblower could contemplate it without a tremor or a thrill. That was all over. His reason told him that he was the same man as boarded the *Castilla*, the same man who faced El Supremo's wrath, the man who fought to the death at Rosas Bay, the man who had walked decks awash with blood, and yet oddly he felt as if those things had happened to someone else. Now he was a man of peace, a man of indolence, and the cataract was not a thing that had nearly killed him.

It seemed perfectly natural when the Count came in with good news.

'The Count d'Artois has defeated Bonaparte in a battle in the south,' he said. 'Bonaparte is a fugitive, and will soon be a prisoner. The news is from Paris.'

That was as it should be; the wars were over.

'I think we can light a bonfire tonight,' said the Count, and the bonfire blazed and toasts were drunk to the King.

But it was no later than next morning that Brown, as he put the breakfast tray beside Hornblower's bed, announced that the Count wished to speak to him as early as convenient, and he had hardly uttered the words when the Count came in, haggard and dishevelled in his dressing gown.

'Pardon this intrusion,' said the Count – even at that moment he could not forget his good manners – 'but I could not wait. There is bad news. The very worst.'

Hornblower could only stare and wait, while the Count gathered his strength to tell his news. It took an effort to say the words.

'Bonaparte is in Paris,' said the Count. 'The King has fled and Bonaparte is Emperor again. All France has fallen to him.'

'But the battle he had lost?'

'Rumour – lies – all lies. Bonaparte is Emperor again.'

It took time to understand all that this implied. It meant war again, that was certain. Whatever the other Great Powers might do, England could never tolerate the presence of that treacherous and mighty enemy across the Channel. England and France would be at each other's throats once more. Twenty-two years ago the wars started; it seemed likely that it would be another twenty-two years before Bonaparte could be pulled from his throne again. There would be another twenty-two years of misery and slaughter. The prospect was utterly hideous.

'How did it happen?' asked Hornblower, more to gain time than because he wanted to know.

The Count spread his delicate hands in a hopeless gesture.

'Not a shot was fired,' he said. 'The army went over to him *en masse*. Ney, Labédoyère, Soult – they all betrayed the King. In two weeks Bonaparte marched from the Mediterranean to Paris. That would be fast travelling in a coach and six.'

'But the people do not want him,' protested Hornblower. 'We all know that.'

'The people's wishes do not weigh against the army's,' said the Count. 'The news has come with the usurper's first decrees. The classes of 1815 and 1816 are to be called out. The Household troops are disbanded, the Imperial Guard is to be reconstituted. Bonaparte is ready to fight Europe again.'

Hornblower vaguely saw himself once more on the deck of a ship, weighed down with responsibility, encompassed by danger, isolated and friendless. It was a bleak prospect.

A tap on the door heralded Marie's entrance, in her dressing gown, with her magnificent hair over her shoulders.

'You have heard the news, my dear?' asked the Count. He made no comment either on her presence or on her appearance.

'Yes,' said Marie. 'We are in danger.'

'We are indeed,' said the Count. 'All of us.'

So appalling had been the news that Hornblower had not yet had leisure to contemplate its immediate personal implications. As an officer of the British Navy, he would be seized and imprisoned immediately. Not only that, but Bonaparte had intended years ago to try him and shoot him on charges of piracy. He would carry that intention into effect – tyrants have long memories. And the Count, and Marie?

'Bonaparte knows now that you helped me escape,' said Hornblower. 'He will never forgive that.'

'He will shoot me if he can catch me,' said the Count; he made no reference to Marie, but he glanced towards her. Bonaparte would shoot her too.

'We must get away,' said Hornblower. 'The country cannot be settled under Bonaparte yet. With fast horses we can reach the coast –'

He took his bedclothes in his hand to cast them off, restraining himself in the nick of time out of deference to Marie's presence.

'I shall be dressed in ten minutes,' said Marie.

As the door closed behind her and the Count, Hornblower hurled himself out of bed shouting for Brown. The transition from the sybarite to the man of action took a few moments, but only a few. As he tore off his nightshirt he conjured up before his mind's eye the map of France, visualizing the roads and ports. They could reach La Rochelle over the mountains in two days of hard riding. He hauled up his trousers. The Count had a great name – no one would venture to arrest him or his party without direct orders from Paris; with bluff and self-confidence they could get through. There were two hundred golden napoleons in the secret compartment of his portmanteau – maybe the Count had more. It was enough for bribery. They could bribe a fisherman to take them out to sea – they could steal a boat, for that matter.

It was humiliating thus to run like rabbits at Bonaparte's first reappearance; it was hardly consonant with the dignity of a peer and a commodore, but his first duty was to preserve his life and his usefulness. A dull rage against Bonaparte, the wrecker of the peace, was growing within him, but was still far from mastering him as yet. It was resentment as yet, rather than rage; and his sullen resignation regarding the change in conditions was slowly giving way to tentative wonderings regarding whether he could not play a more active part in the opening of the struggle than merely running away to fight another day. Here he was in France, in the heart of his enemy's country. Surely he could strike a blow here that could be felt. As he hauled on his riding boots he spoke to Brown.

'What about your wife?' he asked.

'I hoped she could come with us, my lord,' said Brown, soberly.

If he left her behind he would not see her again until the end of the war twenty years off; if he stayed with her he would be cast into prison.

'Can she ride?'

'She will, my lord.'

'Go and see that she gets ready. We can carry nothing more than saddlebags. She can attend Mme la Vicomtesse.'

'Thank you, my lord.'

Two hundred gold napoleons made a heavy mass to carry, but it was essential to have them with him. Hornblower thumped down the stairs in his riding boots; Marie was already in the main hall wearing a black habit and a saucy tricorne hat with a feather. He ran his eyes keenly over her; there was nothing about her appearance to excite attention – she was merely a lady of fashion soberly dressed.

'Shall we take any of the men with us?' she asked.

'They are all old. It would be better not to. The Count, you, myself, Brown, and Annette. We shall need five horses.'

'That is what I expected,' answered Marie. She was a fine woman in a crisis.

'We can cross the bridge at Nevers, and head for Bourges and La Rochelle. In the Vendée we shall have our best chance.'

'It might be better to make for a little fishing village rather than a great port,' commented Marie.

'That's very likely true. We can make up our minds about it, though, when we are near the coast.'

'Very well.'

She appreciated the importance of unity of command even though she was ready with advice.

'What about your valuables?' asked Hornblower.

'I have my diamonds in my saddlebag here.'

As she spoke the Count came in, booted and spurred. He carried a small leather sack which clinked as he put it down.

'Two hundred napoleons,' he said.

'The same as I have. It will be ample.'

'It would be better if it did not clink, though,' said Marie. 'I'll pack it with a cloth.'

Felix entered with the Count's saddlebags and the announcement that the horses were ready – Brown and Annette awaited them in the courtyard.

'Let us go,' said Hornblower.

It was a sorry business saying goodbye. There were tears from the women – Annette's pretty face was all beslobbered with grief – even though the men, trained in the stoical school of gentlemen's service, kept silence.

'Goodbye, my friend,' said the Count, holding out his hand to Felix. They were both old men, and the chances were that they would never meet again.

They rode out of the courtyard, and down to the road along the river; it was ironical that it should be a lovely spring day, with the fruit blossom raining down on them and the Loire sparkling joyously. At the first turn in the road the spires and towers of Nevers came into sight; at the next they could clearly see the ornate Gonzaga palace. Hornblower spared it a casual glance, blinked, and looked again. Marie was beside him and the Count beyond her, and he glanced at them for confirmation.

'That is a white flag,' said Marie.

'I thought so too,' wondered Hornblower.

'My eyes are such that I can see no flag at all,' said the Count ruefully.

Hornblower turned in his saddle to Brown, riding along encouraging Annette.

'That's a white flag over the palace, my lord.'

'It hardly seems possible,' said the Count. 'My news this morning came from Nevers. Beauregard, the Prefect there, had declared at once for Bonaparte.'

It was certainly odd – even if the white flag had been hoisted inadvertently it was odd.

'We shall know soon enough,' said Hornblower, restraining his natural instinct to push his horse from a trot into a canter.

The white flag still flew as they approached. At the octroi gate stood half a dozen soldiers in smart grey uniforms, their grey horses tethered behind them.

'Those are Grey Musketeers of the Household,' said Marie. Hornblower recognized the uniforms. He had seen those troops in attendance on the King both at the Tuileries and at Versailles.

'Grey Musketeers cannot hurt us,' said the Count.

The sergeant of the picket looked at them keenly as they approached, and stepped into the road to ask them their names.

'Louis-Antoine-Hector-Savinien de Ladon, Comte de Graçay, and his suite,' said the Count.

'You may pass, M. le Comte,' said the sergeant. 'Her Royal Highness is at the Prefecture.'

'*Which* Royal Highness?' marvelled the Count.

In the Grand Square a score of troopers of the Grey Musketeers sat their horses. A few white banners flew here and there, and as they entered the square a man emerged from the Prefecture and began to stick up a printed poster. They rode up to look at it – the first word was easily read – 'Frenchmen!' it said.

'Her Royal Highness is the Duchess of Angoulême,' said the Count.

The proclamation called on all Frenchmen to fight against the usurping tyrant, to be loyal to the ancient House of Bourbon. According to the poster, the King was still in arms around Lille, the south had risen under the Duke d'Angoulême, and all Europe was marching armies to enchain the man-eating ogre and restore the Father of his People to the throne of his ancestors.

In the Prefecture the Duchess received them eagerly. Her beautiful face was drawn with fatigue, and she still wore a mud-splashed riding habit – she had ridden through the night with her squadron of musketeers, entering Nevers by another road on the heels of Bonaparte's proclamation.

'They changed sides quickly enough again,' said the Duchess.

Nevers was not a garrison town and contained no troops; her hundred disciplined musketeers made her mistress of the little place without a blow struck.

'I was about to send for you, M. le Comte,' went on the Duchess. 'I was not aware of our extraordinary good fortune in Lord 'Ornblower's being present here. I want to appoint you Lieutenant-General of the King in the Nivernais.'

'You think a rising can succeed, Your Royal Highness?' asked Hornblower.

'A rising?' said the Duchess, with the faintest of interrogative inflections.

To Hornblower that was the note of doom. The Duchess was the most intelligent and spirited of all the

Bourbons, but not even she could think of the movement she was trying to head as a 'rising'. Bonaparte was the rebel; she was engaged in suppressing rebellion, even if Bonaparte reigned in the Tuileries and the army obeyed him. But this was war; this was life or death, and he was in no mood to quibble with amateurs.

'Let us not waste time over definitions, *madame*,' he said. 'Do you think there is in France strength enough to drive out Bonaparte?'

'He is the most hated man in this country.'

'But that does not answer the question,' persisted Hornblower.

'The Vendée will fight,' said the Duchess. 'Laroche-Jacquelin is there, and they will follow him. My husband is raising the Midi. The King and the Household are holding out in Lille. Gascony will resist the usurper – remember how Bordeaux cast off allegiance to him last year.'

The Vendée might rise; probably would. But Hornblower could not imagine the Duke d'Angoulême rousing much spirit of devotion in the south, nor the fat and gouty old King in the north. As for Bordeaux casting off her allegiance, Hornblower remembered Rouen and Le Havre, the apathetic citizens, the refractory conscripts whose sole wish was to fight no one at all. For a year they had now enjoyed the blessings of peace and liberal government, and they might perhaps fight for them. Perhaps.

'All France knows now that Bonaparte *can* be beaten and dethroned,' said the Duchess acutely. 'That makes a great difference.'

'A powder magazine of discontent and disunion,' said the Count. 'A spark may explode it.'

Hornblower had dreamed the same dream when he had entered Le Havre, and used the same metaphor to himself, which was unfortunate.

'Bonaparte has an army,' he said. 'It takes an army to defeat an army. Where is one to be found? The old soldiers are devoted to Bonaparte. Will the civilians fight, and if so, can they be armed and trained in time?'

'You are in a pessimistic mood, milord,' said the Duchess.

'Bonaparte is the most able, the most active, the fiercest and the most cunning soldier the world has ever seen,' said Hornblower. 'To parry his strokes I ask for a shield of steel, not a paper hoop from a circus.'

Hornblower looked round at the faces; the Duchess, the Count, Marie, the silent courtier-general who had stood behind the Duchess since the debate began. They were sombre, but they showed no signs of wavering.

'So you suggest that M. le Comte here, for example, should submit tamely to the usurper and wait until the armies of Europe reconquer France?' asked the Duchess with only faint irony. She could keep her temper better than most Bourbons.

'M. le Comte has to fly for his life on account of his late kindness to me,' said Hornblower, but that was begging the question, he knew.

Any movement against Bonaparte in the interior of France might be better than none, however easily suppressed and whatever blood it cost. It might succeed, although he had no hope of it. But at least it would embarrass Bonaparte in his claim to represent all France, at least it would hamper him in the inevitable clash on the north-eastern frontier by forcing him to keep troops here. Hornblower could not look for victory; but he supposed there was a chance, the faintest chance, of beginning a slight guerrilla war, maintained by a few partisans in forests and mountains, which might spread in the end. He was a servant of King George; if he could encompass the death of even one of Bonaparte's soldiers, even at the cost of a hundred peasant lives, it was his duty to do so. A momentary doubt flashed through his mind; was it mere humanitarian motives that had been influencing him? Or were his powers of decision becoming enfeebled? He had sent men on forlorn hopes before this; he had taken part in some himself; but this was, in his opinion, an utterly hopeless venture – and the Count would be involved in it.

'But still,' persisted the Duchess, 'you recommend supine acquiescence, milord?'

Hornblower felt like a man on a scaffold taking one last look at the sunlit world before being thrust off. The grim inevitabilities of war were all round him.

'No,' he said. 'I recommend resistance.'

The sombre faces round him brightened, and he knew now that peace or war had lain in his choice. Had he continued to argue against rebellion, he would have persuaded them against it. The knowledge increased his unhappiness, even though he tried to assure himself – which was the truth – that fate had put him in a position where he could argue no longer. The die was cast, and he hastened to speak again.

'Your Royal Highness,' he said, 'accused me of being pessimistic. So I am. This is a desperate adventure, but that does not mean it should not be undertaken. But we must enter upon it in no light-hearted spirit. We must look for no glorious or dramatic successes. It will be inglorious, long, and hard. It will mean shooting French soldiers from behind a tree and then running away. Crawling up in the night to knife a sentry. Burning a bridge, cutting the throats of a few draught horses – those will be our great victories.'

He wanted to say 'those will be our Marengos and our Jenas', but he could not mention Bonaparte victories to a Bourbon gathering. He raked back in his memory for Bourbon victories.

'Those will be our Steinkerks and our Fontenoys,' he went on. To describe the technique of guerrilla warfare in a few sentences to people absolutely ignorant of the subject was not easy. 'The Lieutenant-General for the King in the Nivernais will be a hunted fugitive. He will sleep among rocks, eat his meat raw lest a fire should betray him. Only by being reconciled to measures of this sort can success be won in the end.'

'I am ready to do those things,' said the Count, 'to my last breath.'

The alternative was exile until his death, Hornblower knew.

'I never doubted that I could rely on the loyalty of the Ladons,' said the Duchess. 'Your commission will be ready immediately, M. le Comte. You will exercise all royal power in the Nivernais.'

'What does Your Royal Highness intend to do in person?' asked Hornblower.

'I must go on to Bordeaux, to rally Gascony.'

It was probably the best course of action – the wider spread the movement the greater Bonaparte's embarrassment. Marie could accompany the Duchess, too, and then if the enterprise ended in complete disaster escape would be possible by sea.

'And you, milord?' asked the Duchess.

All eyes were upon him, but for once he was not conscious of it. It was an entirely personal decision that he had to make. He was a distinguished naval officer; let him make his way to England and the command of a squadron of ships of the line was his for certain. The vast fleets would range the seas again, and he would play a major part in directing them; a few years of war would see him an admiral with a whole fleet, the man upon whom the welfare of England would depend. And if he stayed here the best he could hope for was the life of a hunted fugitive at the head of a ragged and starving brigand band; at worst a rope and a tree. Perhaps it was his duty to save himself and his talents for England, but England had able naval officers by the score, while he had the advantage of knowing much about France and the French, and even of being known to them. But all these arguments were beside the point. He would not – could not – start a little feeble squib of a rebellion here and then run away and leave his friends to bear the brunt of failure.

'I will stay with M. le Comte,' he said. 'Provided that Your Royal Highness and he approve of such a course. I hope I will be of assistance.'

'Certainly,' said the Duchess.

Hornblower caught Marie's eye, and a horrid doubt suddenly assailed him.

'*Madame*,' he said, addressing her, 'you will accompany Her Royal Highness, I presume?'

'No,' said Marie. 'You will need every man, and I am

as useful as a man. I know every ford and bridlepath round here. I stay with M. le Comte too.'

'But Marie –' said the Count.

Hornblower made no protest at all. He knew he might as well protest about the fall of an elm-tree branch or a change in the direction of the wind. He seemed to recognize destiny – the utterly inevitable – in all this. And one glance at Marie's face silenced the Count's expostulations.

'Very well,' said the Duchess.

She looked round at them; it was time for the rebellion to begin in earnest. Hornblower put aside his personal feelings. There was a war to be fought; war with all its problems of space and time and psychology. He set himself, almost without willing it, to pick up the tangled threads. Above the desk where the Prefect had sat to execute instructions from the Paris Goverment was a large-scale map of the Department. On the other walls hung even larger scale maps of the sub-prefectures. He looked over at them. Roads, rivers, forests. Goodbye to England.

'The first important thing to know,' he began, 'is where the nearest regular troops are stationed.'

The campaign of the Upper Loire was begun.

19

The forest track which they were following met another at right angles. It was frightfully hot even here in the shade of the pines, thunderstorm weather. Hornblower's feet were badly blistered, and he was hobbling along with difficulty even on the soft pine-needle mould underfoot. There was no wind to call forth any sound from the trees; everything was silent. Even the hoofs of the horses made no sound – the three packhorses that carried food and ammunition, the two horses carrying wounded men, and the one horse that carried His Excellency the King's Lieutenant-General for the Nivernais. Twenty men and two women were shuffling along the trail with Hornblower, the main body of His Most Christian Majesty's army. There was an advance guard of five under Brown out ahead, a rearguard of five far behind.

Where the tracks crossed a man was waiting for them, a connecting file that Brown, like a prudent officer, had left behind so as to leave the main body in no doubt about which track he was following; as they came up he turned and pointed to something hanging beside the trail – something grey and white. It was the dead body of a man, clothed in peasant's dress, hanging by his neck from a pine-tree limb; the white colour was a large printed placard fastened to his chest.

'Frenchmen of the Nivernais!' it said. 'With my arrival

at the head of a large body of troops all foolish attempts to resist the Government of our august Emperor Napoleon must cease forthwith. It is gratifying to me to find that so poor a reception has been given to the Count de Graçay's insane attempt to oppose the Emperor, recalled to his throne by the supplicaton and suffrages of forty million of his loyal subjects. Yet some unfortunate people have been deluded into taking up arms.

'Know, therefore, I am instructed by the clemency of His Imperial Majesty to proclaim that any Frenchman, with the exceptions mentioned below, who hands in his arms and makes personal surrender to any troops under my command before fifteen days from the date of this proclamation will receive amnesty and pardon. He will be free to return to his farm, to his shop, to the bosom of his family.

'Anyone remaining in arms will receive sentence of death, to be carried out immediately.

'Any village offering shelter to the rebels will be burned to the ground, and its leading inhabitants shot.

'Any person giving assistance to the rebels, whether by acting as guide or by giving them information, will be shot.

'Exceptions to the amnesty. The above-named Count de Graçay. His daughter-in-law, known as the Vicomtesse de Graçay. With them are included the Englishman, known as Lord Hornblower, who is required to pay for a life of outrage and crime.

'Signed,

Emmanuel Clausen, Count, General of Division. June 6th, 1815.'

*

The Count looked up at the blackened face of the corpse.

'Who is it?' he asked.

'Paul-Marie of the mill, sir,' said the man who had waited for them.

'Poor Paul-Marie!'

'So they have crossed this track already,' said Hornblower. 'We're round behind them.'

Somebody reached up a hand to the corpse, perhaps to tear off the placard.

'Stop!' said Hornblower, just in time. 'They must not know that we have come this way.'

'For the same reason we must leave the poor devil unburied,' said the Count.

'We must keep marching,' said Hornblower. 'Once over the ford and we shall have time to take breath.'

He looked round at his pitiful little army. Some of them, at the moment of halting, had sunk to the ground. Some were leaning on their muskets, and some were spelling out the placard that hung on the breast of the dead Paul-Marie. It was not the first copy of it they had seen.

'Come on, my children,' said the Count.

The old man's face was white with weariness, and he drooped in his saddle; the wretched horse he rode was hardly in better condition, moving forward reluctantly with hanging head at the prod of the spurs. Shambling, hungry, and ragged, the others followed him, most of them looking up at the dead Paul-Marie as they passed. Hornblower noticed some who lingered, and dropped back to be with them; he had pistols in his belt. Deserters, as well as being a loss of strength, would give information of their intention to cross the ford. Clausen had scored a distinct point with his offer of amnesty, for there were many in the band – Hornblower could list in his mind a number of them – who must already be wondering whether it was worth going on with the struggle. Men with nothing save certain death ahead of them fight far harder in a losing battle than those with a chance to surrender, and his followers must be thinking regretfully of the rapid passing of the fifteen days allowed them in the proclamation. This was 18 June – Sunday, 18 June 1815. He had to keep his men together for three more days to make sure that they would fight on with their necks at stake.

His blistered feet were causing him agony, for the short pause beside Paul-Marie's hanging body had brought back the life into them, and he would have to walk on them for some distance farther before they would be numb again. He had to drive himself to quicken his stride to catch up Marie, walking in the middle of the group with a musket slung across her back and Annette beside her. Marie had cut off her masses of hair – sawed them off with a knife after her first night as a guerrilla soldier – and the ends hung irregularly round her face, which was wet with sweat and streaked with dirt. But both she and Annette were in far better physical condition than Hornblower, stepping out with unblistered feet and still with a certain freedom of stride as compared with Hornblower's leg-weary stagger. They were ten and fifteen years younger than he.

'Why not leave Pierre behind and take his horse, 'Oratio?' asked Marie.

'No,' said Hornblower.

'He will die anyway,' argued Marie. 'That wound will gangrene.'

'Bad for the other men to leave him here to die alone in the forest,' said Hornblower. 'Besides, Clausen might find him before he died and find out from him what we intend to do.'

'Kill him and bury him, then,' said Marie.

Women when they go to war are fiercer than men and inclined to carry the logic of war to still greater logical extremes. This was the tender, gentle Marie, the kind and understanding, who had wept for love of him.

'No,' said Hornblower again. 'We'll capture some more horses soon.'

'Providing we do,' said Marie.

It was hard to keep horses alive in these conditions; they died or went lame while men still lived and marched. Only two weeks had passed since Clausen, marching down from Briare, had forced them to evacuate Nevers, and in the fierce manhunts that had followed horses had died in dozens. Clausen must be an active and energetic officer; his columns had marched hotfoot after them in unceasing pursuit. Only night-march after night-march, stratagems and cunning, had kept them out of his clutches. Twice there had been fierce little rear-guard actions; once they had ambushed a troop of pursuing Hussars – Hornblower remembered the gaily uniformed soldiers tumbling from their saddles as the volley blazed from the roadside – and now here they were with half their strength gone already, marching by day, having marched the night before, to cross the rear of one of Clausen's circling columns. Marie knew of a dangerous and little-known ford across the Loire ahead. Once over that they could rest for a day in the forest of Runes before showing themselves in the valley of the

Allier and causing fresh turmoil there. Clausen would be after them at once, but that was far enough to look ahead; the next move would depend on the new circumstances.

Active and energetic Clausen certainly was – he must have learned about fighting guerrillas in Spain. But he had a considerable force to back him up; Hornblower knew of the 14th Léger and the 40th Ligne – the 14th Light Infantry and the 40th of the Line – and there was another regiment with which he had not yet come into contact, and at least one squadron of the 10th Hussars. Nine battalions or more – six or seven thousand men – all chasing his ragged thirty. He was doing his duty, for those seven thousand men could be better employed on the Belgian frontier, where undoubtedly some action was stirring. And if he could only keep up the struggle he could wear down even those seven thousand men, wear out their boots and wear down their spirits. He could! Hornblower gritted his teeth and marched on; his feet were numb again now and had ceased to pain him. Only the terrible weariness in his legs distressed him now.

He became aware of a low muttering roar in the distance.

'Guns?' he asked, a little puzzled.

'Thunder,' said Marie.

They had chattered so light-heartedly once; had walked carefree and gay, hand in hand. It hardly seemed as if it were they two who had walked like that, in that breathing space of peace before Bonaparte returned from Elba. Hornblower was too fatigued to love now. The thunder muttered again; the heat was more oppressive.

Inside his clothes Hornblower could feel the prickliness of his sweat. He was thirsty, too, but his thirst was not as severe as his physical weariness. In the forest it was growing dark, not with the approach of evening, which was still far off, but with the massing of storm-clouds overhead. Somebody close behind him groaned, and Hornblower made himself look round and grin.

'Who's that lowing like a cow?' he asked. 'Old Father Fermiac? Five years younger than me, and they call him Father Fermiac and he lows like a cow! Cheer up, Father. Maybe we'll find a bull for you the other side of the Loire.'

That raised a cackle of laughter – some of it pure hysteria, some of it amusement at his not-quite-perfect French, some of it roused by the incongruity of a great English lord cracking jokes with French peasants. The thunder crashed almost overhead, and they could hear the rain beginning to patter on the trees. A few drops found their way down on their sweating faces.

'Here comes the rain,' said someone.

'I've had water underfoot for the past two days,' said Hornblower. 'You ought to see my blisters. Even the good Jesus never walked on as much water as I have.'

The daring blasphemy raised another cackle, got the men along for another hundred yards. The heavens were opening overhead, and the rain was falling in cataracts. Hornblower dropped back to the packhorses, to make sure that the leather covers were securely over the panniers. He had two thousand rounds of musket ammunition there which he did not want spoiled – it would be harder to replace than food or even shoe-leather. They plodded on, in the semi-darkness, their clothes growing heavier with the rain soaking into them. The earth beneath their feet grew spongy and soggy, while the storm showed no sign of diminishing. The thunder still roared and the lightning flashed, lighting up the dark spaces under the trees.

'How much farther?' asked Hornblower of Marie.

'Two leagues and a half, perhaps.'

Three hours more of marching; it would be almost dark, if not quite, by the time they arrived.

'This rain will deepen the ford,' said Marie, sounding the first note of a new anxiety.

'My God!' said Hornblower before he could check himself.

There were eighteen half-battalion columns scattered in pursuit of them, and he was threading his way through the midst of them. He was risking almost everything on being able to cross the river at this unexpected point, which would throw off pursuit for a time at least. Their danger would be extreme if they were unable to pass. This was a rocky country in general, with a shallow topsoil, among the headwaters of the great river, and rain would affect the level of the water after only a short interval. He turned on his weary legs to urge the men to lengthen their stride. That was something he had to do every few minutes during the rest of that dreadful march, as darkness closed in prematurely about them, as the rain roared down upon them incessantly, as the led horses stumbled and plunged and the two wounded men groaned in agony. The Count rode without a word, bowed forward in the saddle with the water streaming from him. He was in the last stages of exhaustion, Hornblower knew.

Someone ahead challenged through the rain and dark; it was a man sent back from Brown's advanced guard. Brown had reached the edge of the forest, and the river lay a short distance ahead across the rocky flood plain. They all halted together under the last of the trees while scouts moved cautiously forward to discover if this lonely stretch of river bank were patrolled – there could not be too many precautions taken, even though any self-respecting sentry would sneak away to find shelter on a night like this.

'The river sounds loud,' said Marie. They could hear it even through the noise of the rain where they lay in the wet mud, and Hornblower dared not think what that implied.

Brown's messenger came back; he had explored the river bank and found no sign of the enemy, as was to be expected. Clausen's division would be sufficiently dispersed guarding likely places, let alone the unlikely ones. They got to their feet, Hornblower feeling new agony as his weight came again on his blisters. He could hardly step at first, and his legs were stiff and weary as well and hardly obeyed his wishes. The Count was able to mount his horse, but the poor brute seemed as leg-weary as Hornblower himself. It was a sorry party that limped and hobbled and stumbled forward in the gathering darkness. The thunder had long ceased, but the rain continued to fall steadily, with every promise of going on through the night.

The turbulent surface of the river gleamed in the half-light ahead of them.

'The ford begins down by those trees,' said Marie. 'It is a ledge under the surface that runs diagonally upstream from there to the middle of the river. That is how you cross the deep part.'

'Come on, then,' said Hornblower. In his pain and weariness he felt as if he would like to cover that last half-mile on his hands and knees.

They came to the water's edge; the rushing river boiled at their feet among the rocks.

'It is too deep already,' said Marie. She was only voicing the suspicion that had formed in every mind. There was no expression in her tone at all; her voice was flat and dead.

'I'll take a horse and try it,' she went on. 'Here, help Pierre down.'

'Let me try, *madame*,' said Brown, but Marie paid him no attention.

She climbed astride into the saddle, hitching up the skirts of her habit to permit her to do so. Then she urged the horse forward into the water. The animal balked, nearly lost his footing among unseen rocks, and went forward with the utmost reluctance under the urging of Marie's heels. The water was almost up to its belly before – as Hornblower guessed – it had reached the end of the ledge of rock that Marie had spoken about. There was another battle of wills between Marie and the horse, and it plunged forward again. Three strides and it was out of its depth, struggling madly over the irregular bottom, almost vanishing from sight, and whirling downstream at frightening speed before it regained its footing. Marie, flung from the saddle, somehow hung on to the pommel, avoiding the lashing hoofs as the horse headed for the shore, and found her footing as it came out from the shallows snorting in fear.

Marie struggled on to the bank weighed down by her dripping clothing. No one had uttered a sound while the trial was being made, not even in the moment of Marie's greatest peril. It was plain now to everybody that the ford was impassable.

'We must all walk on water now besides milord,' said a voice. It might have been a joke, but anyone who heard it knew that it was not.

Hornblower made himself come out of his daze. He had to think and plan and lead.

'No,' he said. 'I'm the only one who can do that. And none of us care to swim. Do we? Then let us keep along the river bank until we find a boat. I'll exchange ten miracles for one boat.'

The suggestion was received in depressed silence. Hornblower wondered if the men were one-half as tired as he was. He forced himself to his feet, by a fierce effort of will ignoring the pain of the blisters.

'Come on,' he said. 'At least we cannot stay here.'

No guerrilla leader in his senses would camp for the night beside an unfordable river against which he could be hemmed in, and with the rain continuing it would be at least twenty-four hours before it would be passable again.

'Come on,' he repeated. 'Come on, Frenchmen.'

Then he knew he had failed. A few stirred reluctantly; more looked to see how their comrades acted, and then deliberately lay down again, some on their backs, some with their faces pillowed on their forearms, with the rain still dropping on them.

'An hour's rest,' pleaded one voice.

Someone – Hornblower guessed it was young Jean,

not yet seventeen – was sobbing unashamedly and loudly. The men had reached breaking point. Someone else, someone with greater powers of inspiration, might have got them to move again, Hornblower told himself, but it was beyond him. Had the ford been practicable they would have crossed it, and staggered on a mile or two the other side, but in the face of this disappointment they were capable of nothing further tonight. And they knew, the same as he did, that there was nothing to go on for. The rebellion was at an end, whether they marched till they died or gave up now. The thunderstorm, the flooding of the ford, had baulked it. The men were realists after this experience of guerrilla warfare, and knew that anything further they did would be only a gesture. They all knew of Clausen's proclamation offering amnesty, too. Brown was at his side, eloquent in his silence, a hand on the butt of a pistol in his belt. Brown, himself, Marie; the Count and Annette, for what they were worth. One or two more – old Fermiac for one – were all he could count on. It would be enough for the moment. He could shoot a couple of the most obstinate of the objectors, and the rest would get to their feet and march, sulkily. But he could hardly keep unwilling men together in a march in darkness. They could slip away too easily; nor would it be difficult for someone more discontented or desperate than the others to slip a knife into his back on the march or put the muzzle of his musket to his ribs and pull the trigger. He was prepared to face that risk, he was prepared to kill a couple of malcontents, but he could see no real benefit from such action. There was one thing left for him to do, the last resource of the hunted guerrilla leader, to disperse his band and hope for better days to come. It was a bitter pill to swallow, especially in view of the desperate danger to Marie and the Count, but it was not a matter of choosing the best of possible alternatives. He had to choose the least bad. But failure was a horrible thing.

'Very well,' he said. 'It is here that we say goodbye.'

Some of the men stirred at those words.

''Oratio!' said Marie, and then ceased abruptly. She had learned the lessons of discipline.

'Your lives are safe,' went on Hornblower. 'You have all read Clausen's proclamation. Tomorrow – tonight if you will – you can make your way to the troops and surrender. You can go to your homes. Madame and the Count and I go on, for go on we must. And we would even if we need not.'

The men were stunned into silence by his words. No one stirred, no one spoke in the darkness. The two weeks of toil and danger and hardship through which they had just passed seemed like a lifetime to most of them, and it was hard to realize that a lifetime had come to an end.

'We shall return,' continued Hornblower. 'Remember us when you are in your homes. Think of us. We shall return with a fresh call to arms. Then we shall all of us gather again in our strength to thrust down the tyrant. Remember that. And now one last cheer for the King! *Vive le Roi!*'

They cheered, feebly enough, but Hornblower had achieved what he set out to do. He had sowed the seeds of a later rebellion; when Clausen's division should move away it would be possible to set the Nivernais in a turmoil once more should a leader arise – should he and the Count ever succeed in in making their way back into the province. It was a desperate, slight hope, but it was all that remained.

'In the name of God!' said Fermiac. 'I come with you now.'

'I also,' said another voice in the darkness.

Perhaps with these Frenchmen it might be possible now to make an hysterical appeal to them, carry them away on a wave of emotion, set them marching once more. Hornblower felt the temptation, and he had to balance the pros and cons coldly. That sort of hysteria would hardly survive the shock of the men's feeling their leg-weariness. Some of the men simply could not march farther. It would not do; by dawn next day he would not have six men with him, and time would have been irretrievably lost.

'Thank you,' said Hornblower. 'I shall remember that in time to come, Fermiac, my friend. But we must ride, and ride hard. Four of us and six horses gives us the best chance. Go back to your wife, Fermiac, and try not to beat her on Saturday nights.'

He even got a laugh by that, at this moment of all moments. It helped to keep the parting on a sane level, the level he was aiming at with an eye to the future. Yet he knew there was no future; he knew it in his soul, in his bones, even while he gave the order for the pack-horses to be stripped of their loads, even while he forced Brown in a bitter argument to leave Annette behind and make her life safe. He was going to die; probably Brown was going to die. And Marie, dear Marie – while his spirit tossed on wave after wave of emotion, of remorse and self-condemnation, of fear and regret, uncertainty and despair, his love for her endured and increased, so that her name was in his mind as a constant accompaniment to his thoughts, so that her image was in his mind's eye whatever else he was picturing. Dear Marie, sweet, beloved Marie.

She was leading a spare horse, and Brown was leading the other; the four of them were mounted on the best of the six. The animals slipped and plunged over the rough surface at the water's edge until they reached the path above the river. They walked dispiritedly through the darkness. Hornblower could hardly sit in his saddle with his weariness; he felt giddy and sick, so that he had to hold on to the pommel of the saddle in front of him. He closed his eyes for a moment and instantly seemed to be swept over some vast smooth declivity, like the boat going over the cataract of the Loire four years before; he was almost out of his saddle before he recovered himself, jerking himself upright and clinging to the pommel like a drowning man. Yet at the foot of the declivity he had known that Marie was waiting for him with the brooding love in her eyes.

He shook off delirium. He had to make plans, to think how they could escape. He called up before his mind's eye the map of the country, and marked on it what he knew of the situation of Clausen's flying columns. They constituted a semicircular cordon, whose diameter was the river, and at whose centre he found himself at present. So far he had buoyed himself up in this danger with the hope of passing the river by Marie's ford. Hard on their heels, he knew, was marching a half-battalion of the 14th Léger, which had apparently been given the duty of direct pursuit while the other columns headed him off. At nightfall that half-battalion was presumably six or seven miles behind, unless – as might easily be the case – its commanding officer forced his men to march on in the darkness. Should he try to pierce the cordon or try to pass the river?

The Count's horse in front of him fell with a crash and a clatter, and his own nearly threw him as it plunged to avoid treading on it.

'Are you hurt, sir?' came Brown's voice in the darkness; he must have slipped down instantly from the saddle despite the handicap of a led horse.

'No,' said the Count quietly. 'But I'm afraid the horse is.'

There was a chink of bridles as Brown and the Count felt about in the dark.

'Yes. He's slipped his shoulder, sir,' reported Brown at length. 'I'll change saddles to the other horse.'

'Are you sure you are not hurt, Father?' asked Marie, using the intimate form of address which was by no means the rule between them.

'Not in the least, dear,' answered the Count, in just the same tone as he would use in a drawing room.

'If we turn this horse loose they'll find it when they come along, my lord,' said Brown.

'They' meant the pursuing troops, of course.

'Yes,' said Hornblower.

'I'll take him away from the path and shoot him, my lord.'

'You won't be able to lead him far,' said the Count.

'A few yards may be enough,' said Brown, 'if you'll be kind enough to hold these two horses, sir.'

They sat and stood while Brown persuaded the

suffering creature to hobble away to his doom. Through the gentle noise of the rain they heard the click as the pistol misfired, waited while Brown reprimed, and then heard the crack of the weapon.

'Thank you, sir,' Hornblower heard Brown say, presumably as he took over the horse the Count had been holding, and then he added. 'Can I take over your led horse, *madame*?'

Hornblower made up his mind at that moment.

'We will keep along the river bank a little longer,' he said. 'Then we can rest until dawn, and try to make a crossing.'

20

They all of them slept a little that night, an hour or so altogether perhaps, in fits and snatches. They were all of them wearing clothing completely saturated, and although in the dark they found a bit of grassy bank on which to lie, the rock was only just below the surface and made itself felt. But such was their fatigue and shortage of sleep that they lost consciousness now and then, forgot the cold and their aching joints. It was the most natural thing in the world that Hornblower and Marie should lie in each other's arms, with his wet cloak beneath them and hers above. It was warmer that way. Probably they would have slept in each other's arms if they had been nothing to each other; and in one way, as a result of their fatigue, they *were* nothing to each other. The great surge of love and tenderness which Hornblower experienced had nothing to do with the contact of his battered body against Marie's. He was too cold and too tired for passion to rouse itself at all. But Marie lay in the darkness with an arm over him; she was younger and less weary than he was, and maybe she loved more dearly. There was one blessed half-hour after the rain ceased, before the coming of light, when Hornblower slept tranquilly with his head on her shoulder, when he was all hers. War was behind them and death in front of them, and nothing could come between them at that moment. Maybe that was the happiest half-hour that Hornblower had ever given her.

Hornblower woke with the first beginning of light. A heavy mist had arisen from the river and the saturated fields, and through it he saw a faint object a few yards away, which with difficulty he recognized as the Count, sitting up enveloped in his cloak. Brown lay beside him snoring gently – apparently they two had slept together as well. It took Hornblower a moment or two to collect his faculties; the roar of the rapid river close at hand was the next thing he recognized. He sat up and Marie woke beside him. He stood up, to be sharply reminded of the pain in his blistered feet and the ache in every joint. The pain was hard to ignore, for every step was torture, as frightful as anything the Middle Ages ever devised, but he said no word about it.

Soon they were on their way, mounted on horses that seemed in no better condition than the night before. This was the life that killed horses. The day was clearing fast; Hornblower expected one of those typical summer days of central France, breezy and sunny together. He could expect the mist to vanish altogether in an hour or less. Beside them the river roared and sang; when the mist thinned they could see its wide grey surface streaked with white. Not far on their right hand was the great road to Briare and Paris; what they were following was the country path skirting the flood plain. With the river beside him Hornblower sketched rapidly what he intended to do to cross. That great expanse of water concealed shallows over much of its width, as they all knew. The main body of water and the main current was to be found in one channel, sometimes on this side, sometimes on that, sometimes in the middle – how well he remembered that phenomenon from the days when he had escaped down the river in a small boat! If they could get themselves across this channel, and swim the horses over, the shallows would hardly delay them. At Marie's ford they had relied on a ridge of rock which crossed the channel near enough to the surface to be passable at low water; as that ridge had failed them they must rely on other means. Even a little rowing-boat such as most riverside farms possessed would suffice. Marie's ford would have been far better, in that the pursuers would have no means of guessing that they had crossed, but anything was better than nothing. Across the river they could steal fresh horses for themselves and shake off pursuit. The Count snorted a little when Hornblower used the word 'steal'; but did not carry his protest into actual words.

The sun had broken through the mist now, and was shining at them almost level over the ridge on their right hand; the river's surface still steamed a little. Certainly it was going to be a hot day. And then they saw what they were seeking, a small farm and outbuildings sheltering below the ridge and above the water's edge. It stood bold and black against the mist with the sun on it. The instinct of war made them wheel instantly into a low basin screened by willows, and dismount for concealment.

'Shall I go ahead, my lord?' asked Brown.

Perhaps it was his way of keeping himself sane, thus to speak formally and with the bearing of the good servant.

'Yes, go on,' said Hornblower.

Hornblower edged himself forward to a position of

advantage whence he could watch Brown carefully worm his way towards the farm. If there were troops anywhere near, they would be quartered here. But then, on the other hand, at this time in the morning troops would be moving about round the outbuildings, and not a uniformed man was visible. A young woman made her appearance, and then an old man, while Hornblower watched. And then he saw something else, something which made him choke with anticipation and hope. Lying on the rocky bank of the river, at the water's edge below the farm, was a boat – the outline was unmistakable. The young woman was on her way towards the vineyard above the farm when Brown, concealed in the ditch, attracted her attention. Hornblower saw the two in conversation, saw Brown rise to his feet, and walk towards the building. A minute later he appeared again and waved an arm to tell them all was well. They mounted, and with Marie leading Brown's horse and Hornblower leading the spare they trotted down to the farm. Brown awaited them, his pistol handy in his belt, and the old man stared at them as they dismounted. They were something to stare at, Hornblower realized, dirty and bedraggled and unshaven. Marie looked like a beggar's wench.

'The Frogs were here yesterday, my lord,' said Brown. 'Cavalry, the same Hussars as we beat last week, as far as I can make out. But they left early yesterday morning.'

'Very good,' said Hornblower. 'Let's get the boat launched.'

'The boat!' exclaimed the old man, staring at them. 'The boat!'

'Why do you say that?' asked Hornblower sharply, wondering with a pang what fresh blow Fate had to deal him.

'Look at the boat!' said the old man.

They walked down towards it. Someone with an axe had struck it four powerful blows; in four different places the bottom was smashed in.

'The Hussars did that,' piped the old man, dwelling on the horrid details with zest. '"Smash that boat," said the officer, so they smashed it.'

The troops had been as fully aware, of course, as Hornblower had been of the importance of keeping the river barred. They had taken all the precautions they could think of to prevent unauthorized persons crossing. That was why Marie's ford would have been invaluable if they had been able to cross it yesterday.

It was a staggering blow; Hornblower looked out over the raging river and the fields and vineyards warm in the young day. Marie and the Count were waiting for a decision from him.

'We can make that boat float,' said Hornblower. 'The oars are still here. Two empty kegs fastened under the thwarts – there'll be kegs to be found here, seeing they make wine. We can patch a little, stuff the holes, and with the kegs to keep her afloat we'll cross all right. Brown, you and I had better get it done.'

'Aye aye, sir,' said Brown. 'There'll be tools in the wagon shed yonder.'

It was necessary to guard against surprise; the repair work on the boat would take some hours.

'Marie,' said Hornblower.

'Yes, 'Oratio?'

'Ride up above the vineyard there. Keep a watch on the high road. Remember to keep yourself and your horse hidden.'

'Yes, 'Oratio.'

Simply, 'Yes, 'Oratio', as Hornblower realized a moment later. Any other woman would have made it clear by word or intonation that the last sentence of his instructions was superfluous to someone who had learned her job. At it was she mounted and rode off in simple obedience. Hornblower caught the Count's eye. He wanted to tell him to rest – the Count's face was as grey as the stubble that grew thick on his cheeks – but he refrained from brutally saying so. It was necessary to keep the Count in good spirits, and that was not the way to do so.

'We shall need your help, sir, soon,' he said. 'Can we call on you when it is needed?'

'Of course,' said the Count.

Brown appeared with barrel staves, hammer, and nails, some lengths of cord.

'Excellent!' said Hornblower.

Feverishly they went to work on the boat. In two places both strakes and frames were smashed. To patch the holes was a comparatively simple matter, but the broken frames presented a more difficult problem. To cross that fast current they would have to row vigorously, and the boat might buckle under the strain. The simplest way to stiffen it would be to strengthen the strakes with one or two diagonal thicknesses of new planking.

'When we turn her over we'll see how she looks,' said Hornblower.

The hammers rang out as they drove the nails home

and clinched them. Hornblower thought of the lusty tugs on the oars necessary to drive the boat through those turbulent waters. Both longitudinally and transversely the strain on the fabric would be severe. They worked furiously. The old man hovered round them. He expected the Hussars back again at any moment, he said – they were constantly patrolling along the river bank. He told them this with that seeming delight in calamity that distinguished his type.

And he had hardly repeated his warning when the sound of hoofs caused them to look up from their work; it was Marie, pushing her horse down the slope as hard as it would move.

'Hussars!' she said briefly. 'Coming along the main road from the south. Twenty of them, I should think.'

It did not seem possible that Fate could be as unkind as she appeared to be. Another hour's work would see the boat ready to float.

'They'll come down here,' said the old man gloatingly. 'They always do.'

Once more it was a matter for instant decision.

'We must ride off and hide,' said Hornblower. 'Nothing else for it. Come on.'

'But the repairs on the boat, sir? They'll see 'em,' said Brown.

'They were only a mile away,' said Marie. 'They'll be here in five minutes.'

'Come on,' said Hornblower. 'Count, please get on your horse.'

'Tell the Hussars if they come it was you who was making these repairs,' said Brown to the old man. Brown thrust his shaggy face close to the wrinkled one.

'Come along, Brown,' said Hornblower.

They rode back to the hollow place where they had hidden themselves before. They tethered the horses to the willows, and crawled back among the rocks to watch. They had hardly settled themselves when a murmur from Marie called their attention to the coming of the Hussars. It was only a small patrol – half a dozen troopers and a non-commissioned officer. The plumed busbies came in sight first, over the ridge, and then the grey jackets. They trotted down the cart-track beside the vineyard to the farm. The old man was waiting for them at the entrance to the courtyard, and the fugitives watched as they reined up and questioned him. There was a catch in Hornblower's breath as he watched the old man, his face raised to the mounted men, replying to the questions. Hornblower saw the non-commissioned officer lean out of his saddle and take the old man by the breast of his coat and shake him. He knew now they would get the truth out of him. Those threats in Clausen's proclamation were not empty ones. A single reminder would make the old man talk – he would only hesitate long enough to salve his conscience. The non-commissioned officer shook him again; a trooper apparently idly walked his horse towards the river and the boat and returned at once with the news of the repairs. Now the old man was talking; excitement was infecting the Hussars' horses, which were moving about restlessly. At a wave from the non-commissioned officer's hand a trooper set his horse up the slope, clearly to carry word to the remainder of the squadron. The old man was pointing in their direction; the Hussars wheeled their horses about, and, spreading out, began to trot towards them. This was the end.

Hornblower glanced at his companions, who looked back at him. In the flying seconds minds worked quickly. There was no purpose in trying to ride away – the fresh horses of the Hussars would overtake them in an instant. The Count had drawn his pistols and looked to the priming.

'I left my musket at the ford,' said Marie, in a choking tone, but she, too, had a pistol in her hand.

Brown was coolly looking about him at the tactical situation.

They were going to fight it out to the very end, then. All the feeling of finality, of inevitability, that had haunted Hornblower from the very beginning of the rebellion – since the interview with the Duchess d'Angoulême – came over him with renewed force. This was indeed the end. To die among the rocks today, or before a firing party tomorrow. Neither of them very dignified ends, but perhaps this one was the better. Yet it did not seem right or fitting that he should die now. For the moment he could not accept his fate with the apparent indifference of his companions; he knew actual fear. Then it passed as suddenly as it came, and he was ready to fight, ready to play out the losing hand to the drop of the last card.

A trooper was riding towards them, not more than a few yards away now. Brown levelled his pistol and fired.

'Missed him, by God!' said Brown.

The Hussar reined his horse round and galloped out of range; the sound of the shot attracted the notice of all the rest of the patrol, which promptly sheered away out of musket-shot and began to circle, spreading out. The forlorn situation of the group in the rocky hollow must have become apparent to them immediately. Any attempt on the fugitives' part to escape must result in their being immediately ridden down, so that there was no need for hurry. The Hussars sat their horses and waited.

It was not more than half an hour before reinforcements arrived, two more troops under an officer whose aigrette and gold-laced dolman displayed the dandyism traditional in the Hussar regiments; the trumpeter beside him was nearly as resplendent. Hornblower watched as the sergeant's hand pointed out the tactical situation, and then he saw the officer's hand indicate the movements he wanted his men to make. The officer could see at a glance the ground was too broken for concerted mounted action; with disciplined rapidity the new arrivals dismounted, and the horses were led off by threes while the remainder of the two troops, carbine in hand, prepared to advance in skirmishing order against the hollow from two directions. For dismounted cavalry deployed as skirmishers, with their long boots and spurs and inaccurate carbines and lack of drill, Hornblower would nominally have felt nothing but contempt, but fifty of them advancing against three men and a woman armed only with pistols meant defeat and death.

'Make every shot tell, this time,' said Hornblower – the first words anyone had spoken for a long time.

Brown and the Count were lying in niches between rocks; Marie was crawling round so as to bring herself to face the flanking column. At a hundred yards the skirmishers grew more cautious, stealing forward trying to shelter themselves behind bushes and rocks, and obviously expecting the musket-shots that did not come. One or two of them fired their carbines, so widly that Hornblower did not even hear the bullets; he could imagine the non-commissioned officers rating the men who were thus wasting ammunition. They were within possible range now of his own rifled pistols – Barbara's gift to him. He lay with his right arm extended, his forearm supported on the rock that sheltered him, and took prolonged and careful aim at the easiest mark before him – a Hussar walking towards him in the open, his carbine across his body. He pressed the trigger, and through the smoke saw the Hussar whirl round and fall, to rise to a sitting position a moment later with his hand to his wounded arm. Hot with a new battle fury, Hornblower fired the other barrel, and the Hussar fell back, limp and motionless; Hornblower cursed himself for wasting a shot and for killing a wounded man who would have been out of the battle in any event. A fierce yell went up from the ring of skirmishers, while Hornblower reloaded his empty pistol, restraining himself as his fever tempted him to hurry. He poured the charges into the barrels, wrapped the bullets and rammed them home, and carefully placed the caps upon the nipples. The sight of their comrade's fall had instilled extra caution into the skirmishers, despite their battle yell – no one wished to be the next inglorious victim. That was a sergeant there, calling to his men to come on. Hornblower sighted again and fired, and the sergeant dropped. This was better. There was a savage satisfaction in killing when he was about to be killed. Carbines were firing from all round the ring; Hornblower could hear the bullets passing overhead.

At that moment a loud fanfare from the trumpet attracted the attention of everyone; it was repeated, and Hornblower looked round while the carbine-fire died away. The officer was walking his horse towards them, a white handkerchief waving from his hand, while the trumpeter rode close behind blowing for a parley in accordance with military etiquette.

'Shall I kill him, sir?' asked Brown.

'No,' said Hornblower. It would be pleasant to take the officer with him to hell, but it would give Bonaparte too good an opportunity to sully his name and thus discredit the Bourbon movement. He knelt up behind his rock and shouted, 'Come no farther!'

The officer reined up.

'Why not surrender?' he shouted back. 'You have nothing to gain by further resistance.'

'What terms do you offer?'

The officer with difficulty suppressed a shrug.

'A fair trial,' he shouted back. 'You can appeal to the mercy of the Emperor.'

The irony of those sentences could not have been greater if it had been deliberate.

'To hell with you!' yelled Hornblower. 'And to hell with the 10th Hussars! Run, or I fire!'

He raised his pistol, and the officer hastily wheeled his horse and trotted back without dignity. Why should it be that with death only half an hour away there should be any satisfaction in thus humiliating the man? He had only been doing his duty, trying to save the lives of his men; why this bitter personal animosity? This insane self-analysis coursed through Hornblower's mind even while he dropped on his stomach again and wriggled into a firing position. He had time to think scorn of himself before a bullet passing close above his head drove him to think about nothing save the business in hand. If the Hussars would only rise to their feet and charge in they might lose half a dozen lives but it would be over quickly. Marie's pistol cracked not far from his right hand, and he looked round at her.

At that moment it happened; Hornblower heard the impact of the bullet, saw the force of it half roll her over. He saw the puzzled look on her face, saw the puzzled look change to a grimace of agony, and without even knowing what he was doing he sprang to her and knelt beside her. A bullet had struck her on the thigh; Hornblower turned back the short skirt of her riding habit. One leg of her dark breeches was already soaked with blood, and while he was gathering himself to act he twice saw the blood pulsate redly – the great artery of the thigh was torn. A tourniquet – pressure – Hornblower's mind hastily recalled all it had ever learned about emergency treatment of the wounded. He thrust his fingers into her groin, unavailingly, the folds of the breeches baulking his attempt to apply pressure to the artery. Yet every moment was precious. He felt for his penknife to rip open her breeches, and at the same time a shattering blow on his shoulder flung him onto the ground beside her. He had heard nothing of the Hussars' charge, nothing of the pistol-shots fired by Brown and the Count unavailingly to turn the charge back. Until the carbine-butt struck him down he had been ignorant of what was going on. Even as it was he struggled to his knees again with only the thought in his head of the urgent need to stop the artery. He vaguely heard a shout beside him as a sergeant stopped a trooper from striking him again, but he thought nothing of it. He opened his knife, but Marie's body was limp and lifeless under his hands. He glanced at her grimy face; it was white under the dirt and sunburn, her mouth hung open, and her eyes stared up at the sky as only the eyes of the dead stare. Hornblower knelt, looking down on her, his open penknife still in his hand, completely numb. The penknife fell from his fingers, and he became aware of another face beside his own looking down on Marie.

'She is dead,' said a French voice. 'A pity.'

The officer rose again to his feet, while Hornblower knelt over the body.

'Come, you,' said a harsher voice, and Hornblower was roughly shaken by a hand on his shoulder. He stood up, still dazed, and looked round him. There was the Count, on his feet, between two Hussars; there was Brown sitting on the ground with his hand to his head slowly recovering from the blow which had struck him senseless, while over him stood a trooper with his carbine cocked.

'Madame's life would have been spared after trial,' said the officer, his voice coming from miles away. The bitterness of that remark helped to clear the fog from Hornblower's brain. He made a wild movement, the two men sprang forward and seized his arms, sending a wave of agony through his shoulder where the carbine-butt had struck him. There was a momentary pause.

'I shall take these men to headquarters,' announced the officer. 'Sergeant, take the bodies down to the farmhouse. I will send you orders later.'

A low moan came from the Count's lips like the cry of a hurt child.

'Very well, sir,' said the sergeant.

'Bring the horses up,' went on the officer. 'Is that man well enough to ride? Yes.'

Brown was looking dazedly around him, one side of his face swollen and bruised. It was all like a dream, with Marie lying there glaring at the sky.

'Come along,' said someone, and they dragged at Hornblower's arms to lead him out of the hollow. His legs were weak under him, his blistered feet resented the movement, and he would have fallen if they had not helped him up and dragged him forward.

'Courage, coward,' said one of his guards.

No one – save himself – had ever called him that before. He tried to shake himself free, but they only held him the harder, his shoulder paining him excruciatingly. A third man put his hands on his back and all three ran him up out of the hollow without dignity. Here were the horses, a hundred of them, moving about restlessly still under the influence of the recent excitement. They shoved him up into the saddle of a horse, and divided the reins, a trooper mounting on each side and taking half the reins each. It added to Hornblower's feeling of helplessness to sit in a saddle with no reins to hold, and he was so exhausted that he could hardly sit upright. As the horse fidgeted under him he saw Brown and the Count made to mount as well, and then the cavalcade moved up to the road. There they broke into a rapid trot, which tossed him about in his saddle as he held on to the pommel. Once he came near to losing his balance, and the trooper beside him put an arm round him and hove him back into a vertical position.

'If you fell in a column like this,' said the trooper, not

unkindly, 'that would be the end of your troubles.'

His troubles! Marie was dead back there, and it might just as well have been his own hand that killed her. She was dead – dead – dead. He had been mad to try to start this rebellion, madder still, infinitely madder, to allow Marie to take part in it. Why had he done it? And a man more skilful with his hands, more ready of resource, would have been able to compress that spouting artery. Hankey, the surgeon of the *Lydia*, had said once (as though licking his lips) that thirty seconds was as long as anyone ever lived after the femoral artery was cut. No matter. He had allowed Marie to die under his hands. He had had thirty seconds, and he had failed. Failed everywhere, failed in war, failed in love, failed with Barbara – God, why did he think of Barbara?

The pain in his shoulder may have saved him from madness, for the jolting of the horse was causing him agony of which he could no longer remain ignorant. He slipped his dangling hand between the buttons of his coat as a makeshift sling, which brought him a little relief, and a short while later he received further relief when a shouted order from the officer at the head of the column reduced the horses' pace to a walk. Exhaustion was overcoming him, too; although thoughts were whirling through his brain they were ceasing to be well-defined and logical thoughts – rather were they nightmare images, terrifying but blurred. He had sunk into a delirious stupor when a new order which sent the horses into a trot again roused him from it. Walk and trot, walk and trot; the cavalry was pushing along the road as fast as the horses could go, hurrying him to his doom.

The château guarded by half a battalion of soldiers

was General Clausen's headquarters; the prisoners and their escorts rode into the courtyard and dismounted there. The Count was almost unrecognizable by reason of the grey stubble thick over his face; Brown, as well as being bearded, had one eye and cheek swollen purple with a bruise. There was no time to exchange more than a look, no time for a word, when a dapper dismounted officer came out to them.

'The General is waiting for you,' he said.

'Come along,' said the Hussar officer.

Two soldiers put their hands under Hornblower's arms to urge him forward, and once again his legs refused to function. There was not a voluntary contraction left in his muscles, and his blistered feet flinched from any contact with the earth. He tried to take a step, and his knees gave way under him. The Hussars held him up, and he tried again, but it was unavailing – his legs floundered like those of a leg-weary horse, and, indeed, for the same reason.

'Hurry up!' snapped the officer.

The Hussars supported him, and with his legs half trailing, half walking, they dragged him along, up a brief marble stair under a portico, and into a panelled room where behind a table sat General Clausen – a big Alsatian with bulging blue eyes and red cheeks and a bristling red moustache. The blue eyes bulged a little wider still at the sight of the three wrecks of men dragged in before him. He looked from one to another with uncontrolled surprise; the dapper aide-de-camp who had slipped into a seat beside him, with paper and pens before him, made more effort to conceal his astonishment.

'Who are you?' asked the General.

After a moment the Count spoke first.

'Louis-Antoine-Hector-Savinien de Ladon, Comte de Graçay,' he said, with a lift of his chin.

The round blue eyes turned towards Brown.

'And you?'

'My name is Brown.'

'Ah, the servant who was one of the ringleaders. And you?'

'Horatio, Lord Hornblower.' Hornblower's voice cracked as he spoke; his throat was parched.

'Lord 'Ornblower. The Comte de Graçay,' said the General, looking from one to the other. He made no spoken comment – his mere glance was a commentary. The head of the oldest family in France, the most distinguished of the younger officers of the British Navy – these two exhausted tatterdemalions.

'The court martial which will try you will assemble this evening,' said the General. 'You have today in which to prepare your defence.'

He did not add, 'if any'.

A thought came into Hornblower's mind. He made himself speak.

'This man Brown, monsieur. He is a prisoner of war.'

The arched sandy eyebrows arched higher yet.

'He is a sailor of His Britannic Majesty's Navy. He was doing his duty under my orders as his superior officer. He is not amenable to court martial in consequence. He is a legitimate combatant.'

'He fought with rebels.'

'That does not affect the case, sir. He is a member of the armed forces of the British Crown, with the grade of – of –'

For the life of him Hornblower could not remember the French equivalent of 'coxswain', and for lack of anything better he used the English word. The blue eyes suddenly narrowed.

'This is the same defence as you will be putting forward at your court martial,' said Clausen. 'It will not avail you.'

'I had not thought about my defence,' said Hornblower, so genuinely that his tone could not but carry conviction. 'I was only thinking about Brown. There is nothing of which you can accuse him. You are a soldier yourself, and must understand that.'

His interest in the present discussion made him forget his weariness, made him forget his own instant peril. The genuineness and sincerity of his anxiety about Brown's welfare had their effect on Clausen, who could not fail to be affected by these pleadings for a subordinate by a man who himself was about to lose his life. The blue eyes softened with a hint of admiration that was lost on Hornblower, keen-witted and sympathetic though the latter was. To him it was such an obvious thing to do to look after Brown that it did not cross his mind that it might be admirable as well.

'I will take the matter under consideration,' said Clausen, and then, addressing the escort. 'Take the prisoners away.'

The dapper aide-de-camp whispered hurriedly to him, and he nodded with Alsatian solemnity.

'Take what measures you think fit,' he said. 'I make you responsible.'

The aide-de-camp rose from his seat and accompanied them out of the hall as the soldiers helped

Hornblower to walk. Once through the door the aide-de-camp issued his orders.

'Take that man,' – indicating Brown – 'to the guard-house. That man,' – this was the Count – 'to the room there. Sergeant, you will have charge of him. Lieutenant, you will be personally responsible for this man 'Ornblower. You will keep two men with you, and you and they will never let him out of your sight. Not for a moment. There is a dungeon under the château here. Take him to it, and stay there with him, and I will come and inspect at intervals. This is the man who escaped four years ago from the Imperial gendarmerie, and who has already been condemned to death in his absence. He is desperate, and you can expect him to be cunning.'

'Very well, sir,' said the lieutenant.

A stone staircase led down to the dungeon, a relic of the not so distant days when the lord of the manor had the right of the high justice, the middle and the low. Now the dungeon showed every sign of long disuse when the clashing bars opened the door into it. It was not damp; on the contrary, it was thick with dust. Through the high barred window came a shaft of sunlight, just sufficient to illuminate the place. The lieutenant looked round at the bare walls; two iron chains stapled to the floor comprised the only furniture.

'Bring some chairs,' he said to one of the men with him, and, after a glance at his weary prisoner. 'And find a mattress and bring that too. A palliasse of straw at the least.'

It was chill in the dungeon, and yet Hornblower felt sweat upon his forehead. His weakness was growing with every second, his legs giving way under him even while he stood still, his head swimming. The mattress had hardly been laid upon the floor before he staggered to it and collapsed across it. Everything was forgotten in that moment, even his misery regarding Marie's death. There was no room for remorse, none for apprehension. He lay there face downward, not quite unconscious, not quite asleep, but oblivious; the throbbing in his legs, the roaring in his ears, the pain in his shoulder, the misery in his soul – all these were nothings at that moment of collapse.

When the bars at the door clashed to herald the entrance of the aide-de-camp Hornblower had recovered somewhat. He was still lying face downward, by now almost enjoying the lack of need to move or think, when the aide-de-camp came in.

'Has the prisoner spoken at all?' he heard the aide-de-camp ask.

'Not a single word,' said the lieutenant.

'The depths of despair,' commented the aide-de-camp with facile sententiousness.

The remark irritated Hornblower, and he was further annoyed at being caught in such an undignified attitude. He turned over and sat up on his palliasse and glared up at the aide-de-camp.

'You have no requests to make?' asked the latter. 'No letters you wish to write?'

He did not wish to write a letter upon which his gaolers would fall like vultures upon a corpse. Yet he had to be exigent, had to do something to remove that impression of being in despair. And with that he knew what he wanted and how desperately he wanted it.

'A bath,' he said. He put his hand to his hairy face. 'A shave. Clean clothes.'

'A bath?' repeated the aide-de-camp, a little startled. Then a look of suspicion came into his face. 'I cannot trust you with a razor. You would try to cheat the firing party.'

'Have one of your men shave me,' said Hornblower, and seeking for something to say to irritate he added. 'You can tie my hands while he does it. But first a bucket of hot water, soap, and a towel. And a clean shirt at least.'

The aide-de-camp yielded.

'Very well,' he said.

A queer mood of light-headed exaltation came to Hornblower's rescue. It was nothing to strip himself naked under the eyes of four curious men, to wash the filth from his body and to towel himself dry, ignoring the pain in his injured shoulder. It was not the legendary and strange Englishman that they were interested in so much as in the man about to die. This man soaping himself was shortly to pass through the gates ahead of them all; this white body was soon to be torn asunder by musket bullets. Telepathetically he felt his gaolers' morbid curiosity, and proudly and disdainfully he would indulge it. He dressed himself again while they watched his every movement. A trooper came in with his hands full of lather-bowls and razors.

'The regimental barber,' said the aide-de-camp. 'He will shave you.'

There was no suggestion now of tying his hands; as Hornblower sat with the razor rasping over his throat he thought of reaching suddenly up and grasping the blade. His jugular vein, his carotid artery were there; one deep cut at the side and he would be out of his torment, and there would be the additional satisfaction of having completely outwitted the supercilious aide-de-camp. The temptation was momentarily keen; he could visualize his corpse collapsing in the chair, blood pouring from his throat, to the consternation of the officers. So clear was the vision for the moment that he dallied with it, enjoying it But the fate of a suicide would not arouse nearly as much resentment as a judicial murder. He must let Bonaparte kill him, he must make that one last sacrifice to his duty. And Barbara – he would not like Barbara to think of him as a suicide.

The barber held a mirror before him just in time to break this new chain of thought; the face he looked at was the same familiar one, deeply sunburned. The lines about his mouth were perhaps more noticeable. The eyes were perhaps more pathetic than ever, more appealing. Disgustingly the forehead was a little higher, the scalp more visible. He nodded his approval to the barber, and rose to his feet as the towel was taken from under his chin, making himself stand firm despite the pain of the blisters on his feet. He swept his glance imperiously round, abashing the curious stares. The aide-de-camp pulled out his watch, most likely to conceal some embarrassment.

'In an hour the court martial will assemble,' he said. 'Do you wish for food?'

'Certainly,' said Hornblower.

They brought him an omelette, bread, wine, cheese. There was no suggestion that anyone should eat with him; they sat and stared as he carried each mouthful to his lips. He had not eaten for a long time, and now that he felt clean he was ravenously hungry. Let them stare;

he wanted to eat and drink. The wine was delicious, and he drank of it thirstily.

'The Emperor won two great victories last week,' said the aide-de-camp suddenly, breaking into Hornblower's mood. Hornblower paused in the act of wiping his mouth with his napkin to stare at him.

'Your Wellington,' went on the aide-de-camp, 'has met his destiny at last. Ney beat him thoroughly at a place south of Brussels called Les Quatre Bras, and on the same day His Majesty destroyed Blücher and the Prussians at Ligny, which is the old battlefield of Fleurus, according to the map. It was a pair of victories as decisive as Jena and Auerstadt.'

Hornblower forced himself to complete the wiping of his mouth apparently unmoved. He addressed himself to pouring himself out another glass of wine; he felt that the aide-de-camp, annoyed by his apparent indifference to his fate, was telling him this news in an endeavour to penetrate his armour. He tried to think of a riposte.

'How did this news reach you?' he asked, apparently all polite attention.

'The official bulletin reached us three days back. The Emperor was in full march for Brussels.'

'My felicitations, monsieur. For your sake I hope the news is true. But is there not a saying in your army about "to lie like a bulletin"?'

'This bulletin is from the Emperor's own headquarters,' said the aide-de-camp indignantly.

'Then there can be no doubt about it, of course. Let us hope that Ney informed the Emperor correctly of the facts, for his defeat of Wellington is a remarkable reversal of history. In Spain Wellington defeated Ney several times, as well as Masséna and Soult and Victor and Junot and all the others.'

The aide-de-camp's expression showed how much the speech nettled him.

'There can be no doubt of this victory,' he said, and he added viciously, 'Paris will hear the same day of the Emperor's entry into Brussels and of the final suppression of brigandage in the Nivernais.'

'Oh,' said Hornblower politely, with raised eyebrows. 'You have brigands in the Nivernais? I commiserate with you, sir – but I met none in my travels through the country.'

The aide-de-camp's mortification showed in his face more plainly than ever, and Hornblower sipped his wine and felt pleased with himself. What with the wine and his light-headed elation he could find little to fear in the prospect that soon he would be condemned to death. The aide-de-camp rose and clanked out of the cell, while Hornblower pushed back his chair and stretched his legs with an elaborate pose of well-being that was only partly assumed. They sat on in silence, himself and his three watchers, for some considerable time before the clash of the bars told of the door being opened afresh.

'The court is waiting. Come,' said the aide-de-camp.

No sense of well-being could disguise from Hornblower the soreness of his feet. He tried to walk with dignity, but he could only limp grotesquely – he remembered how only yesterday he had found that the first hundred yards after a halt was acutely painful until his feet grew numb. And today it was far less than a hundred yards to the great hall of the château. As Hornblower and his escort came up on to ground level they met the Count, walking between two Hussars, and the groups paused for a moment.

'My son, my son,' said the Count, 'forgive me for what I have done.'

There was nothing odd to Hornblower's mind in being addressed as 'son' by the Count. Quite automatically he made the equivalent reply.

'There is nothing for me to forgive, Father,' he said, 'but it is I who ask forgiveness.'

What compelling motive was it that made him drop on his knee and bow his head? And why did an old freethinker and Voltairean like the Count extend his hand to him?

'Bless you, my son. God bless you,' he said.

Then he passed on, and when Hornblower looked back the grey head and spare figure turned the corner and disappeared.

'He is to be shot at dawn tomorrow,' explained the aide-de-camp, as he opened the door into the great hall.

Clausen at his table was now flanked by three officers on either side, and at each end of the table sat a junior officer with papers before them. Hornblower hobbled towards them, struggling and failing to walk with any dignity. When he reached the table the officer at one end rose.

'Your name?' he asked.

'Horatio, Lord Hornblower, Knight of the Most Honourable Order of the Bath, Commodore in His Britannic Majesty's Navy.'

The court exchanged glances; the officer at the other end of the table, who was apparently acting as secretary, scribbled furiously. The officer who had asked the question – clearly the prosecutor – turned to address the court.

'The prisoner has admitted his identity. And I understand that he had previously already done so, to General Count Clausen and to Captain Fleury. His appearance also corresponds with his published description. It is submitted, then, that his identity is proved.'

Clausen looked round at his fellow judges, who nodded.

'It only remains, then,' went on the prosecutor, 'to submit to the court the verdict of a court martial held on 10 June 1811, wherein this said 'Oratio 'Ornblower was condemned to death, he having purposely absented himself, on charges of piracy and violation of the laws of war; that sentence being confirmed on 14 June of the same year by His Imperial and Royal Majesty the Emperor. The judges will find attested copies before them. I must request that the death sentence be enforced.'

Again Clausen looked at his fellow judges, and received a sixfold nod. Clausen looked down at the table before him, and drummed for a moment with his fingers before he looked up again. He was making himself meet Hornblower's eyes, and when he did Hornblower's strange clairvoyance told him of the repeated orders that had come from Bonaparte to Clausen – 'this Hornblower is to be taken and shot wherever found,' or something to that effect. There was a decided apology in Clausen's blue eyes.

'It is the order of this military commission,' said Clausen slowly, 'that the said 'Oratio 'Ornblower suffer death by shooting at dawn tomorrow, immediately after the execution of the rebel Graçay.'

'Pirates are hanged, Your Excellency,' said the prosecutor.

'It is the order of this commission that 'Ornblower be shot,' repeated Clausen. 'Remove the prisoner. The commission is terminated.'

There it was. Hornblower knew that every eye was on his back as he turned away and walked down the hall. He wished he could stride out, head up and shoulders back, but he could only hobble out, with halting steps and shoulders bent. He had had no opportunity to say a word in his own defence, and perhaps it was as well. He might have stammered and hesitated, tongue-tied, for he had made no speech ready. He hobbled down the steps. At least he was to be shot and not hanged – but would the impact of the bullets on his chest be any less agonizing than the tightening of the rope round his throat? He stumbled into the cell, which was now quite dark. He found the mattress and sat down on it. This was final defeat – he had not looked upon it in that light before. Bonaparte had won the last round of the struggle he had waged against him for twenty years. There was no arguing with bullets.

They brought in three candles, which brightly lit the cell. Yes, this was defeat. With bitter self-contempt Hornblower remembered so recently preening himself on his silly verbal victories over the aide-de-camp. Fool that he was! The Count condemned to death, and Marie – oh, Marie, Marie! He found actual tears in his eyes, and he hurriedly shifted his position on the mattress so that the watchers should not see them. Marie had loved him, and his own folly had killed her. His own folly and Bonaparte's superior genius. God, if only he could have the chance to live the last three months over again. Marie, Marie. He was going to sink his head into his hands, and checked himself when he remembered there were three pairs of eyes stolidly watching him. He must not have it said of himself that he died like a coward. For little Richard's sake, for Barbara's sake, that must not be. Barbara would love and cherish Richard, he could be sure of that. What would she think of her late husband? She would know – she would guess – why he had come to France, and she would guess at his infidelity. She would be deeply hurt. She would be blameless if she held no allegiance to his memory. She would marry again. Still young, beautiful, wealthy, well connected; of course she would. Oh God, that added to the pain, to think of Barbara in another man's arms, laughing with the joy of it. And yet he had lain in Marie's. Oh, Marie.

His nails were hurting his palms, so tightly were his fists clenched. He glanced round to find the eyes still on him. He must show no weakness. If that thunderstorm had not burst and flooded the Loire, he would still be at liberty, Marie would still be alive, the rebellion would still be active. It had called for the direct interposition of fate as well as Bonaparte's genius to defeat him. Those battles that had been fought in Belgium – maybe the bulletins had lied about Bonaparte's victories. Maybe they were not decisive. Maybe Clausen's division, kept inactive in the Nivernais, might have made them decisive had it been present. Maybe – what a fool he was to try to comfort himself with these vain delusions! He was going to die, he was going to solve the mystery that he had only sometimes allowed himself to think about. By this time tomorrow – in a few hours – he would have gone the road so many others had trodden before him.

They were lighting fresh candles; the old ones were burned to stubs. Was the night then passing so fast? Dawn would be here soon, soon – day breaks early in June. He met the eyes of one of the watchers, although the latter tried to evade his glance. He tried to force himself to smile, and knew instantly that the smile was lopsided and forced. A rattle outside the door. That could not be that they were coming for him already! Yes it was, the bars were clashing, the door was opening, the aide-de-camp was entering. Hornblower tried to rise to his feet, and to his horror found that his legs were too weak to support him. He made another effort to stand, unavailing again. He must sit and let them drag him out like a coward. He forced himself to raise his chin and look at the aide-de-camp, trying not to make it the fixed and glassy stare he knew it to be.

'It is not death,' said the aide-de-camp.

Hornblower looked; he tried to speak, but no word came from his open mouth. And the aide-de-camp was trying to force a smile too – an ingratiating smile.

'There is news from Belgium,' said the aide-de-camp. 'The Emperor has been defeated in a great battle. At a place called Waterloo. Already Wellington and Blücher are over the frontier and marching on Paris. The Emperor is there already and the Senate are demanding that he abdicate again.'

Hornblower's heart was pounding so hard that he was still incapable of speech.

'His Excellency the General,' went on the aide-de-camp 'has decided that in this case the executions are not to take place this morning.'

Hornblower found speech at last.

'I will not insist,' he said.

The aide-de-camp went on to say something about the restoration of His Most Christian Majesty, but Hornblower did not listen to him. He was wondering about Richard. And Barbara.

Also available in the Hornblower series by C.S. Forester

A Ship of the Line

Admiral Hornblower

Flying Colours

Hornblower and the Atropos

Hornblower and the Crisis

Hornblower and the Hotspur

Hornblower in the West Indies

Lieutenant Hornblower

Mr Midshipman Hornblower

The Commodore

The Earthly Paradise

The Happy Return

The Ship